CAGE

The La Rouge Triplets

ELLIE MASTERS   USA TODAY BESTSELLING AUTHOR
OF ROMANTIC SUSPENSE

JEM Publishing

Editor: Erin Toland

Proofreader: Roxane Leblanc

Published in the United States of America

JEM Publishing

This is a work of fiction. While reference might be made to actual historical events or existing locations, the names, characters, businesses, places, and incidents are either the product of the author's imagination or are used fictitiously, and any resemblance to actual persons, living or dead, business establishments, events, or locales is entirely coincidental.

ISBN: 978-1-964261-17-1

Dedication

This book is dedicated to my one and only—my amazing and wonderful husband.

Without your care and support, my writing would not have made it this far.

You pushed me when I needed to be pushed.

You supported me when I felt discouraged.

You believed in me when I didn't believe in myself.

If it weren't for you, this book never would have come to life.

Also by Ellie Masters

The LIGHTER SIDE

Ellie Masters is the lighter side of the Jet & Ellie Masters writing duo! You will find Contemporary Romance, Military Romance, Romantic Suspense, Billionaire Romance, and Rock Star Romance in Ellie's Works.

YOU CAN FIND ELLIE'S BOOKS HERE:

ELLIEMASTERS.COM/BOOKS

Military Romance

Guardian Hostage Rescue Specialists

Rescuing Melissa

(Get a FREE copy of Rescuing Melissa

when you join Ellie's Newsletter)

Alpha Team

Rescuing Zoe

Rescuing Moira

Rescuing Eve

Rescuing Lily

Rescuing Jinx

Rescuing Maria

Bravo Team

Rescuing Angie

Rescuing Isabelle

Rescuing Carmen

Rescuing Rosalie

Rescuing Kaye

Cara's Protector

Rescuing Barbi

Charlie Team

Rescuing Rebel

Rescuing Stitch

Military Romance
Guardian Personal Protection Specialists

Sybil's Protector

Lyra's Protector

The One I Want Series
(Small Town, Military Heroes)
By Jet & Ellie Masters

EACH BOOK IN THIS SERIES CAN BE READ AS A STANDALONE AND IS ABOUT A DIFFERENT COUPLE WITH AN HEA.

Saving Abby

Saving Ariel

Saving Brie

Saving Cate

Saving Dani

Saving Jen

Rockstar Romance
The Angel Fire Rock Romance Series

EACH BOOK IN THIS SERIES CAN BE READ AS A STANDALONE AND IS ABOUT A DIFFERENT COUPLE WITH AN HEA. IT IS RECOMMENDED THEY ARE READ IN ORDER.

Ashes to New (prequel)

Heart's Insanity (book 1)

Heart's Desire (book 2)

Heart's Collide (book 3)

Hearts Divided (book 4)

Hearts Entwined (book5)

Forest's FALL (book 6)

Hearts The Last Beat (book7)

Contemporary Romance

Firestorm

(KRISTY BROMBERG'S EVERYDAY HEROES WORLD)

Billionaire Romance
Billionaire Boys Club

Hawke

Richard

Brody

Contemporary Romance

Cocky Captain

(VI KEELAND & PENELOPE WARD'S COCKY HERO WORLD)

Romantic Suspense

EACH BOOK IS A STANDALONE NOVEL.

The Starling

~AND~

Science Fiction

Ellie Masters writing as L.A. Warren

Vendel Rising: a Science Fiction Serialized Novel

To My Readers

This book is a work of fiction. It does not exist in the real world and should not be construed as reality. As in most romantic fiction, I've taken liberties. I've compressed the romance into a sliver of time. I've allowed these characters to develop strong bonds of trust over a matter of days.

This does not happen in real life where you, my amazing readers, live. Take more time in your romance and learn who you're giving a piece of your heart to. I urge you to move with caution. Always protect yourself.

ONE

Ava

———

THE FIRST LIGHT OF DAWN CREEPS OVER THE HORIZON, CASTING A golden glow across the vast, untamed Alaskan wilderness. In the distance, the mountains stand as silent sentinels, their peaks capped in eternal snow as the rising sun splashes hues of pale pink, faint yellow, and the first blush of blue across the sky.

The crisp, invigorating air carries the promise of a new day as I draw in a breath that delves deep, caressing the essence of my soul.

All around me, the wild is waking; the distant call of an eagle, the gentle rustle of small mammals in the underbrush, and the ever-present burbling of the nearby stream where a mother elk brings her young one to drink.

"Amazing, isn't it?" Justin Tanner, the Youth Services Outdoor Program Coordinator from the Department of Juvenile Corrections, my *twinsie* brother from a different mother, brings me a steaming cup of coffee. His breath forms small clouds in the cold.

"Thanks." I take the coffee and inhale its robust scent. "This never gets old. These teens remind me how small my problems are."

My sentiments are for the dozen troubled teens Justin entrusts to my care—entrusted.

Today is our last day together.

"They're lucky to have you." Justin stands beside me, my rock and strongest supporter.

This isn't our first trip in the wilderness together. We're the same age—exactly the same—having been born in the same hospital on the same day, at the same hour and minute, separated only by the adjacent rooms of our mothers.

Who are best friends.

Nuclear besties for life.

Sisters bound by choice rather than genetics, which means Justin and I grew up together.

Siblings by choice, if not birth, and he's my best friend.

My fiercest supporter.

My rock.

My everything.

"And you." The steel cup of coffee warms my hands. It's typical of him to downplay his influence on these teens.

"I'm just their court-appointed warden." He shrugs, uncomfortable with the praise, as light as it is.

Behind me, the morning stillness is interrupted by the awakening of once-troubled teens. Their groans and muffled conversations pierce the crisp dawn, subtly altering the tranquil silence. The rustle of nylon and the thud of gear being methodically packed echo around us, each sound a testament to the dawning of a new day and a new beginning.

"You're far more than that. They look up to you." I'll never stop showering Justin with the praise he deserves.

He's a positive influence on these teens, a man willing to take one last stab at helping them turn their lives around.

"Maybe now, after you've shown them how to survive the wilderness. Six weeks ago, they hated my guts." He rocks back on his heels and spares a glance at the teens.

"That's a bit extreme."

Six weeks ago, these teens entered the wilderness, burdened by the weight of their struggles, their young souls chipped and fractured by life's harsh trials.

I took them on a journey through the rugged land and helped

them navigate the tangled wilderness within themselves. Under my watchful eye and steady hand, I taught them more than survival skills; I imparted resilience, teamwork, and inner strength to the teens.

Life skills they will take with them to carve out a better future.

Now, as they break camp for the last time, there's a palpable change in them: a newfound steadiness in their movements, a purposeful cadence in their steps, and light in their eyes.

The once sullen and distant teens stand taller, filled with glimmers of hope and determination.

"Maybe." He bumps my shoulder. "Regardless, we're really lucky to have your help. Finding a guide willing to take on a dozen unruly teens for six weeks at the end of the season is hard. Let alone a…"

"Don't say it."

"Woman." Justin's eyes glint with mirth.

"Sexist bastard," I tease him right back and jab him in the ribs with my elbow.

Justin is the least sexist man on the planet. He judges each person based on individual merits rather than gender. Not to mention, I'd kick his ass if he really meant it.

I turn my attention to the teens, observing them with pride as their once rare and strained laughter rings freely.

"I don't care how it sounds," he says. "This program is as effective as it is because of you. At first, all they see is a female. They make all these preconceived judgments that you blow out of the water on the first day. Let alone what you teach them in the first week and the next five. It's transformative."

"Well, I'm always willing to help out."

They're no longer troubled teens. Today, they stand on the cusp of reentering the world as young adults equipped with the tools to survive a different kind of wilderness.

Nature's challenges have reshaped them into self-reliant adults ready to face whatever life throws them.

The transformation is palpable. It's evident in how they communicate less with words and more through meaningful glances and small, supportive gestures. It's in how they tackle tasks, no longer alone but as part of a team. As they fold their tents and secure their packs, an unspoken camaraderie binds them, a silent acknowledgment of the journey they weathered together, the internal battles fought, and the personal victories won.

I have the best job ever.

I take a deep inhale. It's one of those breaths that reaches deep down to invigorate and renew.

"We've got you on the books come spring. Is this your last expedition for the season?" Justin asks. "They say winter is going to come in harsh and biting."

"I've got one more client before closing up shop."

"Anyone interesting?"

"Some hotshot photographer."

"I sense trouble."

"Not trouble, just…"

"Just what?"

"He's an outdoor enthusiast and mountaineer. His photography is world-renowned."

"Then what's the problem?"

"I've heard he's relentless in his pursuit of the perfect shot."

"Relentless? Sounds like you went digging."

"Guilty as charged."

"Tell me, what did you find?"

"Cage La Rouge has scaled the Seven Summits. Captured Everest's daunting majesty, braved Aconcagua's icy winds, and endured Denali's unforgiving cold. He's stood atop Kilimanjaro, witnessing dawn break over Africa, traversed Elbrus's treacherous slopes, and battled Vinson Massif's isolation. Even Puncak Jaya's rocky face couldn't deter him."

"Wow, took a deep dive on this one. Memorized all that?" Justin gives me a look saying he knows there's more to it.

"What can I say? He's booked for a three-week expedition, four if required. You bet your ass I checked him out. Took the time to drill into the details of his life. The man is rough and rugged, an adventure seeker, a skilled climber, and a phenomenal photographer, and he's soon to be a thorn in my side."

"Your memory never fails to amaze me, and three weeks? That's a stretch."

He speaks to my nearly eidetic memory. It's not a perfect recall, but if there's a rhythm to what I've read, things get stuck in my head.

"His lens has seen the extremes of this world, but it's never enough. He's always searching for the next, even more perilous peak." I turn to Justin as if my hesitation should be clear.

"I don't see the problem. Sounds like the perfect client. He comes equipped with survival skills. Makes your life easier."

"That's the problem." I huff an exaggerated sigh, then bring my hands to my mouth to blow on them for warmth. "His track record, impressive as it is, means he's cocky and arrogant."

"What are you afraid of?"

Out here, overconfidence can be fatal.

"If he's too headstrong, thinking he knows it all, it could put both of us in danger. That's what worries me. I don't need some Alph-A-hole thinking he knows everything. Scaling mountains, while impressive, is nothing like surviving the wilds of Alaska. That's what I'm afraid of."

"It has to be easier guiding him than taking on a dozen troubled teens who know nothing about the outdoors." Justin gestures to the teens breaking camp.

"I'll take the teens any day over this client."

"Why is that?"

"Because men like him think they know it all. They don't listen. They do their own thing, and when he sees me…"

"He's not likely to listen to a woman? Is that what you're worried about?"

"That and more. Not that I can't handle him. I've been blowing stereotypes out of the water since I was a kid. I'm just over it. Hopefully, he'll fall in line, do as he's told, and not cause me too much grief."

"Good luck with that."

"At least it pays well."

"Has to be better than what we pay."

"His company is paying triple my usual fee."

"Wow."

"Everyone pays better than the Department of Corrections."

"Same deal, Ava." Justin folds his arms across his chest and gives me his stern *brother* tone. "Every morning by eight and every night by ten. If I don't hear from you, I'm bringing the cavalry to your last known location."

"Protective much?"

"Not nearly enough."

"You know that's not necessary."

"I know."

"But you're going to do it anyway."

"Yup." He rocks back on his heels. "Big brother prerogative."

"By ten seconds." It's our usual bit. He technically entered the world ten seconds before me.

"Enough for me to worry about you spending three weeks in the bush with a man you don't know. Not to mention lions, tigers, and bears." He grins at his Oz reference while I shake my head. The thing is, Justin's serious.

If I don't do my daily check-ins with him, he'll lead the charge to rescue me. Big brothers are a major pain in the ass.

Two of the older teens, Mia and Lucas, approach with their backpacks slung on their backs. A smile plays on my lips. Mia was initially the worst of the bunch when it came to waking up with the dawn. Now, she's first to rise and last to bed.

"I never knew the sky could have so many colors." Mia's eyes widen, taking in the pastel pinks and oranges stretching across the sky.

"I'm going to miss this." Lucas adjusts his backpack, his voice filled with wonder. "It's a different world out here." His expression is troubled, and for good reason.

Lucas is less fortunate than the others, who will face parole after this expedition. Despite Justin's best efforts, the teen will return to

Juvenile Detention and serve the remaining thirty days of his sentence.

"Every day is a new day to make things better." Sullen, hostile, and combative the first time I met him; there's been a significant change in Lucas. A change for the better, I hope. "It's only thirty days. Take them one by one and when you get out, take me up on my offer."

Out of all the others, Lucas shows an innate talent when it comes to handling himself in the wilderness. My guide business is booming. Rather than turning clients away due to a lack of staff, I want to hire him as a guide.

The boy has no one, and I want to give him a chance to turn his life around and start new.

"Sure." He hangs his head, but there's less of a slump in his shoulders. Used to rejection and lies from the adults in his life, he's not one to trust easily.

"I mean it. The job is yours if you want it. How about you and Mia get the others ready to head back to the lodge? You can lead us back."

We've got ten miles ahead of us. Our last day won't be easy, but at least it's mostly downhill over level ground. It'll be a good test of Lucas's leadership skills; see if he will take off and leave the group or if he'll monitor his pace to account for the slowest hiker.

It's a rugged hike, and Lucas leads the way with innate skill. He stands taller with the challenge of leading us home. We stop for breaks, then lunch, sharing our last meal together in the wilderness, and then he brings us home as the sun slips down toward the horizon.

With dusk on our heels, the lodge comes into view. Its windows glow warmly, welcoming weary travelers home. Unfortunately, it signals the end of my time with this group of teens.

I will miss them.

Justin glances at me. "You did good, Ava. Damn good for this group."

"Every group teaches me something new. I hope it helps."

"It helps more than you know." Justin clamps his hand on my shoulder, giving a reassuring squeeze. "Same place this spring?"

"Wouldn't miss it for the world."

"Don't stress about your next booking. I'm sure this guy won't be as bad as you think."

"Let's hope." Unfortunately, doubt threads through my voice.

Alpha men, like this Cage La Rouge, tend to be assholes who think women can't handle anything that might break a nail.

"But he could be an axe murder." Justin's like a dog with a bone. "DO NOT skip the check-ins."

"I won't."

As the last teen disappears into the lodge, a sense of profound accomplishment washes over me. The Alaskan wilderness has once again worked its magic, leaving behind a group of transformed teens ready to face the world with fresh eyes and a profound new understanding of what they can accomplish once they put their minds to it.

I look at the breathtaking landscape; the fading hues of the sunset cast a warm glow on the mountains, and once again, I feel like I need to pinch myself.

I have the best job in the world.

A distant howl echoes through the mountains, a reminder that the wild doesn't yield easily to the presence of humans. The lodge's warmth beckons, signaling the end of one experience and the beginning of another.

The wilderness has a way of testing us, pushing us beyond our limits, and as I prep for the next expedition, I can't help but wonder what lessons nature has in store—for both me and the elusive photographer about to crash into my world.

TWO

Ava

I TRADE THE BITING COLD OUTSIDE FOR THE WARMTH OF HEARTH
and home. My cozy lodge is a stark contrast to the harshness of the
Alaskan wilderness.

Rustic and inviting, the main room is spacious, with high-
beamed ceilings and large windows that offer panoramic views of
the surrounding landscape. Local art adorns the walls, including
paintings of the Alaskan scenery and framed wildlife photographs.

A large stone fireplace dominates one end of the lodge. A fire
crackles merrily along, radiating warmth to the great room. Plush
couches and armchairs are arranged around it, providing both
groups and individuals places to curl up beside the fire. The teens
are already nestled in, sipping hot beverages, their conversation a
gentle hum in the background.

After cataloging their gear and putting it away for the next set of
clients, I spot Mia and Lucas by the fireplace, deep in conversation.
I walk over and catch the tail end of Lucas describing the mesmerizing northern lights.

Mia glances up as I approach, a small smile on her lips. Without
a word, they scoot over to make room for me. Lucas shifts in his

seat, a quiet acknowledgment that I'm welcome. Mia's eyes briefly meet mine, and she nods subtly, continuing the conversation.

"The northern lights are surreal," Mia continues her conversation with Lucas. "Like another world." Her gaze shifts to the window and the darkness outside as she recalls the memory.

"Nature has a way of surprising us when we least expect it." I savor the warmth of the fire and the change in the teens.

Life-altering doesn't even begin to describe what they just experienced.

Lucas chimes in, animated and eager. "I can't believe everything we learned. Challenging, but cool, you know?" He looks at me, a silent question validating my offer for him to work for me in the future.

"Absolutely. Learning to navigate the wild teaches you things you can't find in any textbook." The warmth of the fire heats my face. "And you've got raw talent, Lucas. Something I can use."

"So, you're serious? About the job?"

"I would never lie to you or lead you on. You've got a place here when you finish your sentence, and I've got all winter to teach you everything."

"Thanks, Ava." He hangs his head, perhaps truly believing that not every adult is out to hurt him. "Means a lot."

As the conversation flows, I encourage them to share their reflections on the past six weeks. The room echoes with stories of personal growth, overcoming challenges, and the bonds forged in the face of adversity.

Justin joins us, his coffee cup in hand, and settles into a nearby chair. The shifting dynamics suggest our little gathering has become an impromptu family of sorts.

"I never thought I'd say this…" Lucas leans back and catches my eye.

"What's that?" Justin asks.

"I'm going to miss the early mornings and freezing nights."

"You getting sentimental on us, Lucas?" Justin raises an eyebrow, a wry smile forming.

"Maybe just a little." He smirks in response, but then his tone turns serious. "It's just—good, you know. Knowing there's a future…" He doesn't finish the rest of his thought, but there's hope on his face for the first time.

Mia leans forward, her expression turning thoughtful. "It's weird, but I feel like we've known each other for way longer than six weeks."

"Challenge has a way of fast-tracking friendships." I nod in agreement. "I'm so proud of all of you."

The conversation weaves seamlessly between shared memories, laughter, and unspoken understanding. We discuss the unexpected beauty of the wilderness, moments of triumph, and the inevitable difficulties faced along the way.

As the night progresses, the atmosphere in the lodge becomes one of quiet reflection. The bonds forged through the challenges of the Alaskan wilderness are palpable, and the stories the teens exchange find a common thread in shared glances, nods, and subtle gestures.

Tomorrow is for farewells, but tonight we are family.

We stay up late into the night, but eventually, exhaustion pulls us to bed. I'm the last to retire for the night and take advantage of the quiet to check out my next client online.

In the stillness of the lodge, the fading fire bathes the room in a ruddy glow. I sit alone with my laptop, curiosity driving me to learn more about my new client, Cage La Rouge. With a few keystrokes, his online presence unfolds before me.

A ruggedly handsome man stares back from the screen, brown hair tousled in a way that suggests a familiarity with the outdoors. His eyes, captured in a candid moment, reveal amazing verdant-green eyes that seem to hold stories of their own. I find myself drawn to the way he carries himself in photos—confident, yet not devoid of a certain vulnerability.

The pictures tell a story of a life well-lived, adventures etched into the lines of his face. Cage stands atop majestic peaks, his silhouette against the backdrop of sweeping landscapes. His genuine and unguarded smile hints at a person who cherishes the thrill of exploration. In every picture, he clasps a camera as if it's an extension of him.

As I scroll through more images, I catch glimpses of him navigating dense forests, his expression a mix of determination and awe. Nature is not just a backdrop for him but a canvas on which he paints his experiences. Then, I turn my attention to his impressive portfolio and awards.

The first image to catch my eye is a stunning shot of a black panther, its piercing green eyes gazing directly into the camera. The panther drapes itself over a thick tree limb deep in the Amazon, its dark fur merging into the shadows.

"Wow." Genuine admiration laces my voice.

La Rouge is a phenomenal photographer. The way he captured the panther's gaze makes it feel as if it's staring right into my soul.

Another image gives me pause.

Close to home, it's a breathtaking image of the northern lights. Vibrant hues of swirling green cover the sky and reflect on the dark waters of a lake. The stars are vivid and bright, the sky a canvas of cosmic beauty. At the water's edge is the silhouette of a lone wolf, adding a sense of scale and wildness to the scene.

I pause for one more, a photo of a majestic eagle mid-flight, its wings spread wide against a backdrop of snow-covered mountains. The level of detail is astonishing—every feather is sharply defined, and the eagle's focused gaze as it swoops toward its prey is palpable.

It's as if time stopped for him to capture the moment.

Truly breathtaking.

But there's more to Cage La Rouge than his award-winning photography.

Scores and scores of women fill his personal feed. Clearly, this man is a player, hopping from one bed to the next, which is a shame. Except for that fatal flaw, he might be someone I'd consider dating.

My thoughts linger on the contrast between the untamed beauty of the Alaskan wilderness and the refined ruggedness of Cage's appearance. There's a magnetic quality about him, a blend of adventure and charm that makes me wonder how he'll navigate the challenges ahead of us.

Because there will be challenges.

As I close the laptop, thoughts of the impending adventure swirl in my mind. I perform my nightly ritual of locking down the lodge for the night, then head to bed.

My anticipation lingers as I rise with the dawn. The comforting aroma of fresh coffee and the sizzle of breakfast in the lodge's kitchen bring a smile to my face.

Already up and bustling about, Justin prepares the last meal we'll share with the teens.

In the heart of the lodge, a small corner library beckons, its shelves a treasure trove of Alaskan history, wildlife tales, and survival guides.

A few teens gather there, excitedly flipping through brochures and talking animatedly about their experience. A large, detailed map of the region hangs nearby, becoming a focal point for them to trace their journey.

A reception desk, crafted from polished wood, stands near the entrance to welcome guests. Behind it, my receptionist, Molly, attends to guests' needs and neatly arranges brochures, trail maps, and sign-up sheets for guided tours that await exploration.

I can't help but feel pride in the haven I've created—a place where dreams take flight and adventure begins.

THREE

Ava

Amidst the solitude that follows the farewells to Justin and the teens, I immerse myself in the operational details of my business. While I enjoyed six weeks surrounded by the teens, I miss the quiet solitude of the lodge when we're in between guests.

Suddenly, the lodge's cozy ambiance quivers as the door swings open, unleashing a gust of chilly air that stirs not only the inside, but also the butterflies in my stomach.

In strides Cage La Rouge, a potent force that commands attention. My breath catches as he crosses the threshold, his presence filling the lodge with an undeniable magnetism and virile masculinity. There's an air of confidence about him, a self-assuredness that proclaims his mastery of the untamed.

My gaze lingers as he sheds his jacket, revealing a physique honed by the challenges of the outdoors. The rugged outdoor vest he wears accentuates the broadness of his shoulders and the contours of his chest. There's a quiet strength in how he moves, a savage physicality that suggests a deep connection to the wilderness, hinting at a man who trusts his instincts.

As the lodge's cozy ambiance quivers in response to his arrival, the room shrinks as he strides confidently to the reception desk, each deliberate step asserting his formidable presence. The air changes, responding to the magnetic pull he exudes.

"Cage La Rouge." He confidently approaches Molly, his movements deliberate.

The man is stunning, and I can't help but stare as he runs a hand through his tousled hair.

"I have a reservation," he huffs, "but I need to cancel the guide service. I won't be needing it."

His words cut through the air, breaking the spell of admiration. The declaration lands with a cocky certainty that leaves no room for negotiation.

My initial awe gives way to disappointment.

His rejection of the guide service cements my fears—here's a man who believes he can conquer the wilderness alone, dismissing my expertise.

This doesn't bode well and sets the stage for a clash of wills between the untamed wilderness and a man who sees himself as its master.

Molly glances in my direction, arching a brow. Her expression says it all.

We have one of those again.

I can't help but respond to the silent message in her look. Standing, I approach my client.

"Mr. La Rouge." I offer a polite but firm smile. "In these parts, the wilderness can be unpredictable and dangerous. A guide is strongly recommended."

"And who are you?" He turns to me, his eyes briefly appraising.

"Ava. Ava Livingston." I extend my hand, forcing him to take it. "Your guide. The one you *think* you don't need."

"Ava, is it?" His patronizing tone says it all; my gender is an issue for him. "I'm sure you're skilled, but I don't require babysitting." There's a brief flicker of annoyance, challenging and argumentative in his eyes. "Take some time off."

I hold his gaze, unflinching. "Everyone who ventures out, especially those unfamiliar with these specific terrains, must have a guide. Not to mention, your company requires it. I'm the guide assigned to you."

Cage looks like he's about to argue further, but the set of my jaw and the unwavering tone in my voice seem to give him pause. He exhales sharply, a mix of concession and lingering defiance in his posture.

"Fine," he relents, though his reluctance is palpable. "But I call the shots on my trips. Try not to get in my way."

What a tool.

My fingers curl, nails biting into my palms as I rein in my anger. I'm a professional, and I will act accordingly. However, we play by my rules, not his.

"Of course, within safety guidelines." I recognize the compromise for what it is. The tension in the room is palpable, setting the stage for an uneasy partnership in the vast and unpredictable Alaskan wilderness. "Molly will get you checked into your room. Once you settle in, we can discuss the specifics of your trip."

"Ms. Livingston, I'm more than competent to go alone."

"No doubt about that, but your company…"

"Are assholes. I don't need a guide."

"And yet, you have me." I won't give an inch in this debate.

Rules are rules for a reason, and for some reason, his company cares a whole hell of a lot about his safety. Why else would they pay me triple my going rate to *babysit* a grown-assed man?

After Molly finishes checking Cage La Rouge in, he vanishes into his room, leaving me to the quiet hum of the lodge's nightly routine. I spend the next several hours immersed in bookkeeping tasks, the numbers and figures a stark contrast to the untamed wilderness outside. I also review the calendar for the spring, planning for the re-opening of my guide business after the winter's grip loosens on the land.

As the evening creeps along, the lodge settles into a comfortable silence. I decide to take a moment for myself, settling next to the crackling fireplace with a steaming cup of coffee. The warmth from the flames is a welcome companion, the fire's dance a mesmerizing display of light and shadow.

Just as I begin to relax, Cage reappears. He moves with a quiet confidence, his presence filling the room as he takes a seat across from me at the small table by the fireplace. I keep my expression composed, though I can't help but notice the mix of defiance and amusement in his eyes.

He leans back in his chair, regarding me with a casual yet piercing gaze. Breaking the silence, he speaks first, his voice calm but laced with a hint of challenge.

"Look, I don't mean to make waves, and while I appreciate your concern, I don't need a guide. I've handled far more treacherous terrains than this. Solo-summited more peaks than I can count."

His words, spoken with a blend of assurance and nonchalance, hang in the air between us. They echo the sentiment of many adventurers who have passed through these doors—confident, seasoned, and often underestimating the unpredictable nature of the Alaskan wilderness.

I meet his gaze squarely, my voice steady. "I don't doubt your capabilities, Mr. La Rouge. But the wilderness here is unlike any other. It's not about physical endurance or experience. It's about understanding the land, the weather, and the wildlife in a way that only comes from living here."

Cage shifts slightly in his seat, his expression one of polite skepticism. "I've solo-summitted Everest, Ms. Livingston. I think I can handle a little cold weather and some wildlife." His response comes with a shift in his seat, a hint of impatience and boastfulness edging his tone.

"The Alaskan wilderness has a way of humbling even the most experienced adventurers. It's not a question of if, but when." I can't help but let a small smile break through my professional façade.

He leans back, a mix of defiance and amusement in his eyes. His reluctance to accept guidance in the Alaskan wilderness is nothing new to me; I've dealt with his type before—confident, solitary adventurers who underestimate the land's unpredictability.

"There's nothing out there I haven't faced at one time or another." There's a pause as Cage considers my words, his eyes never leaving mine.

The fire crackles in the background, casting a warm glow over the room. At this moment, the air is thick with tension.

His words hang in the air, a challenge and a dismissal all in one.

I meet his gaze steadily. "Summiting Everest is an impressive feat, but Alaska has unique challenges. The wilderness doesn't care about past conquests, Mr. La Rouge," I reply, my voice steady. "Every journey is different, every trail a new challenge. Respect is earned out there, not assumed."

There's a moment of silence, the crackle of the fire the only sound in the room. Cage's expression shifts, a flicker of something—perhaps respect or realization—crossing his features. The tension between us is tangible, a mix of professional conflict and an unspoken, underlying current of something more.

He smirks, crossing his arms. "And you think you understand the land better than me? Just because you've been playing guide here for a while?"

I resist the urge to react to his patronizing tone. "It's not about playing. It's about respecting the unpredictability of this environment. It's about survival skills, knowledge of the terrain, and experience in handling sudden changes."

Cage leans forward, skepticism clear in his expression. "And you have managed all that? The wilderness doesn't differentiate, but let's be honest, nature can be a bit more challenging for some."

I refuse to yield. "Here, conditions can change in the blink of an eye. Trails disappear under snow, the weather turns deadly, and the wildlife is dangerous. They're the real masters of this land, not to be underestimated."

"I'm aware of that."

I hold back a sigh, familiar with this type of insinuation. "I'm well equipped to be your guide. I've faced and overcome challenges you might not expect. My skills and experience are why I'm sitting here with you now."

He assesses me for a moment, perhaps reconsidering his stance. "I'll take your word for it, but I work best alone. I don't need a guide breathing down my neck."

I smile, just a slight curve of the lips. "I'm not here to hover.

Think of me as your safety net. I'll give you the space you need. My sole job is to ensure you return from your trip in one piece. It's not about limiting your freedom; it's about respecting the force of nature." My gaze locks with his, willing him to understand the gravity of my words.

He doesn't respond immediately, assessing me, perhaps trying to find an angle he can work with, but I don't budge. My resolve is as firm as the mountains outside.

Guiding Cage La Rouge will be as much about navigating his ego as it is about navigating the wilderness.

But I've never backed down from a challenge.

"Fine, you can come; just don't get in my way. Or slow me down. I work best alone and will leave you behind if you can't keep up." He looks out the window, perhaps considering my words or simply unwilling to concede the point.

He'll leave me behind?

Well, I know how to handle arrogant assholes.

"I won't get in your way. Nor will I slow you down. And no matter what happens, I will *never leave you behind*." I can't help but toss his words back at him with that small twist.

This man's arrogance will kill him. Nevertheless, I shake his hand; the deal is sealed.

As our handshake ends, there's a subtle change in the way Cage holds himself. His initial air of condescension seems to falter, replaced by a flicker of curiosity, perhaps even respect.

He studies me momentarily, his eyes narrowing as if reassessing his initial judgment.

"I'll admit," he says, breaking the silence. "I didn't expect you to be so…"

"So, what?" I can't wait to hear what comes next. If I could, I'd cancel this arrogant prick, but I need the money to tide me over until spring.

"Tenacious." His eyes sparkle with amusement.

I feign a smile. He's just blowing smoke up my ass.

Tenacious?

I'll show him tenacious, knock him down a few rungs, and put him in his place.

"The Alaskan wilderness doesn't leave room for anything but tenacity, Mr. La Rouge."

"I'm used to guides who are more—accommodating." Cage chuckles, a sound that breaks some of the ice between us.

"Meaning they let you do what you want?"

"They let me do what I want because I don't need a babysitter."

"As I stated, my role is to guide you, ensure your safety, and bring you back in one piece. You can do whatever you want if it fits within that framework." I maintain a firm yet friendly tone. "As for babysitting you…" I shake my head, already tired of this exchange. "I don't babysit grown men, but I also don't let them speak down to me. Are we going to have a problem?"

There, let's see what he thinks of that.

His gaze drifts to the window, then back to me, still sizing me up, trying to figure out how much control he can exert over this expedition. But there's a new edge of intrigue in his expression, a sign that he's beginning to see me not as an imposition but as someone worthy of his attention, professionally at least.

Personally, I despise his arrogance and elite bravado.

FOUR

Cage

I RISE EARLY IN THE MORNING TO GET IN A RUN AND RETURN
pleasantly winded with my muscles warmed up and my heart
thumping. I stride into the lodge with the crisp Alaskan air clinging
to my jacket. The log cabin lodge could be on a postcard. It's quaint
and reeks of rustic charm.

A far cry from my usual haunts.

I'm here for the thrill of capturing nature's raw beauty through
my lens, but first, there's the matter of dealing with my guide. After
our conversation last night, we're at odds, and I refuse to be side-
tracked by a guide, no matter how competent or unexpectedly captivating she may be.

Ava Livingston.

After our initial meeting last night, she thinks she's in charge.
Today, I'm going to burst that bubble and lay down some ground
rules.

I've heard about her—a legend in these parts. Tough as nails
and with a reputation for dragging city slickers through hell and
back.

Well, I'm no city slicker. A quick glance around the great room reveals no sign of the intriguing beauty, but light spills out of a room off to the side. I approach and place my hand on the warm wood of the door.

The door opens with a soft creak. Inside, Ava Livingston is lost in a world of maps and gear. Leather, pine, and her subtle perfume infuse the room with an oddly captivating scent.

She's a picture of efficiency and rugged beauty. Her hands move over the equipment with the ease of long-term familiarity, tracing routes on the map, checking over the climbing ropes, and inspecting a compact tent. Her outdoor attire, practical and worn, enhances her formidable presence. Her hair, pulled back in a no-nonsense ponytail, frames a face of focused determination, softened only slightly by her femininity.

Her hiking boots, well-worn and reliable, stand next to a backpack equipped for survival. A testament to Ava's expertise is an array of gear arranged neatly on a side table: a well-stocked first-aid kit, a reliable flare gun, robust climbing gear, and a durable sleeping bag.

She doesn't notice me at first, too engrossed in her work. The refined movement of her hands is almost mesmerizing, but then she looks up, and those piercing blue eyes lock onto mine. There's suddenly an electric charge in the air, a mixture of challenge and unspoken attraction I'm reluctant to acknowledge.

She's hot as sin, a fact that doesn't escape me, but there's a sharpness in her gaze—steel beneath the beauty—that tells me my charm won't sway her away from stepping aside as my guide.

I allow my attention to firmly settle on her, taking my time to drink her in and discern why I'm drawn to her.

Bewitched by her.

There's something about her that intrigues me.

Fascinates me.

Tempts me.

Her fiery spirit captivates me the most.

She's a blend of strength and grace, her figure outlined by the rugged attire that speaks of countless journeys through the wild.

This is no delicate, helpless female standing in front of me.

The subtle play of muscles under her shirt is powerful and elegant. It's not just her physical form that's striking; it's how she carries herself with a commanding presence that fills the room.

And yet, she's still wonderfully feminine.

In a nutshell, she captivates me. I'm not used to that. Women come to me. I rarely, if ever, go to them.

In a corner lies my contribution to this expedition—a professional-grade camera rig with a long-range lens. It feels almost alien in this room filled with survival gear, yet it embodies my purpose here.

Her presence is as magnetic as the wilderness, both alluring and formidable, stirring a blend of respect and a reluctant fascination within me. I don't want to be attracted to her. That comes with complications, but those piercing blue eyes radiate fierce intelligence and independence.

How is that *not* sexy?

It's like this woman was made specifically for me.

Her eyes carry a weight that suggests she's seen more of the world than most, and it's not just that. A keenness to her gaze speaks of a mind as formidable as her body.

I find that irresistibly intriguing, but I'm like a little boy with a stick. I can't resist poking her, looking for a reaction.

Any reaction.

"Planning to set up a five-star camp?" I quip, leaning against the doorframe, my usual confidence locked in place.

She barely reacts, just a flicker of annoyance in her eyes. "Just the essentials to survive your company."

Damn, she doesn't miss a beat.

Her voice is steady, her bearing unflappable. I can't help but smirk. This is going to be fun.

Most women melt under my gaze, but Ava… She's different.

A challenge.

And I do love a challenge.

"So, do you always pack like the zombie apocalypse is coming tomorrow?" I saunter closer, curious to see how she'll react.

She turns to face me, arms crossed over her chest.

"Do you always waltz in like you own the place?"

"Touché." I chuckle, amused by her sass.

She's not just a pretty face; there's fire in her, and that flame draws me in despite my better judgment. Women usually come easy to me, a fleeting pleasure, but Ava... She's a puzzle, a mystery I want to solve.

I glance around the room, taking in the neatly arranged gear, the meticulous planning evident in every corner. I've always been a fly-by-the-seat-of-my-pants kind of guy, but Ava's all control and precision.

It's infuriating yet undeniably attractive.

"What's this?" I pick up a harness, examining it skeptically. "In case we stumble upon a vertical cliff?"

"It's called being prepared. You should try it sometime." Her response is quick and sharp.

I smirk, placing the harness back. She's quick; I'll give her that.

And her confidence is—compelling.

It's been a while since I've met someone who didn't immediately fall for my charms. Ava is a breath of fresh air, and I find myself increasingly intrigued and attracted.

What is it about wanting what you can't have that makes things so much fun?

We lean over the map together, and her scent—a mix of pine and something sweet—fills my senses.

"We'll be taking this route." She draws her finger over the map, tracing out a trail.

"That route's for tourists. Where's your sense of adventure?" I tease.

"Right between safety and not getting my client killed," she counters firmly.

Our eyes meet, and there's a spark, an unspoken challenge. Yeah, I'm going to have to work for this one. She's not going to bend easily to my will.

That's fine.

I like a good game of tug-of-war.

We fight over gear for the rest of the morning. I want to travel light, preferring speed over caution. Ava digs in, insisting on thorough preparation.

Her philosophy is rooted in respect for the unpredictable Alaskan wilderness. She moves methodically through the equipment, choosing each piece with a deliberate, practiced eye. Her choices are pragmatic, favoring reliability and safety.

While I argue to pare down our gear to move light and enhance speed, she argues for extra supplies, emergency gear, and contingency plans in flagrant opposition to my impulsive, minimalist approach.

As we debate—some may say argue—she's meticulous, checking and double checking the integrity of every rope, testing each device, ensuring everything is in perfect working order.

Ava's attitude about calculated risks, and her approach to provisioning, speaks to experience.

What I love the most about her is that I'm not sure we're actually having an argument. I mean, I'm arguing and insisting on getting my way, but she's merely humoring me, listening to my words while silently insisting we'll do things her way.

Her attitude is calm, yet firm, as she counters my arguments with logical, well-reasoned points until I give in.

She's not stubborn; she's knowledgeable. A wealth of experience backs her decisions. This frustrates me, as I'm used to making my own decisions, relying more on gut feeling than careful planning.

While I thrive on the adrenaline of the unknown, Ava respects the power of nature. Her approach is a blend of reverence and practicality. She's the embodiment of *preparation meets opportunity*, a lesson in the art of survival against my penchant for seeking thrills and pushing limits.

I'm excited and aroused by our verbal sparring.

Our clash of perspectives becomes a dance of sorts, her methodical planning complementing my desire for speed and efficiency. Ava, grounded and pragmatic, is the complete opposite of my restless, daring spirit.

It's a balance of opposites that, despite my initial resistance, I begin to see as essential for the journey ahead.

We break for lunch, but when I assume we'll be dining together, she surprises me by disappearing.

When I ask Molly, the clerk at the front, where Ava went, she gives me one of those knowing smiles and says Ava's with Justin.

The way Molly says the dude's name makes me hate him instantly. A feral growl rumbles in the back of my throat, but I manage to tamp it down before Molly hears the possessive dominance in my tone.

Don't know where that came from.

I've known Ava for less than a day. She could be married to this 'Justin' with a dozen kids for all I know.

Except I know.

I feel it in my gut.

Ava's not attached.

No way in hell have I misread the tension building between us.

This unexpected break leaves me with nothing to do. I head to my room in the lodge, take a shower, and change into comfortable clothes. With nothing to do, I head outside to explore the small town.

Strolling down the quaint main street, the charm of the old buildings captures my attention. The rustic architecture, marked by time and weather, with their histories etched into the wood, creates a sense of stepping back in time. I soak in the small-town atmosphere, eager to explore.

A cozy diner on the corner emits an inviting aroma of coffee and homemade pie, a reminder of simpler pleasures. The inviting scent draws me in, but before I head in, I spot an elderly gentleman seated outside and angle toward him.

He's deeply engrossed in carving a piece of wood, his hands moving with a skill honed by the years. I approach with a friendly nod, keeping my inquiry casual.

"Good afternoon, beautiful day, isn't it?"

"Every day's a beautiful day up here." The man looks up, his eyes crinkling with wisdom.

"My name's Cage La Rouge." I offer my hand, and the old man pauses his whittling long enough to give a proper shake.

"People around here call me Gramps or Old Man Jenkins." He looks up with a twinkle in his eye.

I take a moment before diving in. "I'm about to head into the wilderness with Ava Livingston. Heard she's the best guide around."

"Ah, Ava." Gramps nods approvingly, his tone warm and friendly. "She knows these lands better than anyone. A real gem. Tough as they come and sharp as a tack. She's as much a part of the wilderness as the pines and the rivers."

"I take it she guides all the time."

"That she does. Word of advice, though… Ava is a lone wolf. Doesn't much care for idle chit-chat or—attachments."

"I figured a woman like her would've been snatched up a long time ago. Hard to believe she's single."

"Single by choice." He almost says more but turns back to his whittling, ending our conversation.

The thing is, I'm not done asking questions about Ava.

"Good to know." Curiosity getting the better of me, I probe further. "You don't come across many female guides."

"Don't worry about Ava. You couldn't be in better hands." He's dismissive but grudgingly answers my questions.

"What's her story?"

"Private. Keeps to herself. Respected by all. Close to few. You know the type." Jenkins chuckles softly. "She's a guiding light for many, but she walks her path alone. Never seen her settle, always moving like the river."

Satisfied with this confirmation of her independence, I thank him and wander toward the diner. In my experience, it's in places like that where the heart of the town beats the strongest.

As I step into the diner, a wave of warmth envelops me, pushing back against the chill of the Alaskan air. The cozy ambiance is immediate—the soft hum of conversation, the gentle clatter of dishes, and the rich aroma of freshly brewed coffee mingling with the scent of home-cooked meals.

The interior is a patchwork of rustic charm: walls adorned with old photographs and local memorabilia, wooden floors worn smooth by countless footsteps, and a long counter lined with stools, each telling its own story.

A small fireplace crackles in one corner, the flames dancing merrily, adding to the room's inviting glow. Around it, a few armchairs and small tables are occupied by locals, their laughter and chatter contributing to the diner's lively pulse.

Martha, the owner, stands behind the counter, a robust woman with a smile as hearty as her cooking. Her presence anchors the room, a maternal figure overseeing this little community hub. She greets me with a warm, welcoming smile, her hands expertly pouring a cup of coffee that she slides across the counter to me.

"Welcome, stranger," she says, her voice rich and friendly. "Where are you from, love? What brings you here?"

I sit at the bar, the stool worn and comfortable beneath me. Around me, the locals engage in animated conversations, a tapestry of stories and laughter. Some sit alone, absorbed in newspapers or books, but still very much a part of the scene.

"I'm from all over these days, but grew up in wine country near Sonoma. I'm headed out with Ava Livingston in a couple of days." I stir my coffee and act nonchalant. "What should I expect? Any advice?"

"Oh, that girl's a gem. Heart as wide as the sky. Expect to be amazed." She wipes her hands on her apron. "Ava's something special."

"I've heard good things. I just wanted to get the scoop before heading out into the bush for a few weeks with a woman I don't know."

"You've got nothing to worry about, honey. Ava's as reliable as the sunrise and as competent as they come, but she's her own person, doesn't let others in easily." Martha cleans the counter. Her smile and the twinkle in her eyes remind me of my mother. "Don't let that scare you. Girl's got a heart of gold." She pours another cup for a regular who introduces himself as Tom and joins our conversation.

"Yeah, Ava's more at home in the mountains and rivers," Tom chimes in. "Her spirit is too wild for any living room, but she's not one for romancing—keeps her heart guarded."

Before Tom can finish his sentence, Martha, with a swift and practiced motion, snaps her towel in his direction. The sharp crack cuts through the air, drawing a few surprised glances from the other patrons.

"Tommy Tuttle," Martha interjects sharply, her voice a mix of reprimand and authority. "Don't be spreading rumors or digging at old wounds." She turns to me, her expression apologetic yet firm. "Ignore him. Tom's the town's gossip, always spreading rumors."

Tom, slightly chastened but undeterred, tries to protest. "Ain't no rumor, Martha…"

But Martha is having none of it. She cuts him off with a look that brooks no argument, her eyes speaking volumes. In that look, there's a stern warning and an unspoken understanding—some stories are better left untold, especially in a small town where everyone knows everyone else's business.

The moment passes quickly, and the diner returns to its usual hum of activity, but the brief exchange leaves an impression. It's clear Martha is more than the owner of this diner; she's a guardian of sorts, protective of her customers and their stories.

As Martha resumes her duties, her movements efficient and practiced, the respect she commands within these walls is palpable. Moments like these reveal the true heart of a place like this—a community bound by unspoken rules and a shared understanding of each other's lives.

"Anything I should know before heading out? Any tips for getting along?"

"She's not one to mix work with anything else." Martha tops off my coffee, and her tone turns protective of Ava.

Her words confirm what I suspect. Ava's a woman of substance, respected and admired, yet fiercely independent. My respect for her grows, mingling with my initial intrigue. I finish my coffee, my mind buzzing with growing interest in Ava.

Maybe too much interest.

I whittle away the hours, getting to know the town and the people who live there, digging for as much information as I can. Ava Livingston is an enigma, a challenge that excites me more than I care to admit.

FIVE

Cage

———————

Later that night, back at the lodge, I settle into the warmth of a roaring fire in the fireplace. It beats back the biting chill of an Alaskan evening while I sink into the comfort of a leather seat.

Soft light spills from rustic fixtures overhead, casting a golden glow over the wooden tables and stone fireplace. The crackling fire adds a comforting soundtrack to the homey atmosphere.

It's the end of the season, which means it's just Ava and me. The other guests departed sometime during the day, leaving us in what would normally be considered a romantic setting.

Ava sits across from me. Firelight dances across her features, enhancing the natural beauty of her face. She changed from her rugged outdoor gear into soft flannel that hints at the gentle curves beneath.

Curves I'm eager to explore.

Her long, brunette hair cascades freely over her shoulders in a shimmer of copper and gold, framing her face in a way that accentuates her intelligent eyes.

Those eyes, reflecting the fire's flicker, are as captivating as they are unreadable.

Her confidence and composed manner reveal an underlying strength that draws me in like a moth to the flame. Exuding a sense of self-assuredness, she's a woman completely in tune with herself and her surroundings. Her presence is commanding, yet there's an easiness about her, a hint of a free spirit that's as intriguing as the untamed landscapes she navigates.

The tension between Ava and me is tangible. A charged current hums in the background. I shift in my seat, trying to find a way to engage her and break through the palpable barrier that her composed demeanor presents.

"So, Ava," I start, watching the flames dance and flicker. "Ever had any close encounters?" The moment the words leave my mouth, my lips twist in a grimace.

Totally not smooth.

I sound like a player spouting cringe-worthy pickup lines.

"Close encounters?" Her eyes sparkle in the firelight. "If you're asking about aliens, sad to say, they leave us alone up here."

"Ha-ha." I lean back, awed by how she makes me speechless. I'm never one at a loss for words. "Come on, you must have a story to share."

She looks into the fire, her face illuminated by its glow. "The wildlife here is as diverse as the landscape. From wolves to eagles, to caribou, moose, and bears, every creature is a part of the ecosystem, but if you respect their domain, you avoid any close encounters."

"I'm calling bullshit. You head out into that wilderness enough times, you're bound to come across something. Come on, Ava, throw me a bone. You've got to have a story or two."

"Fair enough." A smile touches her lips, a hint of adventure sparkling in her eyes. "Once, I was tracking a wolf pack for days. Ended up witnessing an alpha showdown. Nature's raw power is something to behold."

"That sounds incredible." I lean forward, captivated. "That's the kind of shot I'm looking for out there. Nothing like capturing those moments on camera."

"You must have seen some remarkable things through your

lens." She turns to look at me, her gaze assessing. "What's the most unforgettable?"

"Summiting Everest was surreal." I pause, sifting through memories. "Watching the sunrise from the top of the world—it's a humbling experience."

"I imagine it's a different world up there." Ava nods, her expression showing a hint of admiration.

"This place has a beauty you won't find anywhere else."

"What are you planning on photographing here?" Her curiosity about my life's passion gives me hope she may also be curious about me.

"Don't really know."

"Don't know." She leans back, confused and frustrated—almost annoyed by my non-answer. "How can you *not* know? Aren't you doing a spread for a magazine?"

"My editor and I have an understanding, and fortunately, my work speaks for itself. They want me to bring back a story of Alaska. How that will shape up in front of the lens, I won't know until inspiration strikes."

"Wow, they must place a lot of trust in you."

"I've worked hard over the years to earn their trust. My work isn't the same when given an assignment. We've learned that over the years."

"So now they send you out on expeditions with no idea what you'll bring back?"

"Pretty much."

"What does that mean for us? Do you have a specific route or goal in mind?"

"Not really."

"Hmm…" She turns away from me, staring into the fire, with her brows tugged tight together, obviously deep in thought.

With a bit of prodding, our conversation finally begins to flow. We meander from topic to topic, gentle probes that reveal little until the topic shifts seamlessly to small-town quirks.

"I had lunch at the diner. Got to meet some of the locals."

"Then you met Martha. She's amazing but can't help mothering all of us."

"I can see that." I tell her about meeting Gramps and Tom Tuttle and Ava finally begins to open up.

"That's our town," Ava responds with a laugh. "The diner's the local meeting spot where all the good news is shared and the best gossip."

"Martha runs a tight ship."

"Martha's a local legend. She knows everything about everyone." Ava's laughter rings out, warm and genuine. "Just don't believe all her stories."

Our conversation is a stimulating mix of banter and insight, a verbal sparring that keeps me on my toes. Ava's wit is as sharp as her survival skills, her responses laced with a dry humor that challenges and entertains in equal measure.

As we talk, the initial tension begins to ease. It's a dance of words, each of us parrying and advancing, a mutual exploration that's as much about understanding each other as it is about the conversation itself.

I find myself more engaged than I've been in a long time, drawn in by the combination of her striking beauty, keen intellect, and the enigmatic aura that surrounds her.

As the fire crackles along, casting a warm glow inside the lodge, Ava's gaze locks onto mine. There's a playful edge in her eyes, a flicker of amusement that makes me both wary and intrigued.

"You know, it is a small town," she starts, her tone light yet pointed.

"Yes, noticed that with the one main street in town." I can't resist the bait because there's a punchline coming. "Why?"

"Word gets around, especially when a newcomer starts asking questions about me." Her smile widens just a fraction.

"How did you know?" Caught off guard, I try to play it cool.

"Old Man Jenkins and Martha are practically town criers," she replies with a knowing look. "But if you wanted to know more about me, you could've just asked." The slyness of her smile hints at a challenge.

I lean back, a mix of admiration and curiosity stirring within me. "Alright then," I say, meeting her challenge head-on. "Tell me about Ava Livingston. What's her story?"

"Well, for starters…" Ava leans back slightly; the fire creates a play of light and shadow on her face. Her eyes hold a hint of amusement as she processes my words. "I'm not an open book for the casual reader."

"I have to earn the privilege of your story?" I raise an eyebrow, intrigued by her metaphor. "And who says my interest is casual? We're getting ready to spend weeks together in the wilderness. I like to know the person I'm going to be with."

She regards me thoughtfully, a small smile playing on her lips. "Getting to know someone isn't about asking others about them. It's about sharing experiences and facing challenges together. Trust is earned, Cage, not given because you're curious."

Her response strikes a chord in me. It's not a rebuke but a reminder of the depth and complexity of human connections.

"Fair enough. But isn't curiosity the beginning of understanding? I was curious about you, so I asked about you. Nothing wrong with that."

"I don't share my life story with people I don't know, especially not with charming photographers."

"Well, at least that's settled."

"What?"

"You think I'm charming." My tone's smug on purpose.

Her smile broadens subtly. The air between us is charged with an electric mix of tension and playfulness.

"Maybe," she concedes, her voice softening just a tad. "But don't let it go to your head. You're also cocky, arrogant, and dismissive."

"Perhaps. But you said I was charming. Can't take that back."

"I regretted saying that the moment the words tumbled out of my mouth."

Her wit is as sharp as any mountain peak I've climbed, and her laughter, when it finally breaks through, is like music.

I can't help but feel a sense of victory. I managed to crack her composed exterior, if only for a moment.

The conversation flows effortlessly, a dance of words that weaves between teasing and testing.

It's clear that Ava is more than just a guide or a local; she's a force in her own right, a woman of depth and complexity. As we continue our verbal sparring, the connection between us grows, a mutual recognition of the challenge and attraction that lies beneath our banter.

"Come on, surely I've earned one or two tidbits about your life." I lean in, hoping for a morsel from this captivating woman. "We're getting ready to spend several weeks alone in the wilderness together. I don't want to start on the wrong foot."

"You did that when you dismissed me the moment you stepped foot in my lodge."

"That's because I'm a cocky, arrogant, and dismissive fool, but you also said I was charming. Give me a chance to change your opinion of me."

"A chance?"

"Yes, give me one little tidbit about you."

Hopefully, I haven't made such a poor first impression that she'll never open up for me.

Time to lean into the ole' La Rouge triplet charm.

"I've lived here all my life." Ava's expression softens as she speaks. "Grew up exploring these mountains and forests. They're a part of me. I'm passionate about preserving the untouched wilderness and showing others its beauty while teaching them to respect it." Her eyes light up as she talks about her home, her love for the wilderness evident in every word.

"And guiding? How did that start?"

For a moment, a shadow falls over her features, there and gone before I can question whether I saw it at all.

"I guide because I want people to experience this place as I do, see it the way I see it, and understand why it needs to be protected."

"And outside of guiding?" I nod, impressed. "Is there someone special in your life?"

"My personal life is personal. And this is professional." Her bearing shifts, the openness replaced by a guarded expression. "I'm here as your guide. I'm not an open book." Her firm tone leaves no room for further probing.

She might share her knowledge and passion for the wilderness, but her personal life is her own, a boundary she's unwilling to cross.

This only adds to the complexity of the woman sitting across from me, a puzzle that's both intriguing and frustrating.

It means I'm going to get myself into trouble because I grow more and more fascinated with the complex woman sitting before me.

I want to know more.

"Come on, Ava." Undeterred, I lean forward, my tone light yet persistent. "Surely, knowing a bit about each other's personal lives is fair game."

"Is that so? Then let's start with you." She eyes me warily, her defenses still up. "Tell me about your life outside of being a world-renowned wilderness photographer."

"Fair enough." I chuckle, not expecting the turn of tables. "I'm the youngest of three. My family owns a winery in California, run by my brother Asher. My other brother, Brody, is a venture capitalist. As for me, I took a different path. The wild called to me, and I answered."

"A winery? And a venture capitalist?" Ava's expression changes slightly, a hint of surprise flickering in her eyes. She's realizing what everyone eventually finds out, not that it's a big secret.

I come from a very wealthy family.

"Wine is my brother's passion. He's also a hot-shot firefighter." I nod, unbothered by her realization. "I've always been more interested in capturing nature's beauty and tackling its challenges. Photography and mountaineering are my passions."

"That's quite impressive." Ava takes a moment to process this, her gaze thoughtful. "But what drove you from wine to wildlife photography?"

Her question, genuine and curious, shifts the dynamic between us. It's no longer a game of evasion but a sharing of passions and pursuits. I find myself opening up about my journey, the lure of the wild, and the drive to immortalize its untamed beauty through my lens.

"It started as a way to escape. All three of us inherited the vineyard from our father, but three's a crowd when it comes to business. Brody and I are more like silent partners. We let Asher run the show. Brody made some pretty good investments, and those led to other, more successful ventures. Now he spends his time investing in tech startups. I wanted to carve my own path."

I lean back, willing to open up about my past to this amazing woman. "I've always had a connection with nature, a need to capture its untold stories and fleeting moments."

"I've seen some of your photographs. Stunning work."

"Ava Livingston, have you been checking me out?" A thrill runs through me, imagining her interest in my life.

"Not you, but your work. Before you spin that into something it's not, I routinely check out all my clients." She leans back. "You're clearly passionate about your art, and I get the impression it's more than just the photography."

I pause, choosing my words carefully. "It's the thrill of the climb, the rush of pitting myself against nature. Against myself. I honed my survival skills and learned to read the land and the weather. In a way, my experiences," I gesture vaguely toward the wilderness, "are not so different from yours. It's about respecting the environment and understanding it. Probably why my survival skills rival yours."

Ava's eyes narrow slightly, the playful glint replaced by a flicker of irritation. She leans forward, her tone even but firm.

"It's not about who's better. There's no competition about whose skill rivals whose. It's about experience. Not general experience but experience specific to *this* place. When it comes to the wilderness in my backyard, there's no one more experienced than me." Her words carry a weight of confidence, a testament to her years navigating these terrains, but dammit if I didn't step wrong again.

She's pissed.

"Surviving out here, in these mountains," she continues, her voice steady, "is knowledge passed down through generations, understanding subtle cues that nature provides. Knowing when a storm will blow in by smelling the air and watching the animals. It's a way of life. You may have more experience cresting summits. Your survival skills may or may not rival mine, but that's where it ends."

My cocky words shift the tone of our conversation, disrupted by my careless comment challenging her expertise. Ava's walls, which started to come down, are now back up, higher than ever.

Her gaze holds mine, a silent assertion of her authority.

"Fair enough," I acknowledge her point. "I have no doubt about your skills, and I wasn't questioning them. I'm looking forward to learning from you."

The tension eases slightly, her posture relaxing as she recognizes my respect for her experience. Our conversation, though momentarily veering into a contest of skills, finds its way back to a mutual understanding and an anticipation for the journey ahead.

A playful smirk crosses my face. "Every mountain, every expedition teaches me something new, not just about photography, but about living in harmony with the wild. It's a never-ending journey, one that's taken me to some of the most remote corners of the world. Now, it's brought me to your corner of the world. All I was saying, what I meant to say, is that I know what I'm doing."

"Yeah, definitely got that message loud and clear, but your editor hired me to guide you. Maybe they know something you don't."

"And what's that?" I watch Ava's reaction closely. Her interest in me remains despite the callousness of my words.

I find that fascinating.

"Arrogance kills."

"It's not arrogance if it's true. All I'm saying is I know what I'm doing. Don't get twisted because I speak the truth."

"Whatever." The way her eyes roll tells me all I need to know. Yet again, I stuck my foot in my mouth. Not that I'm taking any of it back.

It's the truth.

"Look, you can call me an arrogant prick all you want. I'm just saying it as it is. I would think you'd want to know about my abilities before heading out together. Isn't that your job?"

"My job?"

"To assess my strengths and weaknesses and adjust for them? Cocky, arrogant, or dismissive, I'd think you'd want to know."

"Look…" She lifts her hand, palm facing me, but not looking for a high-five. "It's not worth arguing over something stupid. Your experience is extensive, and I acknowledge that. Yes, it helps me cater to your needs. We've got a lot of time to spend together, and I'd rather not do that bickering with each other the entire time. So, could we please focus on something else?"

"Certainly, and I'm sorry for being a prick. What would you like to focus on?"

Ava's expression softens slightly. Her eyes reflect the flickering firelight, creating an almost ethereal glow around her. The momentary flare of defensiveness fades, replaced by a more thoughtful, contemplative look.

Her gaze lingers on the flames, her thoughts seemingly dancing with the firelight. After a moment, she turns to me, her curiosity evident.

"What are you hoping to capture on this trip? Any specific wildlife shots you're after? If I know what you're hoping for, I can tailor our trip to accomplish it."

"Well, there's the usual suspects—bears, eagles, maybe even a moose if we're lucky." I lean back, considering her question. "But sometimes, it's the unexpected encounters that make the best shots. Like your alpha showdown story—moments of raw, untamed nature."

"Any particular scene you're envisioning?" Ava nods, her interest piqued.

"I'm hoping for something unique," I reply, my mind running through potential images. "Maybe a pack of wolves navigating the fresh snow, leaving trails that tell a story of survival. Or a lone caribou silhouetted against the vast, untouched landscape, a testament to the solitude of the wild."

"Sounds like you don't just take photos; you capture the soul of nature." She smiles, clearly appreciating the imagery.

"That's the idea," I agree. "But the thing about wildlife photography is that you can't always plan your shots. You have to be ready for whatever the wilderness offers, like that moment when the morning mist lifts, revealing a herd of elk grazing in the valley. It's about being in the right place at the right time. Every picture has a story behind it, a piece of the wilderness that I want to share with the world."

The distance between us seems to shrink, bridging not just our shared love for the wilderness but also our approach to experiencing it. The tension from our earlier disagreement slowly fades.

Ava's knowledge of the land and the creatures who live on it, combined with my desire to capture its essence through my lens, reveals a shared passion that drives us both.

We may have more in common than I originally thought.

"That's the beauty of the wild," she muses, her tone softer now. "It teaches us and changes us in ways we never expect. I'm not here to hold you back. My entire goal is to take you where you want to go and bring you back in one piece. Other than that, you're free to go where you will and take the photos your artistic heart desires."

"And I can't think of a better guide to explore it with." The warmth returns to our exchange. I lean in, my voice lowering. "How about a fresh start?"

I hold out my hand, hoping she'll take it.

My words have an underlying current, a subtle acknowledgment of the connection that's slowly forming between us.

Her eyes meet mine, and for a moment, there's a flicker of something more—a shared recognition of the unspoken attraction simmering beneath our professional façade.

"To a fresh start." Her smile is faint, but it reaches her eyes, softening their usual intensity.

She takes my hand, and we shake on it.

"You're in for quite an adventure, Cage La Rouge." She releases some of the tension in her body, finally beginning to relax a little around me. "These mountains have a way of revealing truths about the world and about ourselves."

As we talk, the space around us seems to shrink, the rest of the lodge fading into the background. It's in this flickering light of the fire that our journey truly begins—not through the wild, but through the uncharted territory of whatever is brewing between us.

As Ava speaks, her words weave tales of the mountains and the wilderness, and I'm increasingly drawn to her.

It's not just her knowledge of the wild that captivates me; it's the way her eyes light up when she talks about it and the way her hands paint pictures in the air. There's a passion in her, a fire that seems to match the intensity of the flames flickering in the hearth.

These few weeks with Ava might turn into the best time of my life.

I'm excited, not just for the rugged terrain and the challenges it will present, but the thought of us alone in the vast Alaskan wilderness thrills me.

It's an opportunity to see Ava in her element, witness her skills and knowledge firsthand, and perhaps understand the depths of her character.

I'm intrigued by her, with how she blends strength and softness and how her independence doesn't mask the warmth that occasionally shines through her guarded exterior.

A part of me wonders how our dynamic will evolve. The thought of long days spent trekking through uncharted territory and evenings spent by the fire, just the two of us, offers endless possibilities.

I catch myself staring, lost in thoughts of what lies ahead, and I smile.

Ava, noticing, raises an eyebrow in question. I shake my head slightly, a promise to myself to take this journey one step at a time and savor each moment.

"Here's to the adventure ahead," I raise my glass, toasting the unknown, the wild, and perhaps the possibility of something more between us.

"To an adventure." Ava mirrors my action, her glass chiming against mine; her smile, followed by a shake of her head, says she knows exactly what's going through my head, and it's never going to happen.

Well, game on Miss Ava Livingston.

SIX

Cage

______

Early the next morning, the atmosphere in the lodge feels charged, and the previous night's tension dissipates. Outside, the distant call of an eagle echoes. Inside, sunlight streams through the windows, making specks of dust dance in the air.

Ava and I stand over a large, intricately detailed map of the Alaskan wilderness spread across a rustic wooden table. As I point out a potential route, my hand brushes against hers, and a current zips through me, unexpected and electrifying. It's been a long time since anyone's gotten under my skin like this.

"Focus, La Rouge. The wilderness isn't kind to daydreamers." She pulls her hand away quickly, but not before a flush creeps into her cheeks, betraying her composed exterior.

"Who's daydreaming? I'm fully awake." I try to regain my composure, but the truth is, I'm more awake than I've been in years.

Ava has that effect on me, sharpening my senses more than the brisk morning air. Leaning in close, I can't resist the urge to challenge the woman who's been occupying my thoughts since the moment we met.

"How about we take a break?"

"A break? We still have a lot to plan."

"Yeah, but we've been at it for hours. How about a test of those survival skills you're so proud of?" I lean in close, a mock challenge in my eyes. I'm curious to see if she's as good as her reputation claims.

"You want to test me?"

"Sure." I shove my hands deep into my pockets and rock back on my heels. "Nothing too much, just something to get the blood flowing."

"The blood flowing?" She arches a brow but accepts with a confidence that's both infuriating and attractive. "Ready to eat your words?" Ava meets my gaze, her confidence unshaken—a spark of challenge ignites in the fiery, blue depths of her eyes.

"I prefer my meals with a little more spice." I can't help the smirk that plays on my lips.

The playful banter comes naturally, countering the tension building between us. She rolls her eyes, but her expression has a playful undertone.

"What do you have in mind, hot shot?"

"How about a fire-making competition?" A mischievous grin spreads across my face. "Old school style—no lighters or matches."

"You sure you're ready to lose?" Ava glances at me, a skeptical eyebrow raised.

"Oh, I'm ready," I retort with a playful smirk. "Just don't be too hard on yourself when I win."

We head outside, and the crisp morning air hits us like a splash of cold water, instantly invigorating.

The ground is a mosaic of autumn leaves and pine needles, and the forest surrounding us is a symphony of greens and browns.

The land feels alive, almost as if it's holding its breath in anticipation. Ava and I stand in a clearing, the sun casting dappled shadows through the tall pine trees. I take a deep breath, inhaling the scent of earth and pine.

"Let's set up here." Ava points to a spot where the morning sun filters through the canopy, creating a patchwork of light and shadow.

We choose a clearing, the ground flat and open, perfect for our challenge.

We split up to gather our materials. I head toward a cluster of birch trees, collecting dry moss and fine wood shavings, confident in my choice of the flint and steel method. I feel Ava's eyes on me, her gaze analytical, perhaps even slightly amused.

"Hope you're not getting cold feet over there," I call out to her, my tone teasing.

"Just focusing on winning. You should try it sometime." Ava, busy selecting the perfect softwood for her fireboard and spindle, replies without looking up.

I can't help but laugh. Her confidence is both infuriating and incredibly attractive. I return to the clearing with my arms full of tinder, ready for the challenge.

Ava joins me shortly after, her equipment for the bow drill method meticulously organized. She looks prepared, her expression one of calm determination.

"I hope you're ready to be humbled, La Rouge." Ava arranges her fireboard and spindle with precise movements, and a hint of a challenge rises in her voice.

"I was born ready." I can't help but watch her; her hair catching the sunlight creates a halo effect. Her focus and confidence are mesmerizing.

"We'll see about that."

"How about a little wager to make things interesting?" I propose, the excitement of the challenge adding a spark to my voice.

"What kind of wager?" Ava pauses, her hands stilling over her fire-making setup. Her expression is a blend of curiosity and guardedness.

"If I win, I get a kiss." The words leave my lips before I can second-guess them, my grin widening with the thrill of the challenge.

Ava's reaction is immediate and complex. At first, there's a flash of interest, a hint of a smile tugging at her lips, but as quickly as it appears, it's replaced by a shuttered expression, her eyes narrowing.

"You're that confident, huh?" Her voice is edgy, a blend of amusement and offense. "Would you make the same wager if I were a man?"

Laughing off her retort, I lean against a nearby tree, my stance relaxed. "If you were a man, Ava, I assure you, I wouldn't be interested in kissing you."

"Fine, I accept your wager. If I win, however…" A mischievous spark lights up her eyes, "You'll have to do something for me that's a bit—out of your element."

"And what would that be?" I'm intrigued yet apprehensive.

She thinks for a moment, then smirks. "If I win, you'll have to sing a song of my choosing at the diner tonight. In front of everyone."

"Sing? You realize I'm a photographer, not a performer, right?" I balk at the thought of singing in public, but I've got an ace up my sleeve.

"Scared of a little spotlight, La Rouge?" she teases, her eyes dancing with mirth.

"Fine, but when I win, remember you agreed to this." I sigh, realizing that backing down isn't an option. "And I'm not talking a quick peck on the lips. I'm going all in."

"All in?" Ava nods, a satisfied grin on her face. "Better be prepared to go all in with your singing."

The woman is fabulous. I love her tenacity.

"Deal." The word leaves my lips with a mix of excitement and apprehension.

I extend my hand toward Ava, the challenge set, the stakes higher than ever. As I wait, there's an eagerness in me, an anticipation not entirely about the bet.

Ava looks at my outstretched hand, a hint of a smile playing on her lips. She reaches out, her hand sliding into mine, and the moment our skin touches, a jolt of electricity courses through me.

It's a simple handshake, but it feels like so much more.

Her hand is strong. Confident. The grip is firm yet not overpowering.

Her calloused hands are a testament to her life outdoors, a stark contrast to the softness of her smile. My heart beats a little faster, and my palm tingles where her skin meets mine. It's a sensation that's both new and exhilarating, stirring something within me that I hadn't anticipated.

As we shake hands, our eyes lock, and there's an unspoken acknowledgment of the tension between us. Her eyes are piercing, a deep blue that seems to see right through me, challenging yet playful. I find myself not wanting to let go, wanting to hold on to this connection, this electric charge that's buzzing between us.

Finally, we release our hands, but the energy remains, hanging in the air like an unsaid promise. I'm left with a lingering warmth and a curiosity beyond our playful banter. In the short time since I met her, Ava has gotten under my skin in a way no one else has, her touch igniting an interest that's about more than just the thrill of the challenge.

"Cage…" Ava takes a step back, her cheeks somehow flushed again.

"Yes?"

"Better prepare your vocal cords; I'll be picking a real crowd-pleaser."

"I'm not planning on losing our bet."

"The cocky ones never do." She pivots sharply and takes a look around us. "Shall we begin?"

The challenge is set, and the stakes are higher than before. As we continue with our fire-making task, I can't help but feel a twinge of nervousness at the prospect of singing in front of a crowd.

Ava, on the other hand, seems more focused than ever, perhaps already imagining her victory and my impending performance. The air is thick with competition, but underneath it all, there's a sense of playfulness, a connection that's growing stronger with each shared glance and quip.

The banter continues as we prepare our fire-making stations, the air between us charged by friendly competition and an undeniable undercurrent of attraction.

I strike my flint, focusing on the sparks. "Just be gentle with me when you brag about your victory."

Ava, methodically working her bow drill, doesn't look up. "Oh, I'll be sure to be very gracious in my victory. You, on the other hand, will have to live with the knowledge a girl bested you."

"A girl I'm eager to kiss."

"You have to win the bet, Cage La Rouge, and I don't see that happening anytime soon."

The teasing continues, each of us throwing playful jabs at the other. The tension builds not from the competition but from the unspoken possibilities that lie beyond it.

As we focus on our respective tasks, I'm increasingly captivated by how she seamlessly blends strength and grace.

She's a puzzle, one that I'm finding increasingly intriguing. I strike my flint against the steel. Sparks fly teasingly close to igniting the tinder.

"Just don't fall too hard for me when I win and take that kiss," I quip, glancing over at her.

"Keep dreaming," she fires back, her bow drill moving in a steady rhythm. "You might need those dreams to keep you warm tonight."

The forest clearing becomes our arena, the morning sun casting long shadows over the ground strewn with autumn leaves.

Ava, with the composed focus of a seasoned outdoorswoman, works her bow drill. Her setup is meticulous: she chooses a piece of softwood for her fireboard, carefully carving a precise notch in the center. She selects a sturdy yet flexible branch for her bow, attaching a cord from her survival kit. Each element is chosen carefully, reflecting her deep knowledge and respect for the craft.

Her movements are the seamless perfection of efficiency and skill. She positions herself comfortably, her foot firmly on the fireboard to hold it in place. Her left hand steadies the top of the spindle while her right hand works the bow back and forth with a rhythmic, fluid motion. The bowstring wraps around the spindle, creating tension and friction as she moves. The wood begins to speak, a soft whispering sound that promises the birth of fire.

Gradually, wisps of smoke rise from the fireboard, curling up into the crisp morning air. Ava's concentration is unwavering, and her breathing is controlled as she meticulously nurtures the growing heat.

A small pile of fine, powdery wood dust accumulates in the notch, turning darker as the friction increases. Then, like magic, a tiny ember glows amidst the dust, a flicker of life born from her relentless effort.

Meanwhile, I struggle with my flint. I strike the steel against the flint, aiming for the bundle of dry moss and fine wood shavings I've gathered. Sparks leap from the collision, bright and ephemeral, but they dance away from the tinder as if playing a cruel game of keep-away.

I adjust my angle and strike harder, more desperately, but the sparks remain elusive, teasingly close to igniting the tinder, yet always just out of reach.

I glance at Ava, who is now gently blowing on her ember, coaxing it into a larger flame. Her eyes are bright with the thrill of success. The ember catches the tinder, and a small flame springs to life, growing steadily as she feeds it more wood.

My fire, however, is still stubbornly nonexistent. The flint feels rough and cold in my hands, and my strikes are becoming more erratic as I try to match Ava's success. The irony isn't lost on me—here I am, a man who's conquered mountains, struggling to light a simple fire.

The contrast between us couldn't be more stark: Ava, calm and methodical, a master of her environment, and me, increasingly flustered, fighting against nature rather than working with it.

It's a humbling realization, one that deepens my admiration for Ava and the skills she possesses. Her victory in our little competition is undeniable, but it feels like more than just a win against me. It's a testament to her connection with the wilderness, a bond I'm only beginning to understand and appreciate.

"You know, if you need tips on fire-making, I'm sure I could give you a few pointers," Ava says, a playful glint in her eye as she gently blows on her flame, nurturing it with tiny sticks as it grows.

"I'll keep that in mind." My frustration mounts as I strike the flint harder, but my tinder refuses to ignite. "You just got lucky."

"Or maybe—it's skill," she retorts, her focus unbroken.

Finally, a spark catches in my tinder, and a small flame flickers to life. I look up triumphantly, only to see her fire already well-established.

She nurtures a steady flame, feeding small branches now, letting her fire grow into a real blaze. Ava looks up, her eyes meeting mine, a triumphant glimmer in them. She stands, brushing off her hands, a look of satisfaction on her face.

"Skill always wins over luck."

"I guess I owe you one," I concede, my respect for her growing. I can't help but admire her and the way she took on the challenge with such poise and expertise. "I underestimated you."

"That's not the first time, but hopefully, it'll be the last. Don't let this—" she gestures to her body, "confuse you. I may be a woman, but I'm a master of my craft."

The air between us crackles with a tension that's more than just competitive. I'm drawn to her, not just by her beauty but by her strength, skill, and sheer presence.

It's a pull that's becoming harder to resist.

I can't shake the feeling that this bet, though lost, has opened a door, a chance to explore the connection that's undeniably growing between us. Ava may have won the challenge, but the game, it seems, is far from over.

"If you're done measuring dicks, how about we head inside and plan our expedition?" She gestures back to the lodge.

Ava's sharp words, laced with a confidence that borders on arrogance, catch me off guard. There's a moment when I'm rendered speechless, her directness leaving me momentarily disarmed. The way she stands there, victorious not just over the fire but seemingly over the situation, leaves me puzzled and oddly more attracted to her.

Insanely attracted.

Her challenge—*"If you're done measuring dicks"*—hits me with a mixture of surprise and amusement. It's not just the words but the way she says them, with a no-nonsense directness that's as refreshing as it is disconcerting. Her ability to keep me on my toes only heightens the intrigue.

"One thing you'll learn about me, Cage La Rouge, is that I win because I plan, and I never take a bet unless I'm going to win. Preparation beats chance every single time." Her words ring with truth, a reminder of the skill and foresight she's demonstrated.

I watch her, a mix of respect and a budding sense of challenge stirring within me. "Now, put out my fire and meet me back inside," she commands, nodding toward the lodge. "We've got a lot to plan before we leave in the morning."

As she walks away, her stride confident and purposeful, I'm left standing there, looking at the small fire she so skillfully created. I can't help but smile despite my bruised ego. Ava Livingston is a puzzle, a series of contradictions that blend into a compelling and captivating whole.

I follow her instructions, dousing the flames carefully, ensuring no embers remain. Her words echo in my mind, a challenge and a promise all wrapped up in one. Anticipation of what's to come, the hunt for Ava's affection, fills me with an excitement I haven't felt in a long time.

SEVEN

Cage

As a self-confessed player, I typically find women a pleasure, not a challenge. As I watch Ava move with grace and confidence that's as compelling as it is infuriating, I can't help but feel that the game has changed this time.

And I'm not prepared.

The planning sessions for our expedition are intense. We argue over every detail, tension rising with each word. Every heated glance intensifies the undeniable pull growing between us.

It's quickly becoming a magnetic force that's increasingly hard to ignore. Ava is unyielding in her approach, and her knowledge of the wilderness is evident in every word she speaks. I find myself grudgingly respecting her, even as I push back against her control.

The air between us crackles with tension, a blend of professional conflict and unspoken attraction. I can't remember the last time I've felt this alive, this engaged.

It's as if Ava has woken something in me, something I didn't know was asleep.

She challenges everything I thought I knew about women.

She's fierce.

She's a fighter.

She's unstoppable.

She's so fucking sexy.

We argue over routes, gear, and tactics. With each word, each glance, the space between us seems to shrink. There's heat, explosive energy, and an undeniable pull that I'm finding harder and harder to ignore.

I don't do complicated.

I don't do entanglements.

But I want more of this incredible woman.

It's become increasingly harder to remind myself I'm here for the beauty of the wild and not Ava Livingston. Yet, as I sit across from her, watching her argue her point with a passion that matches my own, I can't help but feel that maybe, just maybe, I've found something worth chasing after all.

It's going to be fun unraveling the mystery that is Ava.

Hunched over the map, our discussion shifts to gear, a critical part of our upcoming venture. I point to the list I've made.

"We should travel light. Speed over everything." I detest lugging excessive gear. My photography equipment is burden enough.

Ava looks up from the map, her expression a mix of amusement and exasperation. "Being underprepared is not an option. This is Alaska, not a walk in the park."

"Never said it was, but I didn't take this much gear on my ascent up Everest. I think we can ditch a thing or two. Besides, I don't like the route you picked."

"Why?" She huffs out another breath of frustration.

"That route is too well traveled."

Ava looks up from the map, a hint of triumph in her eyes. "I told you. I know these mountains like the back of my hand. If you want to go here, we must travel this path." She points stubbornly at the map.

"All the hikers scare off all the wildlife and push them from the trail. I have no chance of getting any shots if we go that way. When it comes to photography, I know what works best, and it's not by traveling well-known trails. We must go overland."

"That's more risk than I'm willing to allow."

"Look, Ava, I'm not one of your juvenile delinquents who knows nothing about survival in the wilderness. We're both highly skilled. It should be a walk in the park for the two of us, but the presence of humans pollutes that route," I argue, pointing to a trail on the map.

"Predictable can save your life out here." She leans in, her breath a whisper away. "And with winter on our heels, a snap storm overland may be the last storm you see. We stick to the trail."

I hold her gaze, the air crackling between us. There's a vibrancy in this exchange I haven't felt in a very long time. Ava has ignited something within me, a spark that's been dormant for far too long.

"Fine. We stick to your route, but there's preparedness, and then there's over-preparedness." I lean back, crossing my arms, trying to appear nonchalant. "We'll need pack mules to take everything you want."

"I know these mountains." She glances up from the map, a hint of irritation in her eyes. "I'd rather be prepared than get caught out there without the gear I need to bring your sorry ass home." Her voice is firm, leaving no room for argument.

"Then how about ditching these? Keeps our load lighter." I pick up two compact, single tents from the pile. "A double tent is sturdier, more heat efficient."

"It's also bulkier and heavier than the singles. Not to mention, there's no backup if we lose one. With those," she points to the single tents, "if we lose one, we have a backup. Trust me, you don't want to go without shelter out there."

"Close quarters might not be so bad." I hold up the double tent, a glint of mischief in my eyes.

"In your dreams, La Rouge." She places the double tent back on the shelf, her smile reluctant but present.

"Just thinking practically. Body heat is a valuable resource." I sigh theatrically, feigning disappointment. "If you're worried about bulk or weight, I'll carry it."

No fucking way is she carrying more than me.

"Personal space is also a precious commodity out there." Ava's response is quick and sharp, yet there's a hint of humor in her voice. "I'd rather have separate tents."

We continue our discussion, the air growing thick with unspoken tension and attraction. With each piece of gear we debate bringing with us, the challenge becomes more about navigating our growing connection than surviving the wilderness.

When I suggest ditching the ice picks, she vents another frustrated sigh.

"It's better to have it and not need it than to need it and not have it." Ava's gaze is steady as she insists on extra provisions.

The intensity of our exchange is palpable, a dance of words and wills. Ava's fiery spirit matches my own, creating a dynamic that's as exhilarating as it is challenging, but finally, after a long afternoon, packing is complete.

"Hungry?" she asks.

"Starving."

"The whole town's waiting for your debut." Ava's tone is teasing, her eyes twinkling with mischief as we head to the diner.

Ava's reminder about our bet brings a sense of playful dread.

I can't hide my surprise. "The whole town? How do they know about our bet?" My curiosity piques as I give her a suspicious glance.

"I told you it is a small town," she replies, her voice laced with amusement. "Word travels."

"Yeah, but I've been with you the entire day. When did you sneak off and tell anyone?" I try to piece together the puzzle.

Ava smiles, a knowing look in her eyes. "La Rouge, there is so much I have to teach you. Here, word travels faster than you think. And besides, Martha knows everything that happens in this town."

I shake my head, baffled but amused by our impending visit to the diner.

"Now, come on. Grab your coat. We're headed to the diner for dinner."

Seizing the opportunity, I throw in a playful tease. "So it's a date, then?"

Ava pauses, turning to give me a look that's both stern and playful. "Not a date," she asserts firmly, but the corners of her mouth betray her, curving into a reluctant smile.

The lights of the diner glow invitingly as we approach. Laughter and boisterous conversation spill out into the street. The thought of performing in front of the whole town is daunting, yet there's an undercurrent of excitement I can't deny. I take a deep breath, ready to embrace whatever the night has in store.

Sensing an opportunity to keep the playful banter going, I throw in a quip aimed to tease Ava and test the waters.

"You know, in my book, if I end up paying for dinner, that technically makes it a date."

"Is that so?" Ava glances at me, a smirk playing at the corners of her mouth, her eyes alight with a teasing spark. "Well, La Rouge, in my book, it's only a date if both parties agree, and right now, you're just a man paying his debts."

"Alright, fair enough." I can't help but laugh at her quick-witted response. There's an ease to our exchange, a dance of words that feels both challenging and flirtatious. "But for the record, I make an excellent dinner companion."

I make an even better partner in bed, but Ava's not ready for that.

She steps inside, pausing to look back at me with a playful glint in her eye. "I'll be the judge of that. Let's see how you handle your spotlight first."

As we enter the diner, the warmth from the room and the welcoming smiles from the locals make the place feel inviting. The atmosphere is charged with a sense of community and anticipation. This evening is about more than just a bet—it's a chance to connect with Ava and the people of this small town, to be a part of something that feels unexpectedly special.

Whether it's a date or not, one thing is clear: an undeniable chemistry is building between us, and I'm curious to see where it might lead.

But Ava's twitchy.

She's equally likely to fall into my arms as she is to run from them. I can't put my finger on it exactly, but she's skittish.

EIGHT

Cage

THE DELICIOUS AROMA OF COFFEE AND FRESHLY BAKED PIES FILLS THE air, mingling with the sounds of laughter and conversation to create an unforgettable combination. The locals, some I recognize from earlier, including Martha, Tom, and Old Man Jenkins, turn to look as we enter. Their expressions form a curious mixture of surprise and amusement.

"Looks like you're the star tonight," Ava says, her eyes sparkling with mischief. "And your song is 'I Will Survive.'"

"You're kidding me? I'm not singing that."

"A bet's a bet, Cage La Rouge." She makes a sweeping motion toward the makeshift stage where an old karaoke machine waits.

"Fine." I take a deep breath, steeling myself. "Let's get this over with."

The atmosphere in the diner shifts palpably as I take the stage. A buzz of excitement and a sense of anticipation fills the air. Ava watches with amusement as I grudgingly step up to the microphone, ready to fulfill my end of the bet.

The diner falls silent, expectant eyes on me. I clear my throat. "So, as part of a bet I lost to Ava, I'll be performing a special number she picked out." I pause for dramatic effect. "I hope you enjoy my rendition of 'I Will Survive.'"

The first chords of "I Will Survive" echo through the diner, and I grasp the microphone with a confidence that's second nature to me.

A hush falls over the crowd, the locals perhaps expecting a comedic effort and terrible singing, but my voice rings out, clear and precisely controlled. The room fills with the smooth, rich timbre of a seasoned singer.

I'm no stranger to the art of performance. My voice weaves through the lyrics with a professional ease, each note perfectly pitched.

The song, known for its empowering message, becomes an instrument in my hands, a means to showcase not just my vocal talent but also the charisma that's always been a part of my allure.

Ava's expression shifts from anticipatory amusement to something akin to bug-eyed bewilderment. As the chorus approaches, I ramp up the energy. My movements blend precision and flair—a nod here, a wink there, engaging the audience with a performer's magnetism.

The locals, initially taken aback, now tap their feet and nod their heads in time with the music. Martha, behind the counter, can't help but smile, thoroughly enjoying the unexpected quality of the performance.

I play with the lyrics, injecting a hint of humor here and there, making the song my own. It's not just a performance; it's a statement—a statement to Ava about how I will always turn things around to my advantage. As the final notes die down, I hold the last line with a flourish, my gaze meeting Ava's.

The diner erupts into applause, the atmosphere electric with surprise and admiration. People cheer and whistle, and some stand to give an ovation. As I step down from my impromptu stage, the crowd's energy is palpable, their reactions a mixture of delight and respect.

Ava meets me as I return to our table, her eyes betraying a

newfound appreciation. "I didn't know you were holding back a secret weapon," she says, a playful yet impressed tone in her voice.

I lean in, a smirk playing on my lips. "Just keeping you on your toes, Ava. Never underestimate a man with hidden talents."

The evening continues with a lively buzz, our table becoming a mini-hub of attention and conversation. The performance has not only shifted the dynamic in the room but also between Ava and me.

There's a new layer to our interaction now, a blend of playful competitiveness and mutual respect that adds depth to our burgeoning connection.

It's too early to call it anything more.

The promise of our upcoming expedition seems even more enticing, filled with possibilities and the thrill of the unexpected.

The atmosphere in the diner, already buzzing from my performance, shifts to a keen curiosity about our impending journey into the Alaskan wild.

"So—" Tom starts, leaning over from the next table with a grin, "what's a big shot photographer planning to snap in the wilds of Alaska?"

I chuckle, taking a sip of my coffee. "Well, that's the million-dollar question, isn't it?"

"You must have some idea, something that's caught your eye?" Martha chimes in from behind the counter, wiping her hands on her apron. "What's the plan? What are you hoping to photograph?"

"Honestly?" I pause, considering how to articulate the undefined nature of my quest. "Part of the beauty of photography is not always knowing what you'll capture. It's about being in the moment, letting the wilderness reveal its secrets. I let the land tell its story. Nature guides me. I'm hoping to capture the essence of Alaska—its landscapes, its wildlife. The unexpected moments that you can't plan for."

"But there's gotta be something, something specific you're aiming for with your camera?" Old Man Jenkins, sitting at the end of the bar, nods sagely. "Like bears, or maybe the northern lights?"

"My goal is to raise awareness of Alaska's fragility, her raw beauty, and the importance of protecting the land for future generations. It's more than just the big-ticket items like bears and the northern lights. It's about the smaller details, too—the way the light falls through the trees, the patterns of the rivers, the life in a single drop of morning dew. The beauty of photography is in finding the extraordinary in the ordinary."

"Like a storyteller with your lens." Tom nods sagely, and he's not wrong.

"That sounds amazing." A younger local, perhaps in her twenties, pipes up from the back, her eyes wide with interest. "But aren't you worried about the dangers?"

"We take every precaution, of course," Ava interjects, her voice confident. "But part of respecting the wilderness is acknowledging its power and unpredictability."

I have no idea what will catch my eye, only that I'll find it once Ava and I are on the trail.

"You'll find some incredible sights out there, and Ava knows that land like the back of her hand," Martha adds. "We'll be waiting to see what you come up with."

"Here. Here." Tom raises his coffee mug in a salute.

"Thanks." I nod, appreciating their interest and support. "I hope to share some amazing shots with you all."

"You look like you've got a good head on your shoulders, son." Old Man Jenkins, from his usual spot at the end of the bar, leans forward. "The wilderness is a beautiful thing, but it can turn on you in a heartbeat."

"That's why I have Ava." I turn to my wilderness guide, eager to spend time alone with her during our adventure.

The conversation in the diner takes on a richer depth as the locals, familiar with Ava and protective of one of their own, lean in with increased interest.

Martha wipes at the counter and looks up with a knowing glance. "How long are you planning to be out there in the wild?"

"Several weeks," Ava answers casually, but with a professional tone. "We've got a thorough plan and route, but we're allowing ourselves the flexibility to explore."

"Several weeks, huh?" Tom, leaning back in his chair, raises an eyebrow. That's a long time out in the wilderness, even for a seasoned guide like yourself, Ava. And with winter coming sooner than we thought. Sure, that's a good idea?"

"Cage is more than capable, and if there is an early storm, we're prepared to deal with it." She glances at me, almost as if vindicated for her insistence on being over-prepared.

"I couldn't be in better hands." I lighten my tone. "Who better to guide me through the Alaskan wilderness than Ava?"

"Just make sure to look after each other." Old Man Jenkins chuckles softly, his eyes twinkling. "The wilderness is a beautiful place, but it demands respect. Look after our girl out there."

"I will."

The locals nod in agreement, their expressions a blend of admiration and concern. Their protective nature toward Ava is clear, but it's also evident that they have a deep respect for her skills and judgment.

The conversation meanders into other topics, but the excitement about the potential discoveries of our expedition lingers in the air. Despite the unpredictable nature of this trip, there are untold stories waiting to be captured through my lens.

I'm eager to begin.

The energy in the diner is electric, and riding on the wave of my unexpectedly successful first performance.

"Who wants another song?" I'm not an entertainer, but these people protect Ava, which means I need them on my side if I decide to pursue her.

The locals' resounding chorus of "Yes!" fills the diner with a warm, communal energy. Their enthusiasm is contagious, and I'm swept up in the spirit of the moment.

"Alright then, another song it is." A genuine smile spreads across my face. The crowd's reaction is a reminder of the power of music to bring people together.

As I step back up to the karaoke machine, I glance at Ava. Her eyes shine with amusement and something else—a hint of pride, perhaps. It's clear that her community's acceptance means a lot to her, and their growing approval of me seems to bring her a sense of ease.

I pick songs that not only echo the call of the wild but also carry a subtle seduction, each lyric subtly aimed at Ava. Soon, songs that resonate with a sense of adventure and camaraderie fill the room. The first chords ring out, and I lose myself in the music, my voice blending with the melody.

The locals join in, some singing along, others tapping their feet or nodding their heads in rhythm.

"Into the Wild" by LP is my first choice. The powerful melody and lyrics about adventure and freedom echo the spirit of our upcoming journey.

I pour passion into every word, occasionally locking eyes with Ava, inviting her into the song's embrace.

Next, I shift gears to "Hungry Like the Wolf" by Duran Duran. This classic track lets me infuse the performance with cheeky playfulness. My glances toward Ava are laden with innuendo, matching the song's theme of a primal chase.

Then, I slow it down with "The Look of Love" by ABC. This song is a smooth, romantic turn, and I sing it as if each word is a message directed across the room to Ava.

During the set, amid cheers and applause, I step down from my impromptu stage and walk over to Ava, my heart racing with adrenaline and anticipation.

"How about a dance?" I ask, challenging her with my gaze.

Spurred on by her friends, Ava can't help but accept. I find a spot near the fireplace, the crowd making room for us. As we dance, I sing softly, the words of a love song meant only for her. Around us, the locals watch, their expressions ranging from amusement to gentle teasing.

We keep the music flowing; some songs I lead with my voice, and others turn into lively group sing-alongs. In the spirit of the evening, I invite Martha for a dance, guiding her through a cheerful spin around our makeshift dance floor, which we've carved out by nudging a few tables aside to create space.

This is part of a subtle strategy to draw Ava into dancing more with me without making my interest in her too obvious.

The diner slowly empties until it's just Ava and me, the dying embers of the fire casting a soft glow around the room. The evening, which started with a sense of obligation, becomes one of the most enjoyable nights I've had in a long time.

As Ava and I prepare to leave, the warmth of the diner and its inhabitants stays with me. The experience has added a new layer to our journey—a connection not just with the wilderness we're about to explore but also with the people who are close to Ava.

Leaving the diner behind, Ava and I step out into the crisp night air. The sky above glitters with countless stars. The town is quiet, and the vibrant energy of the diner fades into a serene stillness that envelops us.

As we stroll back to the lodge, our footsteps crunch softly on the frosted ground, leaving footprints in the snow. The night is clear, and above us, the aurora borealis begins its ethereal dance across the heavens.

Ribbons of green and violet light twirl across the sky, bathing the world around us in an other-worldly glow.

It's a breathtaking sight, a surreal scene that feels as if we've stepped into a realm where time stands still. We halt in our tracks, our eyes drawn upward, captivated by the celestial display. The colors ripple and flow, illuminating the night with a ghostly beauty. It's as if the cosmos is staging a show just for us, a grand finale to an unforgettable evening.

"This is incredible," I whisper, my voice barely audible under the vast, starlit sky.

"The northern lights never get old." Ava nods, her eyes still fixed on the sky. "It's like watching the earth's heartbeat."

We stand in silence, shoulder to shoulder, sharing this moment of awe. The connection between us, already charged from the evening's events, now feels deeper, as if solidified by the magic of the aurora.

Emboldened by the night's events and the beauty surrounding us, I turn to Ava, wanting to capture this moment, to seal it with something tangible. I lean in, hoping for a good night kiss, a perfect end to a perfect night.

Ava's hand on my chest is a gentle yet unmistakable barrier, her message clear under the soft glow of the heavens. Her eyes, usually full of fire and challenge, hold a softer, more contemplative expression.

"Cage," she begins, her voice low and sincere, "this trip, it's professional, first and foremost. I keep a clear line between my work and personal life. I'm not looking to change that."

I listen, taking in her words and the earnestness in her tone.

"I respect you as a photographer, as an adventurer," she continues, "and I won't deny there's something—unexpected happening here, but I can't let that get in the way of my job. I'm serious when I say the wilderness demands our full attention. Distractions are deadly."

"Can't say I'm not disappointed, but I understand." I absorb the weight of her words. "The last thing I want is to complicate things."

I totally want to complicate things.

"Thank you." She smiles, but it's a smile tinged with wistfulness. "It's best not to rush into anything that might cloud our judgment and distract us."

Her words are like a compass, realigning our course. The boundaries she sets aren't walls; they're guidelines, ensuring that what's important remains in focus. As we resume our walk back to the lodge, the aurora borealis shimmers above us.

Ava's right.

The wilderness awaits.

"We have all the time in the world," I reply, my voice laced with promise.

NINE

Ava

———

Dawn greets us with a crisp, invigorating chill, the kind that awakens the senses and heralds the start of something new. The air, rich with the scent of pine, carries with it the undeniable thrill of impending exploration.

I go through my mental checklist, immersed in my process to ensure we're fully prepared for whatever the wilderness might throw at us.

The tents are checked for their integrity, ensuring no tear or broken zipper could compromise our shelter. The sleeping bags are rolled tightly, their material scrutinized for any signs of wear that could fail us in the cold nights ahead. Cooking gear is arranged precisely, every utensil accounted for, and every pot and pan inspected for functionality.

As I work, Cage observes me, a slight grin playing on his lips. He finds my thoroughness amusing, perhaps different from his own approach.

But I pay little mind to his amusement; this level of detail and organization is not just a preference but a necessity.

In the wilderness, overlooking even the smallest detail can mean the difference between comfort and hardship, or in extreme cases, life and death.

I double-check the first aid kit, ensuring every essential item is in place—bandages, antiseptics, pain relievers, and emergency equipment. I verify the presence of our navigation tools—maps, compass, and GPS device—all crucial for orientation in the vast, unmarked expanse of nature.

I set the beacon on the sat phone, a dedicated broadcast sent out once a day, and then check the charge in the spare battery. Justin insists I carry the sat phone and check in regularly. He can be a bit over-protective, but I don't mind.

"Check. Check." I make the first of many calls to my brother from a different mother.

"Hey, Ava, how's it going?" Justin's voice rings out loud and clear.

"Just going over last-minute prep. We'll be heading out within the hour."

"Heard you two made a splash at the diner last night. What's the scoop on La Rouge?"

"No scoop."

"The way Martha says it, the two of you are hitched with five kids already."

"Hardly." I scoff at his comment and move into the other room where Cage can't overhear this particular conversation.

"Hardly?" Justin pauses. *"The stories I hear say otherwise."*

"Well, he's a tool, and I'm not interested." I'm also not interested in being the topic of town gossip. "This is just another job."

"If you say so." From his tone, Justin doesn't believe me.

"Hey, I gotta go." And get off this damn line before Justin realizes I'm lying about my interest in Cage.

"Have a great trip. Be safe, and remember to check in."

"I know, by eight in the morning and no later than ten at night. I'll check in. In the meantime, I've got to finish packing before we lose the day."

"Lose the day?" Justin laughs. *"It's six in the morning."*

"And I wanted to be on the trail already. I'll check in with you tonight. Don't worry about me."

"Never worried about you, but I don't know this La Rouge character. He could be an axe murderer for all I know."

"I don't think that's the case."

"We'll see. Talk to you later."

"Bye." I end the call and put the satellite phone into standby mode.

"Who was that?" Cage peeks out of the gear prep room.

"Just a friend."

"A friend?"

"Yes."

"As in a friend-friend or a boyfriend?"

"Ewww, Justin's like a brother to me."

"Like a brother?"

"We grew up together, and our mothers are best friends, and we're best friends."

"Good to know."

I brush past Cage, troubled by his interest, and pack my backpack. Why did that brief exchange annoy me?

"Planning to bring the whole lodge with us?" Cage winks at me.

"You'll thank me later." I look at him, half-annoyed and half-amused. We've had this conversation before.

Cage chuckles, stepping closer to help. "I guess every expedition needs its master planner. Lead on, Commander Livingston."

"Commander?"

"A great expedition demands a great leader."

"What's that make you?"

"The talent?" His grin is infectious. "I'd say Sherpa, but you're carrying almost as much gear as I am."

"In my defense, half your gear is photography equipment. I'm happy to carry the food. My burden will only lighten as we continue."

"Well…" he stops and looks around. "I'm ready when you are."

"Let's head out."

Maybe my annoyance comes from the late start. I wanted to be on the trail before dawn, but Cage's constant questions about gear slowed down final packing.

With our backpacks shouldered and our spirits high—his are high, mine are troubled—we set out, heading northeast. The land stretches before us, an expanse of rolling tundra giving way to dense forests and towering mountains in the distance.

The air is crisp and clean, filling my lungs with each breath. The flat, open terrain stretches endlessly, and the horizon blurs where earth meets the sky.

The sense of freedom is exhilarating—out here, we're just two souls against the vastness of nature.

As we walk, the lodge and its familiar comforts shrink away, becoming just a memory. The wild engulfs us, its beauty stark and unforgiving. Birds call from above, their songs a wild symphony accompanying our trek.

We hike across the tundra, the first part of our expedition into the wild. Our boots crunch against the frost-laden ground, the only disruption in the silence. We rarely speak, each seeming content to enjoy the sound of silence.

The sky above is a canvas of deep blues and grays, and the sun casts a pale light that bathes the land in a golden glow.

I set a demanding pace, keen to cover as much ground as possible before nightfall. At times, Cage seems taken aback by my speed. This is my favorite part of my job, heading out into the vastness of nature and becoming part of its raw, untamed beauty.

The landscape stretches out in all directions, an endless sea of open, flat terrain. The horizon blends seamlessly into the sky, a symphony of blues and whites. The ground beneath our feet is a mixture of hard-packed permafrost and soft, spongy moss, each step a reminder of the wildness we're traversing.

"I'm learning not to underestimate you, Ava Livingston." Cage laughs, a sound that blends easily with the rustle of leaves and the crunch of earth beneath our boots. "You set a rigorous pace."

"I can slow down if you want."

"Nah, I can keep up."

We encounter wildlife—caribou grazing in the distance, their movements slow and graceful.

"You see that?" He points toward a distant herd of caribou, his camera already in hand.

The way he captures each moment, finding the extraordinary in the seemingly mundane details of the landscape, is fascinating.

"Beautiful, isn't it?" I respond, watching him as he works. His eyes are keen and focused, finding angles and compositions that speak of a deep understanding and appreciation for the wild around us.

"You ever get tired of this?" He gestures toward the vast expanse around us.

"Never. How about you?"

"Not in a million years." His eyes scan the horizon with an artist's appreciation. "Every angle, every moment is a story waiting to be told."

His camera is always at the ready, a natural extension of his being. He stops frequently, capturing scenes with a meticulous eye. The click of the shutter is a steady accompaniment to our journey, a rhythmic beat that echoes the heartbeat of the wilderness.

"Look at that light." He points to how the sun filters through a passing cloud, casting a golden glow on the tundra. He works his camera, framing the scene and capturing fleeting beauty with a practiced eye.

Midway through the day, we are greeted by the sight of a crystal-clear, fast-flowing river. The gentle sound of rushing water is a soothing symphony in the quiet expanse of the tundra.

"Time for a break," I announce, feeling the weight of my backpack growing heavier on my shoulders. "And maybe catch our dinner if we're lucky."

As I unhook the straps of my pack, preparing to set it down, a sudden hush falls over him. His hand shoots up, signaling me to stop.

"Quiet." When he whispers, his voice is a low, urgent caress in the wind.

I halt, my movements stilled, my backpack half-slung over my shoulder.

His intense focus fixes on a point in the distance. Following his gaze, I see them—Arctic foxes, their brilliant white fur a stark contrast against the earthy hues of the tundra. They dart playfully, weaving in and out of sight, their quick, fluid movements a mesmerizing ballet.

He drops to one knee, an instinctive movement. His camera, an extension of his being, raises in a fluid, seamless motion. I find myself inexplicably drawn to him. There's a grace to his posture, a focused intensity that radiates from him.

A force so strong, it's palpable.

It's sexy as hell.

As he adjusts his lens, the subtle flex of muscles in his arms catches my eye. Each movement is a testament to a strength that speaks of both power and control.

Watching him, my breath catches slightly. His focused form exudes a raw masculinity, a presence as compelling as the wilderness around us. There's an undeniable allure in how he immerses himself in his task.

His fingers, skilled and sure, work the camera with expert precision, capturing the foxes' fleeting beauty.

The way his sandy hair falls slightly over his forehead, the lines of concentration etched on his face, the unwavering steadiness of his hands—all of it captivates me, drawing me in. I'm observing not just his skill as a photographer but the essence of the man who is as much a part of this wilderness as the creatures he passionately captures.

The moment stretches on, timeless, as the foxes continue their play, unaware or uncaring of our presence. His camera clicks in a rhythmic pattern, echoing the heartbeat of the wild around us.

My admiration for him deepens, tinged with a growing, undeniable attraction—a pull toward him that's becoming harder to rationalize as mere professional respect.

There's something about him in this element, a raw, unguarded side that he reveals only to the wilderness and, inadvertently, to me.

The foxes vanish suddenly, spooked by something, and leave the wind whispering across the tundra and the water rushing along the banks of the river.

Cage lowers his camera, and a satisfied smile plays on his lips, the kind of smile that hints at secrets shared only with the wild.

"Got it," he says, more to himself than to me.

The intensity of the moment dissipates, replaced by the serene calm of the river beside us. He stands, stretching his back, the movement fluid and natural. The light catches in his green eyes and reflects a spark of triumph from the successful capture of the wild.

I can't help but smile back, feeling a shared sense of accomplishment in his success. His passion for his craft, his connection with the environment—it's alluring in a way that's hard to articulate.

"We should take that break now." I finally set my backpack down.

As we prepare to rest, my thoughts linger on him more than they should. There's a depth to our journey, a shared experience that goes beyond mere exploration.

The river, with its clear waters, becomes our companion as we rest, its steady flow a reminder of the ever-changing yet constant nature of the wilderness we traverse.

As I watch him unpack his gear for a short break, I feel a sense of comfort and rightness in this place, in this moment, with him by my side.

I pull out my compact fishing gear, assembling it with practiced ease. Cage watches, then follows suit, casting his line into the river with a hopeful expression.

As we fish, the silence between us is comfortable; the only sounds are the gentle flow of the river and the distant call of an eagle.

I live for moments like these—the simplicity, the connection with nature, and the peace that comes from being exactly where you belong.

After a while, Cage's line jerks.

"Got something." He reels in his line with excitement. It's a decent-sized trout, its scales glinting in the sunlight.

"Nice catch," I compliment him, genuinely impressed. "We're going to skin and gut it here. Leave the innards for the bears. That way, tonight, we won't have to worry about them sniffing around camp."

"Smart." Cage sets to work gutting the fish.

"You've done that a time or two." I admire his skill and speed.

"My brothers and I spent our summers fishing when we weren't getting into trouble."

"I bet." He leaves the guts behind, and I take the fish, wrapping it tight to eliminate the smell and any curiosity from roaming bears.

As we trudge through the ever-changing landscape, our conversation ebbs and flows as easily as the river we leave behind. Our chatter combines professional knowledge with personal insights, interspersed with Cage's well-timed humor.

"So, what's your favorite part about being out here?" Cage asks, his eyes scanning the horizon.

I think for a moment, the endless expanse of wilderness stretching out before us.

"The solitude, I guess. It's peaceful. You get to know yourself better. What about you? What draws you to places like this?"

"The challenge." He smiles, looking thoughtful. "There's something about pitting yourself against nature, and I love capturing nature's beauty through a lens. It's raw and real."

"Speaking of which, you asked me, but have you ever encountered dangerous wildlife on your trips?"

"I once had a close call with a bear in Yellowstone." Cage chuckles, a gleam in his eye. "Let's just say I learned the value of bear spray the hard way."

"Well, out here, bear encounters are a real possibility." I laugh, imagining the scene. "So, keep that spray handy."

"Thought that's what the pistols were for."

"I'd rather use nonlethal ways of repelling a bear. The pistols are a last resort."

"As long as you don't hesitate."

"I never hesitate."

Out here, hesitation kills, and while I prefer nonlethal means of protecting myself from a bear attack, I know not to trust my life to bear spray.

As night falls, we set up camp under the vast Alaskan sky. The stars emerge like tiny pinpricks of light, then brighten into a brilliant tapestry above us. The Milky Way stretches across the heavens, a swirling path of light in the dark expanse.

The air is crisp, and the silence of the wilderness envelops us, a reminder of our smallness in the face of nature's grandeur.

Sitting by the campfire, the warmth of the flames is a comfort against the chill of the night.

"Makes you feel small, doesn't it?" I comment, staring up at the stars.

"In the best way possible," he agrees, his voice a whisper in the darkness. "It's humbling."

Our conversation flows easily, meandering like the trails we've traversed. It's casual, filled with laughter and anecdotes, a natural flow that bridges the gap between guide and photographer. Eventually, we say good night and retreat to our separate tents, where we sleep alone.

The first three days pass in much the same way. The bond between us strengthens as we get to know each other better, a chaste but undeniable connection forged by shared experiences and the awe-inspiring beauty of Alaska.

It's as though the wilderness itself is drawing us closer, its majestic presence a backdrop to the unfolding story between us.

TEN

Cage

I'M UP BEFORE AVA, SURPRISINGLY. THE QUIET OF THE MORNING IS A stark contrast to the chaos of my usual life, filled with city lights and fleeting encounters of gratuitous sex with strangers.

I've been gifted with many things in life, including my good looks and no concerns about money. That kind of thing is like honey when it comes to women.

They swarm around me, eager to get a piece of me. It's both a curse and a blessing, but with Ava, I don't know where I stand.

She's not affected by wealth and seems to care even less about my looks. I'm a job to her, and I don't like that.

Not one damn bit.

I brew coffee over the campfire, the aroma blending with the earthy scents of the forest.

Ava emerges from the tent, eyes still heavy with sleep. For a moment, she looks vulnerable, a far cry from the confident guide I know.

She joins me by the fire and holds out her hands for warmth. She may start a fire quicker than me, but I brew better camp coffee. As a gesture of peace, I hold out a steaming cup of the bitter brew.

"We're heading into rougher terrain today," she says.

"Worried I'll slow you down, Livingston?" I can't help but tease right back.

"Just don't want to have to carry you." She meets my gaze, unflinching. There's a challenge in her eyes, one that I'm all too eager to accept.

"Pffft…"

"I'll give you this." She blows on the coffee, but all I can see is the pink perfection of her lips.

Carefully, she takes a sip. Her eyes close, and the most delicious moan escapes her mouth.

My dick gives a little twitch.

Down, boy.

The eager fucker.

"Definitely better than what I make." There's a smirk on her lips, a smile in her eyes, and a tiny drop of coffee on the cupid's bow of her upper lip.

My fingers twitch, and I resist the urge to lick the coffee off her lip.

Damn, if she's not the most beautiful thing.

"I figured you'd need a bit of a pick-me-up if you were going to *keep up* with me today."

"Ha-ha!" She shakes her head and takes time to fully enjoy the dark brew.

I join her, but the coffee is gone all too soon, which means it's time to hit the trail.

We break camp, the air between us charged with an unspoken competition. As we hike, I push myself, keeping pace with her effortlessly.

I'm Cage La Rouge, an adventure seeker, mountaineer, and all-around outdoor guy. I've faced more than tough trails. I've climbed mountains and summited the highest of peaks.

I can keep pace with a woman.

But Ava? She's something else.

She moves with a purpose, every step calculated and sure. It's infuriating, admirable, and sexy as hell.

I watch her navigate through the dense underbrush with awe, a part of me wanting to see her falter and prove she's not as perfect as she seems.

Another part of me, the rascal in me, wants to haul her over my shoulder and find a sturdy tree to fuck her against. Or maybe a soft bed of needles or moss. What about bending her over a log and plowing into her from behind?

Fuck, my brain's stuck on sex with my wilderness guide.

We reach a steep incline that she climbs easily, her strength evident in her every move. I follow, my own breath coming in quick bursts. It's a challenge, but I won't let it show. I'm too close to her now, close enough to catch the faint scent of her, something wild and untamed.

At the top, the view takes my breath away. Mountains stretch out before us, their peaks touching the sky. For a moment, everything else fades away.

It's just me, Ava, and the endless wilderness.

"Beautiful, isn't it?" she says, her voice soft.

I nod, unable to find the words, and grab my camera. We spend the next twenty minutes in silence as I capture the perfect shot. The tension between us shifts as we rest from the strenuous hike, turning into something else.

Something I can't quite name.

But then the moment passes. A thick bank of clouds rolls through, ruining the light. I pack my camera, and Ava turns, ready to continue the trek.

Like always, I'm left to follow.

A part of me wants to reach out and bridge the gap between us —to feel her hand in mine—but I hold back.

The day wears on, and the terrain becomes more challenging. Her pace is daunting, but I keep up, matching Ava step for step. There's a grudging respect growing between us, a recognition of each other's strengths, but there's also something more, a pull that's becoming harder to ignore.

The simmering chemistry growing between us can no longer be ignored. Don't know about her, but I'm ready to explode.

In my fantasies, I've fucked her twenty times to Sunday by the time she calls it quits and discovers a lovely place to set camp in a small alpine meadow ringed with conifers and pine.

As we set up camp, our movements are in sync, a silent partnership in the fading light. The air is cool, the sky a blanket of stars. Ava sits by the fire, her face illuminated by the flames.

I join her; the warmth of the fire a welcome reprieve from the chill.

As dusk falls, Ava nudges me in the ribs and gestures toward the trees. A moose steps tentatively into the clearing to nibble on the tender grass. I capture its elegance before it notices us and disappears in a flash of hooves and impossibly long legs.

Ava looks on, her appreciation of the moment matching mine.

"We make a good team." The words slip out before I can stop them.

"We do." She looks at me, a hint of gentleness in her tone. It's a subtle recognition of how things between us have changed.

The fire crackles between us, the only sound in the vast silence. I want to say more, to break down the walls between us, but I hold back, afraid of what might happen if I do.

Afraid of ruining things by moving too fast.

I've always been in control, but here, in the heart of the Alaskan wilderness, I'm starting to wonder if maybe, just maybe, it's time to slow down the fast life I've been living.

ELEVEN

Ava

As I step out of my tent, the chill of the pine-scented morning air wraps around me like a comforting blanket. The tundra stretches behind us, a vast expanse we're leaving for the winding embrace of the Silverthorn River and the thick pine forests that climb toward the mountains.

We break camp and make a quick meal of trail mix and black coffee.

"Ready for a change of scenery?" I shoulder my backpack, feeling its familiar weight settle against me.

"Always ready." Cage grins, camera already in hand.

As we trek toward the river, the open land gradually gives way to a denser, more challenging terrain. The underbrush thickens, and the forest canopy closes above us, dappling the ground in light and shadow.

This far from civilization, the forest feels ancient and untouched, a world that breathes and lives around us.

Cage pauses, captivated by the interplay of sunlight filtering through the leaves.

"This light," he says, almost more to himself than to me, "is perfect." The click of his camera softly punctuates his words.

While he takes his pictures, I allow my greedy gaze to get its fill of the masculine energy Cage exudes.

We reach our first river crossing by midday. The water rushes and swirls over and around the rocks, crystal clear and cold.

"Take it slow," I caution Cage as I step into the icy flow.

The current tugs at my legs, stronger than it looked from the shore. A step behind me, Cage crosses the river, his camera half-raised, but he's not focused on a shot.

Nearly on the other side of the river, my footing gives way on a slick stone. I tumble and fall. In an instant, Cage lifts me clear of the rushing water.

"Whoa there." Cage steadies me on my feet, and his breath sweeps across my neck with a whisper of heat. His eyes reflect the unspoken tension that has been simmering between us since the day we met.

The suddenness of the contact sends a jolt of electricity shooting through me, more from his proximity than the threat of a plunge into the chilly waters.

"Thanks." Our eyes lock in that brief, charged moment, a connection sparking between us that goes beyond mere physical support.

For a moment, we're suspended in time, our faces mere inches apart.

Our lips kissably close.

The space between us is charged with a mixture of anticipation and eagerness, yet there is also hesitation.

The air around us thickens with possibilities.

But just as quickly as the moment builds, it breaks and shatters.

The world rushes back in, the sound of the river reminding me of where we are and the journey that lies ahead. I scold myself for the break in professionalism. This is my workplace, and I won't muddy that by getting attached to a client.

"No problem. I'll always catch you when you fall." A slight smile plays on his lips as if he understands the turmoil of feelings that just passed between us.

Reluctantly and almost regretfully, I take a small step back, breaking the spell. The potential of that almost-kiss lingers in the air, an unfulfilled promise that adds a new layer to our relationship. It's slowly becoming less professional and more personal.

"Um… We should keep moving." I can't shake off that moment —the warmth of his body, the steadiness of his arms, and the way my heart raced when he touched me.

"Lead on." He steers me toward the safety of the bank and falls into step behind me.

The rest of the day passes with an easy blend of conversation and companionable silence, but the memory of our brief yet intense contact by the river lingers in the air between us.

It's a moment that hints at depths yet to be explored and feelings yet to be acknowledged.

As we walk alongside the river, the soothing rush of water becomes the soundtrack to our journey, blending seamlessly with the rhythm of our steps and the cadence of our conversation.

"So, what's the most unexpected thing you've ever encountered on one of your trips?" My curiosity is piqued by the array of experiences he must have had.

"Once, in the Amazon, I woke up to find a monkey rummaging through my backpack." He chuckles, a light, easy sound that floats on the breeze.

"No way."

"He was particularly fascinated with my toothbrush." Cage's face breaks into a grin.

It's criminal how sexy that makes him look. I work to swallow and speak before my stare lingers too long on the rugged handsomeness of his face.

Before Cage notices.

"Did he take it?" I laugh, picturing the scene.

"Nah, but we had a bit of a stare-down. I think he realized it wasn't a snack." His eyes twinkle with mirth as he recounts the tale.

Our path takes us over a bed of smooth stones. The river beside us glistens under the sun.

"Your turn. Have you ever had any close calls?" Cage steps carefully over a larger rock that juts out from the river's edge.

"A few," I admit. "Worst was probably getting caught in a sudden blizzard. Had to hunker down and wait it out in a makeshift shelter. That was a long night."

"Sounds intense." He looks over, concern flickering in his eyes.

"It was, but it's all part of the experience, right? The unpredictability. Not to mention, it was a good test of my survival skills."

Cage points at the boulder he just scaled.

"Careful," he says. "That rock's slippery."

As I reach the tricky spot, he extends his hand to steady me.

I nod, accepting his help, but as I step forward, my foot slides on the slick surface.

In a split second, his reflexes kick in.

He steadies me, his arms encircling my waist, pulling me against him to prevent a fall.

"Thanks," I say, a little breathless from the suddenness of it all.

"No problem." His voice is a low, sexy rumble behind my ear. His hands linger a moment longer than necessary before he slowly releases me, ensuring I'm steady on my feet.

I clear my throat, attempting to return to our earlier conversation. "Well, that blizzard was intense. Being at the mercy of nature like that changes you."

"Nature has a way of doing that." His tone reflects a blend of respect and awe.

We continue walking, our conversation ebbing and flowing. We share stories of breathtaking sunsets, challenging climbs, and the serene beauty of nights under the stars. There's a comfortable ease to our exchange, a mutual understanding and respect born from shared passions.

As the day wears on, our talks dive deeper, touching on dreams and aspirations.

"What drives you?" I find myself asking, genuinely curious about what fuels his adventurous spirit.

He pauses, contemplating. "A thirst for seeing the world, for capturing moments that might otherwise go unnoticed. Photography lets me tell those stories."

I nod, understanding the sentiment. "For me, it's about the

connection with nature. The sense of freedom out here is unmatched."

Our gazes meet, holding for a moment longer than necessary. In his eyes, I see a reflection of my own love for the wild, a shared longing for the untamed and unexplored.

The conversation shifts back to lighter topics as we search for our next campsite. The depth of our exchange lingers. It's clear we both seek something beyond the mere physical journey—a quest for meaning, for understanding, for a connection that transcends the ordinary.

We come upon a small clearing next to the Silverthorn River. The riverbank is serene, a perfect spot for a much-needed break. He kneels by the water's edge, focusing his lens on the subtle dance of light on the surface.

Curious, I watch as he captures ripples on the surface. "Why that?" I find his choice of subject intriguing yet puzzling.

He looks up, his eyes reflecting the calm of the river. "It's the small details," he explains, "that tell a story. The way light plays on the water, the ripples—they're all part of the river's narrative."

As he speaks, he reaches into the water, scooping up a handful of sand and pebbles. Sifting through them, he reveals something unexpected—tiny flecks of gold shimmer in the sunlight.

"Look at this." He holds out his palm.

I step closer, examining the specks. "You found gold." My voice is a mixture of surprise and curiosity.

"Yeah." He nods. "This river has a history, stories of exploration and exploitation."

I can't help but be drawn to the tiny glimmers. "It's beautiful. Alaska's gold rush history is fascinating, but it came with a price."

"True." He washes the gold back into the river, watching it disappear into the current. "At least today, there are strict environmental controls when it comes to mining. Alaska's wilderness is too precious to risk."

Our conversation shifts to the history of Alaska, the gold rush, and the balance between its natural beauty and human desires.

It's a dialogue that's both enlightening and foreboding, hinting at the delicate equilibrium of this vast wilderness.

I love watching Cage work. The ease and passion in his movements and how he sees the world through his lens captivate me.

He's deeply connected to his art.

He finishes his work and joins me in comfortable silence as I set up camp. We fall into what's become a familiar routine.

Our tents go up with practiced ease, and soon, the aroma of cooking fills the air, mingling with the earthy scents of the forest.

"Think we'll catch a glimpse of the northern lights tonight?" Sitting by the fire, his eyes reflect its flickering light.

I join him, warming my hands by the flames. "Maybe. The sky's clear enough."

Dinner is a simple affair, but out here, every meal feels like a feast. We eat, talk, and laugh, the land around us a silent witness to the bond growing between us.

He reaches into his backpack and pulls out a soft blanket. With a thoughtful gesture, he spreads it out beside the dying fire.

"Come." He gestures to a spot on the blanket next to him. "Let's get a better look at these stars."

I join him, lying down on the blanket. The ground beneath is firm yet comfortable, and as we settle back, the expanse of the night sky opens above us.

It's a breathtaking canvas. The stars twinkle like diamonds, and the Milky Way, a celestial river of light, arches across the sky.

"There's the Big Dipper," I point out, tracing the constellation with my finger.

"And there," he adds, his arm extended, "is Orion, the hunter. The star at its shoulder is Beetlejuice, the closest star, which is supposed to go supernova sometime in the next ten thousand years."

We fall into a comfortable silence, simply gazing upward, letting the awe of the cosmos wash over us. The fire crackles softly beside us, its glow a gentle counterpoint to the cool brilliance of the stars.

In the tranquility of the moment, there's a quiet shift in the air between us. His hand inches closer to mine. Its warmth radiates toward mine, an unspoken invitation hanging silently in the cool night air.

Then, with a gentleness that takes me by surprise, his fingers stretch out, brushing against mine. The touch is featherlight, yet it sends a surge of electricity through me.

Every nerve within me awakens, a tingling sensation that starts at my fingertips and spreads through my entire being.

Slowly, almost reverently, he intertwines his fingers with mine. Our hands fit together naturally, comfortably, as if they've found their missing half.

I respond instinctively, curling my fingers around his. The warmth of his hand envelops mine, a secure, comforting presence.

The sensation is electrifying, a silent acknowledgment of the bond growing between us.

The whole thing brings back a rush of youthful emotions, the exhilarating thrill of a first touch, the sweet uncertainty of new affection.

As we lie there, hands clasped under the vast sky, the stars seem to shine a little brighter, and the night turns a bit more magical.

His grip is gentle yet firm, a silent expression of connection that speaks louder than words.

Our conversation drifts to the stars, to the stories they've witnessed. We talk about constellations, about the myths and legends written in the night sky. It's easy, this back and forth between us, as natural as the river's flow.

But we don't talk about holding hands.

As the fire dwindles to glowing embers, the idea of retreating to my tent feels almost like a disservice to the night's beauty.

Cage seems to sense my reluctance to end the night. Rolling onto his side to face me, he props his head up with one hand and gazes deeply into my eyes.

"Why don't we sleep out here tonight? Under the stars?"

I hesitate, the idea appealing yet far too intimate, but the allure of the open sky and the gentle sound of the river are persuasive.

I nod, agreeing. I feel a thrill at the thought of sharing this night in such a unique way.

"I'll be a perfect gentleman." He leans forward, his lips gently pressing a kiss to my forehead.

The gesture is tender and protective, a reassurance of his respect for the boundaries we've implicitly set.

We lie there, side by side, speaking softly of dreams and hopes, occasionally falling into comfortable silences.

Unwilling to break the spell falling over us, instead of a verbal check-in with Justin, I send a series of dots and dashes in Morse code over the phone, telling him I'm alive and Cage has yet to show any axe-murdering signs.

A grin lifts the corners of my mouth before I tuck the satellite phone back into my bag and turn my attention to the majesty around me and the man I'm finding more and more attractive.

Let's just say it.

Enthralling.

That one word encapsulates my feelings well.

Cage notes my check-in over the satellite phone but makes no comment. Instead, he waits for me to rejoin him on the blanket.

The vastness of the sky above envelops us, making the moment feel timeless, as if we're the only two people in the world.

Eventually, our conversation fades, and the sounds of the night lull us toward sleep. I find myself on the edge of slumber, aware of his presence just inches away, thinking of him and the unexpected depth of our connection.

I'm both excited and apprehensive about where it might lead.

TWELVE

Ava

———

THE FIRST LIGHT OF DAWN GENTLY PULLS ME FROM SLEEP. ITS SOFT glow filters through the trees. Beside me, Cage stirs. The chill of the morning air bites at my skin, but it's a welcome sensation, a reminder of this place's raw beauty.

"Good morning." I wipe the sleep from my eyes and run my fingers through my hair.

"Damn, it got cold last night." Cage shakes free the thin layer of frost covering his sleeping bag.

"Nice and nippy. This time of year can be unpredictable. We're as likely to enjoy mild temperatures as we are to be hit with a sudden blizzard. Mother Nature doesn't fool around."

"Damn." He stretches, and together, we pack up camp, with the exception of our sleeping bags.

We shake them free of the thin layer of frost and drape them over branches where they can dry. I check in with Justin, something quick, then gesture to Cage to get his fishing gear.

We then head toward the stream, where I select the perfect spot by the bank. The crisp morning air fills my lungs as I cast my fishing line into the glassy water.

Before long, we've caught enough fish for a hearty breakfast. I gut and descale the fish while he snaps photos, captivated by even these mundane tasks.

We cook the fish over a crackling fire as the rising sun burns away the morning chill.

"Not bad, right?" I prod after he takes his first bite. He may have won when it comes to making campfire coffee, but I'm the queen when it comes to roasting fish over an open fire.

"Incredible," he agrees enthusiastically. "I'm going to be spoiled after this trip, only wanting to eat what I catch myself from now on."

"Well, the fish back home definitely won't taste as good."

"I have a feeling nothing will compare to this…" He looks out over the landscape spread before us.

He doesn't mean the fish or the view. There's an electrifying current running between us. Out here, in the wild, something elemental shifts between us.

After breaking camp, we set out, following the river's meandering path through the valley.

Cage stops every now and then, compelled to photograph whatever strikes his eye. I trail behind, content to pause when inspiration strikes him. His passion for capturing the essence of this place mirrors my own. While our mediums differ, our awe stems from the same source.

We trade playful quips back and forth as we walk, covering more personal ground. He asks about my childhood and what first drew me to the wilderness. I share memories of family camping trips and weekend hikes that left their mark on my young imagination. In turn, he tells me of his globetrotting travels to far-flung locales, always searching for that perfect shot.

By mid-afternoon, we cover several more miles along the Silverthorn's sinuous route. My feet ache slightly, but it's a good kind of soreness, born from a day enriching both body and spirit. When Cage suggests stopping near a curve in the river bank, I'm happy to oblige.

We drink from our water bottles and splash the glacially-fed water on our faces and necks, washing away the day's sweat and dust.

Cage grabs his camera, framing a shot of me with the river's azure-blue glacial water behind me. I give my best mock-serious pose, and he laughs.

"A true explorer," he jokes.

As I lounge on a large, flat rock warmed by the sun, he continues photographing—the river, insects gliding over the water, a family of ducks paddling by, and individual pebbles that catch his eye.

Everything is fodder for his artistic eye.

My own gaze settles contentedly on him. I'm struck again by his rugged capability against the wilderness backdrop, the strength evident in his shoulders and forearms as he moves.

We continue on as the afternoon fades toward evening. Shafts of honey-gold light pierce the canopy, bathing the forest in an ethereal glow. The smell of pine and rain-soaked earth surrounds us. Somewhere nearby, a hawk calls, heralding the closing of another day.

The hawk sweeps into view, and Cage catches its majestic flight with the lens of his camera.

When we find a clearing suitable for camp, I gather kindling as Cage unfurls the tents with practiced ease. We soon have a fire crackling merrily along and two plump trout roasting over the flames.

The stars reveal themselves slowly, the night sky transitioning from dusky purple to jet black, illuminated with what looks like scattered diamonds across the sky.

The aurora borealis is absent, but the night sky remains majestic.

Content and weary from a full day's hike, I settle close to the fire, letting the dancing flames soothe my mind. Cage lowers himself down beside me.

For a while, we gaze skyward in awe-filled silence. There's something humbling about staring into infinity, remembering how small we are against the vast cosmos.

"It's incredible," Cage finally murmurs. "No matter how often I see night skies like this, I'm always left speechless."

"It makes our earthly worries seem trivial."

"I agree." He leans close, bumping shoulders with me.

We talk quietly about the brilliance above us—the stories told in the constellations, the unfathomable mysteries of the universe, the ephemerality of a human lifespan compared to millions of years of stellar cycles.

The air grows cold, thickening with mist. Before long, clouds roll in, threatening rain.

Rather than spending another night under the stars, we pitch our respective tents and retreat to the solitude of individual beds.

I awake to distant booming and ominous skies swirling with iron-dark clouds. The air hangs heavy with the electric charge of an impending storm.

Cage meets my gaze with wordless understanding. We hurry to break camp, preparing to weather whatever nature has in store.

The downpour catches us, transforming swiftly from a gentle shower into a tempest. Gale-force winds whip around us, driving the rain sideways, each drop a needle-prick of icy cold against our skin.

A crack of thunder explodes directly overhead. The sound is visceral and raw, a primal force that resonates through the air and vibrates in our chests. The trees around us shudder, their leaves trembling in the wind that whips through the forest.

Another booming clap of thunder follows. Its reverberations mingle with the relentless assault of the rain, creating a cacophony that envelops us in its fury.

Each lightning flash illuminates the darkened sky with brilliant streaks of white and is followed by more thunder, so close now that each crack and rumble seems to be right on top of us.

"We need to find shelter." The storm forces me to raise my voice to be heard.

I scan our surroundings desperately for any form of shelter, knowing we can't sustain this assault in the open for long.

"Over there!" Cage shouts and points at an up thrusting of rock jutting out of the ground. There, a natural overhang offers a respite from the relentless downpour.

We trudge through the increasingly muddy ground, our boots sinking into the sodden earth, making each step a struggle against the elements.

The overhang is barely more than a shallow cavern, but it's a welcome sight. The rock is cold and unyielding against our backs, yet it provides a barrier against the wind's fury.

We huddle close, our bodies shivering, from both the cold and the adrenaline that courses through our veins.

The deluge pours around us, a relentless barrage drumming on the rock overhead. The sound is deafening, a constant roar that drowns out all else. Water cascades down the sides of the overhang, creating a curtain of droplets that glimmer with the flashes of lightning.

Cage's features are cast in shadow, giving him a rugged, almost wild appearance. Our eyes meet, and there's a moment of unspoken understanding.

He lifts his arm, and I lean into him. His arm wraps around me and holds me tight.

The temperature drops, and I huddle with Cage for warmth. We share body heat as the storm rages.

The air hangs heavy with the scent of wet earth and rain-soaked foliage. Our breaths come out in visible puffs, mingling in the frigid air. Together, we huddle beneath the meager shelter of the over-hanging ledge, pelted by rain even in this relatively protected nook.

"So much for crossing that river," Cage shouts to be heard over the storm's din.

Our planned route involves traversing a wild, unpredictable trib-utary of the Silverthorn River. Even under perfect conditions, it's challenging, but attempting to ford the swollen river after a storm like this is suicide.

I eye the bloated clouds uneasily.

Cage tightens his grip around me, pulling me against his body. Our body heat mingles, and I relax against his sturdy frame.

The rain shows no sign of letting up, continuing its relentless barrage, however, Cage's presence makes the discomfort more bearable.

His steadiness anchors me.

We watch the storm rage around our tiny, sheltered oasis. There is something profoundly intimate about this moment as if we're meant to take refuge in each other's arms.

When the storm lulls, Cage is finally able to speak. "Tell me about your most challenging moment out here. When were you tested the most?"

I pause, thinking back over my many years of guiding in Alaska. One experience stands out that I've never shared with anyone. Taking a deep breath, I answer.

"It was on an early solo expedition. I was miles into the back-country. Had a bad fall. Lost my gear and twisted my ankle so badly that I couldn't put weight on it. The weather turned unexpectedly, and I had to tap into every survival skill I possessed. It was a true life-or-death test."

Cage's arms tighten around me.

The images and emotions flood back as I describe that day—the panic that struck when disaster hit, with no partner or radio to call for help. The desperate struggle not to surrender to despair despite the situation growing graver by the hour.

"After that, Justin convinced me to take a satellite phone when-ever I went out, either alone or with clients. Needless to say, I didn't argue. I wrestled with giving up completely, certain I was going to die alone out there as night fell…" My voice catches at the memory.

Cage reaches out a reassuring hand, his silent support bolstering me.

Drawing a shaky breath, I continue. It feels good to finally confide in someone about that day.

"But, I rallied. Too damn stubborn to quit, I guess. I fashioned a brace for my foot and crutches to walk. It took a few days, but I finally stumbled across other hikers who were able to get help."

I twist to look Cage in the eye. "That was my crucible. It revealed strengths I didn't know I possessed. I discovered I could be tested to the breaking point and still prevail."

Revisiting that brush with disaster still unsettles me years later. Cage gazes back, his expression filled with empathetic respect.

"You're incredibly resilient. I can't imagine persevering like you did..."

"I've never shared those details with anyone."

"Thank you for sharing them with me." Cage's steadfast presence makes him uniquely worthy of my history and battle scars.

Realizing I've dominated the conversation, absorbed in recounting my own near-disaster, it's my turn to ask him about any close calls.

"What about you? I'm guessing you've had some pretty intense brushes with danger climbing those peaks. Any that stand out?"

Cage nods slowly, his gaze drifting out to the rain drifting away over the valleys.

"Well, there was one summit attempt I'll never forget..."

THIRTEEN

Ava

Cage begins his story with a subtle shift of tone in his voice.

"It was on Denali, trying to reach the top. We got caught by a massive storm system rolling in fast."

"How bad did it get?" I prod gently, intrigued by this brush with danger.

"Hurricane-force winds arose without warning," he recounts. "Visibility dropped to zero with this howling whiteness surrounding our tiny, exposed team on the steep, icy slopes. We were clinging to the mountainside for dear life."

I find myself absolutely riveted by his story. Picturing the scene, I twist in his lap until I face him.

We're close.

Too close.

Dangerously—close.

But his story captivates me.

He continues, "I still get nightmares about the hours hunkering behind these tiny outcroppings jutting out. Praying our anchors wouldn't tear loose and send us all tumbling thousands of feet toward the jagged rocks below... We would've been ghosts swallowed by the snow by the time someone found our bodies. If they ever found them. It was sobering." He meets my eyes again.

"I can't even imagine."

"That trip reminded me to respect the power of the elements and that the summit isn't guaranteed. No peak is worth dying over when you're up against nature's whims."

My chest clenches as I envision him braving such relentless forces.

I squeeze his hand in wordless solidarity, knowing that for explorers like us, those lessons underpin why we dare to keep venturing out again and again.

As for our storm, it rages all around us with no sign of abating. To pass the time, we trade stories of scars and near misses earned in the wilds. I point out the pale mark on my forearm where a nylon climbing rope burned through my skin during a high-altitude blizzard. Cage indicates a silvery crescent along his collarbone, a relic of a whitewater rafting misadventure.

"Six stitches," he recalls, "but one hell of a story."

There's something cathartic about this candid exchange. With anyone else, these reminiscences might feel heavy or grim, but with Cage, I discover laughter in the retellings.

Our shared brushes with death reveal overlapping experiences that highlight how well-matched we are.

Well-matched?

When did I start thinking about *us* as *we?*

Late in the day, the rain finally subsides. Shafts of sunlight burst through the clouds and pierce the canopy above us as quickly as the storm overtook us. The air smells fresh and cleansed, the world vivid with renewed color and an unexpected surprise.

Before us stretches a spectacular double rainbow, framing the valley.

I glance over at Cage and find him already watching for my reaction. His eyes crinkle with that irresistible smile that directs a flare of heat straight to my core.

He whips out his camera to capture the brilliance of the double rainbow.

Soggy and wet, we make camp over a bed of pine needles, doing our best to keep our gear from getting waterlogged. Dinner is a cold affair as neither of us has any success making a fire.

We turn in early, cold and exhausted from a day of doing nothing more than trading stories and waiting out that storm.

Fortunately, morning dawns clear and calm. That storm fades to memory as pale sunlight filters through lace-like hoarfrost that coats every branch and needle.

I linger outside my tent, steam rising from a mug of hot tea cupped in both hands. Last night, a subtle but profound shift occurred within me—the strong attraction I feel for Cage deepened into genuine affection. Just looking at him across camp makes my pulse skitter.

He glances up, gifting me with a devastating grin that never fails to kickstart a riot of butterflies swirling through my stomach.

"All packed up. Ready when you are." He cinches down the straps on his pack.

"Almost done." I cup the steaming mug and down the last few drops.

Perfection.

We resume our river-side wanderings. Bloated by the rain from that storm, the Silverthorn churns. In some places, its banks are overrun.

By mid-morning, the forest thickens. The river gleams through the trees to our right, sunlight glinting off its glassy flow. We pick our way carefully around stands of scratchy thorn bushes and across beds of damp lichen and moss.

Suddenly, Cage freezes, throwing out a hand in warning. I halt, peering ahead through the tangle of conifers and undergrowth. At first, nothing appears amiss. Then I see it—a structure visible through the trees.

We exchange a careful look before moving toward what looks to be the remnants of an old prospector's cabin. The rough-hewn wood of its walls is weathered and gray, each plank telling a silent story of years gone by.

"A relic of the gold rush?" That's the only reason a cabin would be out here. This land is protected from prospectors or those looking to live in the wild.

Cage nods and grabs his camera. He veers off to capture the old cabin from a few different angles. We take our time circling the abandoned structure, but I'm curious to head inside.

There's undoubtedly history and tragedy ingrained in that rough-hewn wood, evaporated dreams, and long-dead hopes. Maybe even literal ghosts.

Eventually, I can no longer resist. Each step over the creaking porch feels like a journey through time. The wood groans underfoot, protesting the disturbance of its long-standing slumber. I peer through the gaps in the plank door. With a gentle push, the door yields, its hinges grating, making a tortured sound.

Inside, the cabin consists of a single small room. Dust motes swirl in pale beams of light streaming between holes in the walls and missing roof planks.

The atmosphere feels heavy.

Stepping inside is like entering a time machine as if I've been transported back a hundred years. Rusted pans, their surfaces pitted and tarnished by time, pile haphazardly in a dry-rotted cabinet. They speak of meals cooked over a simple stove and a life sustained by the barest of necessities.

In the corner stands a bed, its frame warped and uneven. The mattress, now little more than a shapeless mass, holds threadbare and moldy blankets. It paints the picture of long nights spent in isolation.

Despite that, it's incredibly well preserved.

While Cage photographs details of this unexpected find, I explore the small space. Kneeling by the mattress, my seeking hands discover something—an ancient leather satchel.

Carefully, I lift it, handling the weathered leather gently, lest it fall apart in my hands. Untying the binding strap reveals a stash of intact letters stuffed inside.

"Look at this…" I glance up at Cage.

He joins me where I sit cross-legged on the dusty floor. I pass him a yellowed sheet of paper, crabbed writing still partially legible in fading brown ink. Skimming the text confirms my guess—this is correspondence from a lonely gold miner, likely intended for a wife or family member left behind.

We take turns peering closely to decipher the old-fashioned script, eager for a firsthand glimpse into this nameless sojourner's experiences. Page by fragile page, I read passages aloud while Cage listens intently:

SEPTEMBER 7, 1898
    Dearest Mary,

OUR CLAIM AT PRESENT SEEMS PALTRY COMPARED TO RUMORS OF strikes downstream. Tomorrow, I depart our valley cabin to try my luck along Quartz Creek. Do not worry about me, my darling wife. Just a few lucky finds and I shall return, our future as golden as our wedding bands...

I GLANCE UP AT CAGE. "EVEN IN 1898, THE GOLD FEVER PUSHED people to extremes out here."

"The lust for fortune has always made fools of men. Read the next one." Cage leans close. Our shoulders touch, and it feels— natural.

OCTOBER 22, 1898
    Beloved Mary,

STILL NO VEIN UNCOVERED, BUT I TOIL UNRELENTINGLY, BE IT DIGGING frozen earth from dawn 'til dusk or panning icy river water through night's blackest hours. This land constantly mocks and thwarts me; its pretend promise of riches is always dancing ahead, just out of reach. But I cannot return empty-handed...

·   ·   ·

Cage sighs, hearing the miner's frustration. "Poor guy. The gold was likely tapped out by earlier prospectors. But he persisted."

"Driven by obsession," I remark. "Unable to walk away empty-handed. The gold rush ruined lives as often as it granted wealth."

January 14, 1899
  My Dearest Mary,

The nights grow ever crueler. I hunker near the embers of my dying fire, envying even the tree stumps not cursed with numb ears and toes. Each day's icy disappointment further steals the warmth from my soul. But I swore I would not return to you unless prospecting enough gold for us to live in comfort. I fear you shall hate me by now or mourn me dead.

Cage shakes his head in empathy. "He put pride over practicality. No gold is worth dying over."

My voice turns solemn as I finish the last letter.

February 2, 1899
  Forgive me…

The next page is too faded, and the sentences illegible and incomplete. I carefully return the letters to their leather home.

"All that suffering for nothing," I say in heavy silence. "He probably died out here alone…"

"And broke his wife's heart waiting back home." Cage's voice resonates with the same sober understanding that we've glimpsed a tragedy born of ego and greed battling against nature's callous indifference.

We take a quiet moment to process the ghost of an old

prospector who seems to hover around us. This nameless miner paid the ultimate price.

It's a sobering reminder.

The wilderness shows no mercy in the end.

Our trespass feels heavy and somber. I say a silent prayer for lost souls like his and for the living who waited somewhere for them to come home.

As we prepare to depart the tragic cabin, a bright crinkle of color catches my eye near the door—a discarded candy wrapper nestled against gnarled roots.

I point it out to Cage.

"Even now, people can't respect the sanctity of the wild. They're supposed to leave no trace, but they leave garbage without thinking about what it does to the environment.

"Who even comes out this deep into the wilderness to litter? Do you run across many hikers this far out?"

"Rarely." My brows furrow because it's exceptionally rare. "The odd hunting party maybe, but they generally stick to their designated grounds." I pause, considering some of the rumors I've heard here and there.

"What is it?" Cage looks at me with concern.

"Probably nothing, just—there've been rumors lately among some guides about illegal prospector activity happening in remote valleys. Old mines reopening under the radar, that kind of thing. But those kinds of rumors are always popping up. Greed makes people stupid."

"And destructive," Cage adds. "Panning for gold is old school. Now, it's about blowing up streambeds, diverting rivers, and causing massive ecologic damage."

The discarded candy wrapper takes on a strange portent, and an ominous chill slithers down my spine.

By late afternoon, we're miles upstream. Dusky sunlight slants against the ridges behind us, burnishing the forest with ripe shades of gold. The river runs glossy as a blue satin ribbon alongside the trail, tranquil compared to the thoughts still churning through my mind after our unsettling detour.

I keep picturing the unnamed miner from the letters, desperate to make his fortune and return to his faraway wife.

FOURTEEN

Ava

———

As Cage and I continue our trek, we come across a serene, crystal-clear lake nestled among the hills. Its surface, mirror-smooth, reflects the azure sky, distant mountain peaks, and the surrounding wilderness. The sight is breathtaking, a hidden gem in the heart of the wild.

"This is incredible," Cage declares, his voice brimming with awe. "I've got to get some shots of this."

He halts, completely taken aback by the pristine beauty of the lake before us.

He quickly sets down his backpack and unpacks his camera gear. I'm mesmerized as he assembles his tripod, his movements precise and fluid.

Cage carefully selects a lens, attaching it to his camera with a click. He surveys the scene, eyes scanning the landscape for the perfect angle. Finally, he positions the tripod at the water's edge, the camera lens pointing toward the lake, capturing its vastness and the reflection of the sky in its mirror-smooth waters.

"There's something about the way the water meets the sky." He peers through the viewfinder. "It's like capturing the essence of tranquility."

I stand back, giving him space to work his magic. He adjusts the settings on his camera, his fingers deftly turning dials and pressing buttons. After a few moments, he pauses, looking up to absorb the scene with his own eyes before returning to the viewfinder.

Click.

The sound of the shutter is crisp in the morning air.

Cage takes a series of photos, each one a careful attempt to encapsulate the beauty before us. He moves around, trying different angles, playing with the light and the reflections on the water.

Watching Cage work his camera is like witnessing a master at his craft. The intensity of his focus is seductive, a virile intensity that comes through in his every movement. He handles his equipment with a confident touch, choosing each adjustment and angle with precision and care.

As he continues to work, lost in his world of angles and light, I grow increasingly entranced by him.

There's something deeply alluring about how he immerses himself in his craft. The focus in his eyes, the slight furrow of his brow as he concentrates—it's a display of passion that's both compelling and sensuous.

His hands move over his camera with a lover's caress, adjusting settings with a confident touch. Those hands, capable and strong, speak of a man who's not just adept at his profession but also in tune with the world around him.

What would those hands feel like on me? Their warmth? Their grip?

Would they be gentle? Firm?

The thought sends an unexpected shiver down my spine and a rush of heat to my core.

There's a certain grace in his fingers as they dance over the camera's buttons and dials, a tenderness in his touch that belies his rugged exterior. In these small, unguarded moments I catch glimpses of a different side of Cage—not just the adventurous photographer but a man with depth and sensitivity.

The way he carefully cradles the camera, ensuring each shot is just right, makes me ponder the care with which he might handle other things.

Like me.

The thought is unbidden, yet it lingers, painting my mind with possibilities that are both thrilling and dangerous. Part of me can't help but be drawn to the mystery of Cage La Rouge.

Deeply absorbed in my thoughts, I don't notice when Cage's gaze shifts from his camera to me. It's only when he speaks, a playful note in his voice, that I snap back to the present.

"Enjoying the view?" Cage raises an eyebrow in amusement.

Heat fills my cheeks at getting caught staring at his ass.

"It's a marvelous sight," I reply quickly, trying to sound nonchalant, but the twinkle in his eye tells me he's not fooled.

Cage's chuckle carries a warmth that seems to echo off the surrounding wilderness, drawing me back from my thoughts. He takes a few steps closer, and there's a softness in his eyes that contrasts with the rugged backdrop.

"Oh, I agree. Absolutely mesmerizing." His gaze lingers on me a moment longer than necessary. "The most captivating scenery is right in front of me." The slight tilt of his head and the earnest look in his eyes leave no doubt about his meaning.

He's talking about me.

His words hang in the air, a bold acknowledgment of the growing attraction between us. A flutter of excitement, mingled with the trepidation of treading into uncharted territory, stirs within me.

"I didn't realize I was part of the Alaskan landscape."

My attempt at maintaining my composure falters. The corner of my mouth quirks up in a half-smile that feels awkward. My gaze darts away, betraying my embarrassment.

Flirting isn't my strong suit, and this playful exchange with Cage is awkward.

Heat warms my cheeks as embarrassment rushes through me.

"Well, you're certainly the most interesting part of it. Nature's got nothing on you." Cage's grin widens, his eyes sparkling with mischief. "Perhaps you'll let me take some photos of you?"

"Me? You're not here to take photos of me."

"Why not?"

"Because I'm not…"

"Ava, You're absolutely stunning."

The banter is light, yet there's an underlying current that's hard to ignore. It's playful yet charged with a sense of something more—a dance around the edges of our growing attraction to each other.

Cage, sensing my discomfort yet undeterred, smoothly transitions the moment by lifting his camera. He peers through the lens, focusing it on me.

"Let's capture some of this Alaskan beauty." With a playful grin, he snaps a few shots.

The camera's clicking serves as a brief respite from our banter, giving me a moment to collect myself. As he lowers the camera, his eyes meet mine again, still holding that playful spark.

"You're an incredible beauty, Miss Ava Livingston, a natural part of the wild that deserves to be documented." He teases with his words, his voice light, but molten heat simmers in his eyes.

"Well, I guess I'll take that as a compliment, coming from a professional photographer." I let out a small, self-conscious laugh, trying to find my footing in this awkward dance with words. "But you're going to have to delete those."

"Why?"

"I'm highly unphotogenic."

"Not from where I stand. You're stunning, and that's more than a compliment. It's a statement of fact." Cage steps closer, his demeanor relaxed. "You fit into this wilderness as if you were made for it. You're a rare beauty."

His sincere and flattering words make my heart skip a beat. It's a strange feeling to be on the other side of a compliment like that, especially from someone like Cage. I find myself at a loss for words, the lines between professional and personal blurring even more between us.

"Keep your focus on the wilderness, Cage La Rouge." I shake my head, a playful retort ready. "That's what we're here for."

"Doesn't have to be the only thing we're here for." His laughter blends seamlessly with the rustling leaves and distant bird calls. "I'm going to get back to work. This light is perfect for catching the soul of this place, and I don't mind if you stare at my ass while I work. Makes me feel less guilty about my dreams about you last night."

My jaw drops.

His what?

Dreams? About me?

How does he do it?

Be so casual about letting me know he's dreaming about me.

Fantasizing about me.

As he turns back to his camera, his words linger in the air, a bold statement about how things might change between us if I let them.

It should worry me that I'm increasingly aware of Cage not as a client but as a man whose presence is becoming more intriguing with each passing day.

"Well, I can't deny the scenery has its perks." I let out a light laugh, conceding to the moment.

"Good to know I rank somewhere close to Alaskan wilderness on the scenic scale." Cage nods, his grin widening.

"Don't let it get to your head." I shake my head, still smiling. "The mountains might still edge you out."

"Ouch, no need to bruise my ego." He pretends to look hurt, placing a hand over his heart. "At least let me pretend you're staring at my ass."

"You're my client. My job is literally to watch your ass and keep it safe."

The banter is light, but there's an undercurrent of something more—a recognition of the tension that's been building between us. It's a dance we've been doing since the start of the trip, a playful back-and-forth that skirts around the edges of something deeper.

"Well, as long as I'm in the top ten of Ava Livingston's wilderness experiences, I'll consider it a win." Sensing the shift in mood, Cage steps back, giving me space.

I appreciate his restraint, the way he catches the moment before it tilts into something more serious.

It's a delicate balance, this push-pull between us, but for now, it remains just that—a gentle teasing that acknowledges the heat building between us without stoking the fire too much.

As he bends to capture a low angle, the muscles in his back flex under his shirt, a subtle display of strength that doesn't escape my notice. His dedication to his art is clear, but it's the raw, masculine energy he exudes while lost in his work that captivates me.

When he straightens to review his images, the light catches his features, highlighting the rugged contours of his face. There's a hint of stubble along his jaw, adding to his outdoor allure.

He looks up, his eyes locking with mine, and in that moment, an electric charge sparks in the air between us.

"Got some great shots," he says, his voice low and slightly husky. "Can't wait to show them to you."

His words stir something within me; the growing attraction I've been trying to keep at bay rushes at me in full force. The way he speaks and the intensity in his gaze is an invitation, a connection beyond the camera and the wilderness.

The moment lingers, laden with unspoken possibilities, before Cage breaks the intense gaze to pack away his camera. The lake, undisturbed and serene, mirrors the sky, but the reflection I'm caught up in is the one I see in his eyes.

"How about a quick swim?" His suggestion holds a new, tantalizing meaning after our charged exchange.

He turns away from me and begins to remove his clothes.

FIFTEEN

Ava

THE CRYSTAL-CLEAR WATERS OF THE MOUNTAIN LAKE BECKON invitingly, promising a refreshing respite from the heat of our hike. Mirror-smooth, it reflects the breathtaking beauty of the mountains around us and the sky, turning them into a shimmering expanse of blues, greens, and grays. It's a sight that never fails to take my breath away.

No matter how many times I've seen it.

Today, however, my attention is drawn to something else entirely.

The Alaskan wilderness is undeniably captivating and dangerous, but my attraction to Cage poses an entirely different threat to my well-being. He stands at the water's edge, his lean, muscular frame a stunning contrast against the serenity of the lake.

He's a force of nature in his own right, embodying a danger just as potent and enthralling as the untamed wilderness all around us.

His fingers deftly unbutton his shirt, and as the fabric slips down his shoulders, it reveals the sculpted contours of his back, muscles shifting sinuously beneath sun-kissed skin as he moves.

A masterpiece of muscle and sinew, I'm lost in the sensual

delight of drinking in his flawless physique and watching the sinuous play of muscles underneath his skin.

He slowly undresses, almost as if making a show of it, revealing a chiseled physique that speaks of rugged adventures. He turns slightly, giving me a view of his chest, the chiseled planes of his pectorals, and the delicious rises and dips of his abdominal muscles.

He's a work of art come to life, each line and curve perfectly crafted by nature and honed by an active lifestyle. Every movement is deliberate and confident, exuding an air of self-confidence that is undeniably alluring. Then, he shucks his briefs, revealing the tight globes of his ass.

This isn't the first time I've noticed how attractive he is, but out here, in the raw, untamed beauty of the outdoors, the perfection of his body hits me with a force that leaves me dizzy.

His legs are strong and defined, the muscles of his thighs and calves flexing as he wades into the water. There's a raw, primal masculinity to him, a strength and vitality that seems to emanate from every pore.

It's not just his physical form that captivates me, but an aura of confidence and capability that surrounds him. He moves with the grace and surety of someone completely at home in his own skin and the wild landscapes we traverse.

It speaks to something deep within me.

A wave of desire sweeps through me, leaving me unexpectedly breathless. I'm utterly captivated by the man standing boldly before me, revealing a sculpted form that demands admiration. I hungrily take in every detail, contour, and ridge of muscle.

"Well, are you coming?" He turns to me, his grin playful and teasing. "Or are you going to stand there with your mouth gaping?"

The invitation to join Cage is tempting. It's a chance to cool off not just from the hike but also from the smoldering tension that's been building between us. Yet, I hesitate, conscious of the professional boundaries I've set.

The man's not in the least bit self-conscious about his nakedness. Not that he should be with that physique and the impressive member between his legs.

"I'm not…" I snap my mouth shut, feeling embarrassed and overwhelmingly drawn to him.

"You are, and I don't mind." His wink is devastating, powerful enough to make my knees wobble.

"I'll pass on the swim." I shake my head, trying to push aside the rush of desire that courses through me.

"It's okay, Ava. I don't mind if you stare. Just don't be surprised when I return the favor." Cage dives into the water, breaking the spell.

I watch, transfixed, as he dives beneath the surface. The water ripples out in concentric circles from his point of entry, but I feel a ripple of something else entirely deep in my core.

It's a pull, a yearning, a visceral response to the sheer masculine beauty before me.

Exhaling shakily, I turn my gaze to the serene landscape around us.

The wilderness, with its endless sky and sprawling beauty, reminds me of the vastness of the world we're exploring—a world that's both exhilarating and humbling in magnitude.

But my thoughts keep returning to Cage. To the things I want him to do—to me.

With me.

My desire for him burns hot as I try to maintain a professional distance, but it's impossible to resist the allure of his adventurous spirit and his chiseled form.

When he resurfaces, water sluices off his skin in tantalizing rivulets that follow every ridge and bulge of muscle. He pushes his hair back with one hand, and the droplets clinging to him catch the light like tiny diamonds.

He's a vision of raw, elemental power, a force of nature given human form, and he turns all that power on me.

A grin spreads across his face and beckons for me to join him.

I hesitate, feeling not only self-conscious but torn by the professional boundaries I've set for myself.

Lines I've sworn not to cross.

I'm no stranger to the wilderness, but the thought of being so exposed and vulnerable in front of him sends a flutter of nerves through me. When he looks back at me with warmth, affection, and that irresistible twinkle in his eyes, my reservations melt away.

Those boundaries I've placed begin to blur as my desire to explore this connection between us continues to grow and deepen.

He swims in the crystal-clear lake while I remain mesmerized by the graceful way he cuts through the water, taking long, lazy strokes. The ripples he creates dance around him as he makes his way toward the center of the lake.

"Are you sure you don't want to join me?" Cage's playful, yet persuasive, voice carries over the water. "The water's chilly but not too cold. Perfect for a quick dip."

"No, I'll pass." I shake my head, feeling self-conscious about my body.

Cage shrugs and continues his swim, disappearing into the depths of the lake. I take a deep breath and sit on a nearby rock, watching him with fascination. He resurfaces after a few minutes, his hair slicked back.

Droplets of water glisten on his skin.

He floats effortlessly, his gaze fixed on me. "Come on, Ava. You need to get out of your head and have some fun."

I hesitate, torn between the professional boundaries I've set and the spontaneous urge to join him.

"No, I'm good here." I try to sound more convinced than I feel.

My mind wanders to forbidden thoughts. Cage is not just a skilled photographer and fearless explorer—there's a primal sensuality to him that ignites my desires.

He oozes sex.

"I dare you." Cage's eyes sparkle with mischief.

"You what?" He catches me off guard with his challenge.

"I dare you." His smile is broad and inviting—maybe a bit lecherous as well. This is Cage La Rouge, after all, where everything has a second meaning. "I promise I don't bite. Unless that's what you like?"

His playful persistence is like a gentle nudge, pushing me toward a decision. He floats there, waiting, a look of anticipation on his face.

"I think I'm good."

I want to join him. The water looks amazing. No doubt chilly, but swimming in a remote lake in the Alaskan wilderness is something to experience. There's a pristineness to it—a connection to our primal roots as humans on this land.

"Come on, Ava, just a quick dip. It's refreshing, you'll see."

"I don't know. The water looks—chilly." I raise an eyebrow, maintaining a semblance of resistance.

"You're not scared of a little cold, are you? I mean, if one of us should be worried, it would be me."

"How do you figure?"

"With the shrinkage." He grins, splashing water playfully in my direction. "I don't want you thinking I'm lacking in certain departments."

I sidestep his splashing, pretending to be unimpressed.

"Come on. Are you scared to join me?"

"Scared? Never. I'm just—strategically assessing the situation." My strategy is a debate with myself.

What are the chances this swim turns into something more?

What if that's what I want?

You want it.

"Strategically assessing? Come on, where's my fearless adventurer?" Cage laughs, and the sound echoes across the water. "I double dog dare you."

"You what?" I stand, appalled by the challenge.

"You heard me, Miss Ava Livingston. I double dog dare you to strip and join me in this pristine jewel of a lake."

SIXTEEN

Ava

CAGE'S WORDS HANG IN THE AIR, A CHALLENGE WRAPPED IN HUMOR. I look at the serene lake, then back at him, his expression full of challenge and amusement.

"Fine. You win," I finally concede, a playful smirk forming. "But just so you know, I'm only doing this because you double dog dared me, and nobody turns down a double dog dare."

"That's the spirit." His triumphant grin is infectious.

Feeling a sense of recklessness overcome me, I quickly strip off my shirt and pants, leaving on my panties and bra. A crisp, cool mountain breeze caresses my skin.

Taking a deep breath, I ready myself for the plunge. It's going to be shockingly cold. Which may be exactly what I need to douse the fire he ignites within me. This isn't about taking a swim; it's about diving into the moment and embracing the possibilities of life.

Unlike Cage, I'm not brave enough to skinny dip. With a running start, I leap into the lake; the water envelops me in its refreshing embrace. It's cool against my skin and sends shivers down my spine.

Cage looks surprised as I join him in the center of the lake.

"Thought you weren't coming in," he says with a smirk.

I brush off his comment and try to focus on swimming instead of the knowledge he's completely naked and within arm's reach.

But Cage doesn't push and maintains a respectful distance.

"I knew you couldn't resist a dare," Cage teases..

We swim together in silence, taking in the sheer beauty of our surroundings. The sun, now high in the sky, casts its warm rays upon us. I'm completely at peace, weightless within this vast expanse of nature.

Cage suddenly splashes me with water, breaking our peaceful reverie.

"Oh, it's on." I splash him back.

Before we know it, we're locked in an all-out splash war. Water flies everywhere as we try to outdo each other's antics. For a moment, all worries and responsibilities fade away as we play like carefree children.

We swim around each other, trying to dodge the water attacks and devise new ways to surprise each other, but then he reaches out. Breathless with anticipation, his hands settle around my waist.

With us both treading water, he pulls me to him. The contact sends a shiver through me that has nothing to do with the chill of the water.

"You're beautiful." His gaze roves over my face with an intensity that makes my stomach flutter. If we were standing on solid ground, my knees would buckle—they feel that weak.

A flush creeps up my neck and down to my core. That warmth has nothing to do with the sun overhead.

"You're not so bad yourself." My voice comes out huskier than I intend, sounding sexy and inviting.

He laughs, the sound rich and warm, then tugs me closer. We float there, wrapped in each other's arms, the rest of the world falling away until it's just us, the water, and the endless expanse of sky overhead.

I let my hands roam over his back, feeling the strength of his muscles. Any moment, he's going to lean in and kiss me, and I don't know if that's what I want.

You want it.

That tiny voice in my head isn't wrong.

What's the worst that could happen if I let myself surrender to the pull between us, to the undeniable attraction that's been simmering beneath the surface since the day we met?

But I'm scared and pull back.

Cage senses my unease and releases me from his embrace.

With that twinkle in his eyes, he cuts through the sexual tension.

"Race you to the shore," he challenges.

"Race?"

"On three?" His brow arches with another dare.

"Fine," I concede, but I'm not waiting for three.

"One… Hey!"

Without waiting for him to count it down, I take off at full speed. It's exhilarating. My arms slice through the water, and my legs kick strongly.

Despite that, Cage closes the distance.

We reach the shore at almost the same time, both out of breath from our sprint. Laughing and gasping for air, we collapse on the shore. Cage turns to me with sparkling eyes, a mischievous glint dancing in them.

"You know," he says between breaths, his voice husky. "I never imagined you would join me in the water. It seems like you have hidden depths, just like this lake. You, Miss Ava Livingston, are a wonderful mystery I can't wait to unwrap."

My cheeks flush at his words, and a mixture of embarrassment and excitement courses through me.

As I catch my breath, I prop myself on my elbows and meet Cage's gaze. His playful grin fades into something more tender, more vulnerable. My heart flutters as he reaches out and brushes a strand of wet hair away from my face.

Cage's presence, so close, overwhelms me. His whispered words hold a sincerity that touches something deep within me. His finger, gently tracing my jawline, leaves a trail of heat in its wake, stirring emotions I've tried and failed to keep at bay.

"You're different, you know?" His warm breath grazes my cheek. The proximity sends a wave of shivers cascading through me.

"There's depth to you that I admire. A fire within you that matches mine."

His intense, green eyes reveal a longing that mirrors mine. The world around us seems to melt away, leaving only this moment suspended in time. Our faces draw closer, the space between our lips diminishing, charged with the anticipation of a kiss that is inevitable.

The air around us thickens with tension.

With want.

With need.

Every breath shared.

Every heartbeat felt.

As his lips hover just a whisper away from mine, a small, knowing smile plays at the corners of his mouth. It's as if he's savoring the slow build of our shared desire.

My heart races, pounding against my rib cage like a frantic drum; its rhythm is the only sound in my ears. The anticipation is exquisite, a sublime mixture of fear and excitement that makes me feel more alive than ever.

Cage traces the contours of my face with his finger, sending delightful tingles of electricity down my spine. He heightens my senses to every subtle movement, every shared breath.

In this bubble of time, with the soft rustle of leaves and the distant call of a bird, the world beyond us fades into insignificance. It's just Cage and me, on the brink of crossing a line that will change everything.

Without another word, he leans close, our lips draw together in a slow and deliberate dance. The kiss is gentle yet electrifying, igniting a wildfire of emotions within me.

Cage's firm and confident lips take the lead. My heart beats wildly as he deepens the kiss. His hands cup my face, and the world around us fades into oblivion, replaced by the warmth of our embrace and the intensity of our kiss.

His lips move in sync with mine, each touch sending waves of pleasure coursing through me. His hand slides down from my cheek to my neck, his fingers tangling in my hair as he pulls me closer.

I wrap my arms around his neck, melting into his embrace as our bodies press against each other. The connection between us feels electric, every touch igniting a fire within me.

Suddenly, Cage pulls away slightly and looks into my eyes with a small smile on his face.

"I've wanted to do that since the moment I saw you, and you taste exactly the way I imagined."

"How's that?"

"You taste like sin."

For a moment, all thoughts evaporate from my mind as I become lost in the sensation of his touch. His lips move slowly and expertly against mine, sending waves of pleasure through my body.

As we break apart to catch our breaths, Cage's forehead rests against mine. His eyes search mine with an intensity that makes my heart race even faster.

"Fuck professionalism, Ava Livingston." His voice is thick, husky, and full of desire. "I won't tell if you don't."

Heat fills my cheeks, and I can't help but smile at his admission.

He chuckles before leaning in for another kiss, this one more urgent and filled with raw passion.

Our bodies press together as we melt into each other's embrace, our kisses growing more intense with each passing moment. Heat builds between us as our bodies press closer together, and my heart races with desire.

Cage's hands explore every inch of my body, sending shivers down my spine with every touch. Our breaths mix together as we kiss, our bodies melding into one.

With one swift motion, Cage rolls me to my back and climbs over me, propping himself up on his elbows.

The cool grass beneath me adds another sensation to this already intense moment. We break apart briefly to catch our breaths before our lips crash back together in a frenzy of desire.

The last vestiges of my control slip as Cage's hands move down my body, igniting a fire within me that I never knew existed. Every touch from him is like an electric shock, setting my nerves on fire.

His mouth travels from my lips to my neck and down to my

collarbone, leaving a trail of fire in its wake. My fingers grip his shoulders as he explores my body with his lips and tongue.

"Cage," I moan out his name without thinking, giving in completely to this intoxicating pleasure.

"I've been dreaming about this from the moment I first saw you," he whispers against my skin before continuing his trail downwards.

My heart pounds in anticipation as Cage slowly removes first my bra and then my panties. He takes in every inch with his gaze. He looks at me with a hunger that leaves me breathless.

"Are you sure?" he asks softly, giving me one last chance to back out. But there's no doubt in my mind. I want this just as much as he does.

"Yes," I reply without hesitation.

The world around us fades to a mere whisper. Cage delicately traces the contours of my body, and heat builds within me, a longing intensified by every tender touch and smoldering look. His eyes, dark with desire, drink in every inch of me, leaving a trail of unspoken promises in their wake.

A guttural huffing, deep and resonant, shatters the moment. It's a sound primal and raw, tearing through the fabric of our intimate bubble.

SEVENTEEN

Ava

Instinctively, we freeze, a cold dread replacing the warmth of our embrace. Our heads turn as one toward the source of the sound.

There, at the tree line, looms a large grizzly bear, an embodiment of the wilderness, untamed and unpredictable.

Its massive head sways from side to side, nostrils flaring as it sniffs the air. The scent of our presence, so stark against the natural backdrop, has drawn its attention. The bear's eyes, small dark pools in its massive skull, fix on us with unsettling intelligence.

Rising onto its hind legs, the grizzly towers over the landscape, a specter of raw power and terrifying might. Its sheer size is breathtaking, a reminder of our own fragility in the face of one of nature's apex predators.

Cage's hand finds mine, a silent pact in the face of danger. Our clothes, a scant few feet away, might as well be miles from us. We're exposed, vulnerable, with nothing but our wits and courage to protect us.

Every instinct screams to flee, yet running only invites a chase we will lose. The bear's presence commands the clearing, a ruler surveying its kingdom, and we are at its mercy.

The grizzly lets out a deep, rumbling roar that vibrates the air and strikes a chord of fear deep within me. My heart pounds in my chest, a rapid drumbeat echoing the bear's growl. The sound is primal, a declaration of dominance that sends icy tendrils of terror down my spine.

"My gun's by my pack. Where's yours?" Cage's body tenses, his muscles coiled and ready for action.

Our situation is dire. The bear, its massive bulk a testament to raw, untamed power, shifts its weight, its muscles rippling beneath its thick fur. Each movement is calculated, a display of strength and agility that belies its size.

"With my clothes." I point toward the pile of my discarded clothes, my voice tight with tension.

I keep my pistol on me at all times except when I'm naked and being unprofessional. Now, I curse my lapse in judgment.

The bear's gaze locks on us, its black eyes piercing and calculating. With a sudden, earth-shaking thud, it drops to all fours. The ground vibrates under its weight as it takes a deliberate, lumbering step forward. Its nostrils flare, scenting the air, honing in on our vulnerability.

My pulse races, every instinct screaming danger. The bear's proximity is suffocating, its presence an overwhelming force.

The bear watches us, its head tilting slightly, assessing our movements. My mind races, calculating our chances and strategizing our next move. Each second feels like an eternity, stretched taut with the anticipation of the inevitable.

Our deaths.

"I'll distract it," Cage murmurs under his breath. His eyes are wide, his body coiled like a spring ready to unwind. The determination in his voice is palpable, a willingness to risk everything to protect me. "You get your gun."

The bear's attention shifts to our gear, which is temptingly close to the water's edge—too close to where we lie on the grassy shore. Its eyes glint with a predatory gleam, a hunger that goes beyond mere curiosity.

"Cage, no." It's suicide, but before I can argue, the bear lowers to all four and charges.

In a burst of terrifying speed, the grizzly devours the distance between us. It's a nightmare come to life: a surge of muscle and fury, its massive paws slamming the earth with each stride. The ground shakes beneath its weight, a testament to its raw, unstoppable power.

"Run!" Cage's shout is a command, pushing me into action. He darts in the opposite direction, drawing the bear's focus away from me. His movements are swift and purposeful, a desperate gamble to buy me time.

My heart hammers in my chest, and adrenaline pumps through my veins. Cage risks his life to create a diversion for me, a selfless act of bravery that terrifies and humbles me.

I sprint toward my clothes, my mind racing. I need to get to my gun. Every step feels like an eternity, the distance stretching out before me in a mocking challenge.

The bear's heavy paws thud against the ground, the steady drumbeat terrifyingly close. I feel it closing in on Cage, a vivid reminder of how thin the line is between life and death.

I reach for my clothes, fumbling frantically for the pistol. My fingers wrap around bear spray, a non-lethal deterrent.

Shit.

Where's my gun?

I'm reluctant to harm the bear. The animal is more curious than aggressive, a wild animal drawn by the scent of food, but with Cage's life on the line, I have no choice.

"Catch!" I shout to get Cage's attention and hurl the can through the air, my aim true.

The moment the bear spray is out of my hands, I search for my pistol with renewed urgency.

There.

Under my jeans.

My fingers close around the cold metal, a lifeline in the face of mortal danger.

Cage catches the bear spray and immediately unleashes a cloud of noxious chemicals toward the charging beast. The spray billows out, a caustic barrier between him and the grizzly.

I steady my shaking hands. I have to get this right.

I only have one chance.

I aim for a shot that will kill the bear, my finger hovering over the trigger. The weight of the moment settles on my shoulders, a burden of responsibility and survival.

The bear, caught off-guard by the painful spray to the eyes, nose, and mouth, recoils. Its roar of pain and confusion splits the air, a sound that chills my blood and sets my nerves on fire.

It rears back, confusion and pain etched in its wild, flailing movements. A guttural huff of discomfort escapes its throat as it backs away from Cage, violently shaking its massive head in an attempt to rid itself of the stinging irritant.

Unfortunately, Cage is also hit in the face by the irritating spray. His eyes water and he coughs, his own discomfort evident, but he stands his ground in the face of overwhelming danger.

The scene is a tableau of chaos and tension, a snapshot of the raw, untamed power of the wilderness. We're caught in a dance with death, our fates hanging in the balance of the next few heartbeats.

Will the bear retreat, driven back by the painful deterrent?

Or will its instincts override its discomfort, urging it to press the attack?

I hold my breath, my finger tight on the trigger, ready to take the shot if needed, but I pray it won't come to that.

I pray we'll walk away from this encounter with a newfound respect for its dangers. Out here, we are not apex predators. We're small players in a grand, unforgiving drama.

I stand my ground until the bear decides its fate.

Fortunately, the bear retreats, roaring in pain and shaking its head, while Cage stumbles backward. His hands go to his face in a reflexive attempt to shield his eyes, temporarily blinded by the very thing that saved him.

Saved us.

"Don't rub them." I react instantly, my heart pounding with a new surge of adrenaline. I rush to him. "It'll only make it worse."

I guide him to the water's edge and grab a water bottle and clean cloth from my pack. Sitting Cage down, I tilt his head back on my lap and rinse his eyes with water, flushing out the irritant as best as possible.

Cage tries to keep his eyes open as the water flows over them, hissing in discomfort but cooperating. After a few minutes of continuous rinsing, he blinks a few times and looks at me, his eyes puffy, red, and watering but slightly less pained.

"Are you okay?" My voice is laced with worry as I flush the irritant from his eyes.

Despite the pain and the precariousness of our situation, he manages a small, strained smile, his characteristic humor shining through even in adversity.

He nods, his breathing heavy, still trying to regain his bearings.

"Yeah, just—give me a moment." He winces but maintains that wry smile, embodying his innate resilience. "That was—intense."

"Just rest your eyes for a bit." I nod, relieved that he's okay.

He chuckles softly, the sound surprisingly light given the circumstances.

"Talk about being naked and afraid. Not to mention, that bear is one hell of a cock-blocker."

His words, delivered with a half-laugh, cut through the tension like a knife slicing through butter.

I can't help but laugh, a genuine sound that feels like a release valve for my pent-up fear and tension.

"*Naked and afraid?*" I shove him playfully. "Good one."

There's something liberating in our laughter, a sense of camaraderie and mutual respect that only grows stronger by the day.

We find ourselves relaxing, the laughter easing the strain of the past few minutes.

As Cage sits there, blinking away the last of the discomfort from his eyes, a playful glint returns to them. Despite the harrowing situation we've just endured, his humor remains undiminished, a buoyant force in the face of adversity.

"You know, I've always wanted to hug a bear, but that was a bit too close for my taste." His face fills with a lopsided grin.

I can't help but chuckle, shaking my head at his irrepressible spirit. "I think you got a bit closer than recommended for wildlife encounters."

"You know, in all the excitement, I realized something crucial." Cage, blinking away the discomfort, looks at me with a wry grin, a playful twinkle in his eye.

"What's that?" A smile tugs at my lips despite the lingering adrenaline.

"Well, in my backpack, which I meticulously packed for every eventuality, I have condoms. But guess where they are?" He raises his eyebrows comically.

"Where?" I'm curious despite myself and very interested in the fact he packed them at all. The man definitely has a one-track mind.

"They're shoved all the way at the bottom. Just my luck, right?" His chuckle is infectious, and I can't help but join in.

"At the very bottom, under everything else. So, in the heat of the moment, they might as well be on the moon." His laughter is light, a welcome sound amidst the tension.

I can't help but join in, the absurdity of the situation hitting me. "That's just perfect. Prepared for a bear attack, but not for… Other encounters."

He nods, his smile broadening. "Exactly. Ready for every wilderness challenge, except romance, it seems. Talk about being caught with my pants down—figuratively speaking, of course."

"At the moment, it's quite literal," I tease, gesturing to his still-naked state with a playful smirk.

We're both naked, but all the heated passion from a few minutes ago is gone.

Cage glances down at himself and laughs, unabashed and free. "Well, that just adds to the stories we'll tell our friends, doesn't it?"

"Definitely makes for a memorable story." I shake my head in amusement.

He looks up, his eyes glinting with humor and an unspoken

promise. "That bear kind of ruined the mood, and I'm guessing you'll suggest we move."

"Exactly. I want as much distance between us and that bear as possible."

"We'll have to wait for the right moment then."

"What?"

"You and I, Ava Livingston, have—unfinished business."

"I suppose we do."

Our laughter mingles and dances through the trees, a testament to Cage's ability to find lightness in even the most intense situations.

It's a reminder that sometimes, life throws unexpected challenges our way—and sometimes, those challenges include being caught quite literally with your pants down.

"For the record, I prefer my nature a little less—grizzly." His eyebrows wag comically, pleased with his own pun.

I laugh, the sound echoing amidst the trees. "You're impossible."

He takes a step back slightly, feigning a hurt look. "Hey, I just survived a bear attack and a pepper spray facial. I think I've earned the right to a few bad jokes."

"Fair enough," I concede, smiling. "But let's avoid any more wildlife encounters. My heart can't take the excitement. Get dressed." I grab his clothes and toss them to him.

Cage snatches them out of the air and begins to get dressed. "Agreed. From now on, the wildest thing I want to encounter is a squirrel. Maybe a rabbit if I'm feeling adventurous."

"You know, it's not every day you need bear spray *and* condoms at the same time." I shake my head at the weird direction our day has taken.

From almost having sex to surviving a grizzly bear encounter, this is definitely going down as one of the oddest animal encounters I've ever experienced.

"Next time, I'll put the condoms on top."

"You're assuming there will be a next time."

"Oh, dear Ava, there will definitely be a next time. It's inevitable."

As I lace my boots, the encounter is a stark reminder of how a momentary distraction can turn deadly in the blink of an eye. It reminds me to remain alert and not let passion overcome reason.

The moment I drop my professionalism, my client is nearly killed by a bear. We may be *inevitable*, but there will be no sex for the remainder of this journey.

I can't allow distraction.

Out here, it's deadly.

We set off again. Cage, still recovering, continues to crack jokes, each one lightening the atmosphere a bit more.

His ability to find humor in the face of danger is more than just a coping mechanism; it's a testament to his character and his strength.

It makes him that much more attractive, and my lady-bits tingle in anticipation of doing exactly what I just swore I wouldn't do.

EIGHTEEN

Cage

———

OVER THE NEXT FEW HOURS, MY VISION GRADUALLY IMPROVES. THE world around me—a hazy blur of pain and indistinct shapes from the bear spray—slowly comes back into focus.

Lush pines and rolling hills emerge from the mist of my impaired sight, their details sharpening as if coming into focus through a camera lens.

It's a relief to see the world around me regaining its vividness. Each tree and bush stands crisp against the backdrop of the vast Alaskan expanse. The Silverthorn River, a ribbon of silver and blue, winds through the land, catching the sun. It glints as if hinting at hidden secrets.

Gold runs in the veins of this land—it's everywhere here, not just in the riverbeds but in the very heart of this land. It's a treasure that, for centuries, has lured souls both noble and nefarious.

I never know where my assignments will take me, which is why there's no solid plan or scheduled shoots. I'm fortunate to have an editor who knows how I work best. I'd never have the story I'm slowly piecing together if I kept to a rigid script.

This shoot is quickly becoming more than a focus on Alaska's untouched wilderness. Every photo I take is a testament to the glory and the plight of this untamed land, but when I found those flecks of gold in the river and then we stumbled upon that abandoned cabin back in the woods, the story began building itself.

Ava and I continue our journey along the riverbank, our steps cautious and measured. The storm has left its mark here, and with each step, we uncover more evidence of human interference, a silent testament to the illegal activities hidden within this remote paradise.

Ava and I take a break by the river. We've been walking for hours, content to meander slowly, captivated by elegant hawks soaring high above in the search for prey and the scurry of red squirrels busy among the underbrush hiding from the hawks. Our relaxed pace feels suited to the beauty around us.

My camera gets a vigorous workout, capturing the primitive splendor around each bend. I find myself framing shots not just of the soaring mountain peaks and glassy lakes but studies of minute details—the riverside stones polished smooth by relentless currents, the knots and whorls in weathered pine concealing secret inner worlds.

Ava indulges each impromptu stop, waiting with that trademark half-smile that conveys amused tolerance of my artistic compulsions. I appreciate her patience and the guiding role she slips into as naturally as donning her worn leather boots each morning.

Out here, she's fully in her element.

Strong. Determined. Resilient.

By late morning, we halt beside a meadow strewn with wildflowers offering views that rob me of both breath and words. Snow-draped peaks loom in the distance, more real and magnificent than hours earlier when they were shrouded in mist.

Ava drops her pack, stretching lithely, while I catch the microscopic reflection of our world in dewdrops clinging to the tips of delicate flowers.

Her innate grace reminds me of the lynx we spotted two hours back—lethal grace coiled beneath casual nonchalance, primed to pounce on unfortunate prey.

I force my gaze from Ava, raising my camera to admire the majestic landscape around us. My fingers work their magic, adjusting F-stops to maximize lighting effects and enhance the luminance glittering off a distant glacier's cracked façade.

But my concentration wavers.

My awareness keeps drifting back to the enigmatic woman at my side who outshines even nature's brilliance.

Back to that kiss.

With each passing day, my attraction to Ava intensifies. It's a geological event with subtle rumbles that will eventually give way to violent upheaval.

We're an inevitability.

That fleeting kiss leaves me craving more.

That grizzly bear ruined the perfect moment.

Cock-blocked me when I was right on the cusp of finally claiming Ava as mine.

Each night, my dreams transform into fevered fantasies of Ava's lithe limbs intertwined with mine. I can't get her out of my head.

She's in my blood, in my very bones. Her smile, her laughter, and the fire in her eyes when she looks at me ignite flames that threaten to consume me whole.

I ache to pull her fiercely into my arms, to feel her melt against me as our passion ignites into an all-engulfing inferno. One searing kiss, and I know she'll be as lost to this craving as I…

Ava suddenly whirls, alertness widening her eyes. I exhale raggedly, trailing her belatedly as she goes to investigate. Crouched upon the trail, she traces a boot print barely detectable against wild grasses and stones. This far into the backcountry, evidence of previous human passage makes her instantly wary.

An emotion I share.

"What's wrong?" The question escapes me before I can yank it back, and my protectiveness surges to the surface.

"We're not alone." She turns to look at me, and our gazes lock.

Slowly, she reaches for her belt and goes to the holster where she keeps her gun. The tightness of her jaw brooks no argument. She senses a threat, not comprised of fang and claw but two-legged and highly unpredictable.

"They could just be hikers." I hope for the best, but trust her instincts.

"Hikers rarely venture this far." She shakes her head, and her fingers curl around the pommel of her gun. Without another word, she follows the direction of the bootprint.

"The prints could be days old. Weeks old."

"Not after that storm. These prints are fresh." She traces the outline of the print. "See how the sides are sharp? The rain would've worn down older tracks. These are less than a day old. They were placed after that rain, when this ground was wet."

Ava exchanges a loaded glance with me.

She brings a finger to her lips and shakes her head, determination flashing. The subtext isn't hard to parse—she needs to know who trespasses here and why.

Crouching low, breaths measured and controlled, she advances. I trail behind her warily and scan left and right.

We try to follow the trail but lose it in the underbrush. Frustrated, Ava gives up, and we continue our journey along the Silverthorn River, the water's murmur a constant companion to our steps.

The recent storm transformed the landscape, and with every step, we uncover more of its aftermath.

Usually a gentle, meandering ribbon of water, the Silverthorn River churns violently, swollen from the downpour. The river's banks, previously well-defined and stable, are transformed. Where there once was a smooth continuity of sand and mud, now there are jagged edges and abrupt interruptions.

Eroded embankments expose layers of earth that have remained hidden for years, if not decades. The rich browns and dark grays of the soil form a stark contrast against the lighter sand, revealing a history of the river's path.

As we progress, it's not just the natural shifts that catch our eye. Unnatural patterns emerge in the mud and sand—linear imprints and geometric depressions that disrupt the river's organic flow. These alterations are jarring, an abrupt deviation from the natural order of things.

I can't help but pause at these signs, a sense of foreboding growing within me. The wilderness I came to capture and celebrate through my lens now reveals a hidden narrative, one that speaks of human interference and greed.

Ava, with her expert knowledge of the land, moves ahead with a determined stride, her eyes scanning the ground. She crouches beside one of the more pronounced imprints, her hand hovering above it as if to feel the story it tells without disturbing its tale.

"These aren't natural formations." Her voice holds a complex blend of anger and sadness. Her eyes, usually bright with the thrill of the wild, now darken with worry. "Look at this. It's too structured, too deliberate. Someone's been using heavy equipment here."

I kneel beside her, my camera hanging forgotten around my neck. Once pointed out, the imprints are unmistakable—the legacy of machinery likely used for excavation.

"You think it's related to mining?" I ask, although I already suspect the answer.

Ava nods. She stands and surveys the area with a practiced eye. "It's the only explanation that makes sense. But why here? This part of the river is remote, far from any legal mining sites."

"I think that's the operative word." My teeth grind as the muscles of my jaw bunch.

"What's that?"

"Legal."

We follow the disturbed riverbanks, the evidence becoming more apparent with each step. The storm's ferocity inadvertently exposed activities meant to remain hidden.

Continuing our exploration along the river, we find further evidence of human activity, each discovery more disheartening than the last. We scramble over a grouping of boulders and come upon a startling scene.

Half-buried in the silt and debris left behind by the storm's fury are remnants of mining tools. Metal pans, their edges bent and worn, lie scattered among the stones. Shattered sluice boxes, which play a crucial role in sifting through river gravel, are busted fragments of their former utility. Frayed lengths of hose, once vital for directing water, lie twisted and abandoned.

I pause, my camera in hand, and document the intrusion. The twisted metal and broken wood stand in stark contrast to the river's natural beauty. Each photograph I take feels like an indictment, a silent testimony to the careless disregard for this wilderness.

As we move on, our path takes us through a thicket where the storm left yet another mark. Tangled amongst the branches and roots, we find fragments of heavy-duty canvas and rope. These pieces, torn and weather-beaten, are evidence of a temporary but significant human presence.

Ava examines the scene and points to a clearing nearby. The ground is flattened and bare, and the grass and underbrush are trampled by frequent use.

"Looks like they had a camp here." Frustration tinges her voice. "This isn't just a few tools left behind. They set up here for a while."

I nod, taking in the scene. "But why here? And where are they now?" The question hangs in the air, unanswered.

Ava walks over to the flattened area, her eyes scanning the ground. "They were hiding. Far enough from the river to avoid detection but close enough to mine it." She kicks at a small pile of rocks, uncovering more traces of their stay.

I capture the scene, my camera clicking repeatedly. This is a sophisticated operation.

The remains of the camp and the discarded tools suggest hasty abandonment. "They must have fled when the storm hit," I muse aloud. "Or maybe they were spooked by something else."

Ava dusts her hands. "Either way, they left in a hurry. And they didn't care what they left behind."

This wilderness, which I came to capture in its natural state, is caught in the crossfire of human greed. It reminds me that even in the most remote corners of the world, the impact of human actions is ever-present.

As Ava and I push further along the riverbank, the signs of human intrusion become even more pronounced. We reach a stretch of the river where the earth itself tells a story of disturbance and disruption.

Here, the soil and gravel along the water's edge look freshly turned, the layers unmistakably disturbed.

"This is recent," I comment, kneeling to take a closer look. The ground under my knees is soft, the soil loose and unsettled. I run my fingers over the surface, feeling the granularity of the freshly moved earth.

Ava joins me, her gaze scanning the area with a trained eye. Her voice holds a note of concern. "They were digging right here, along the river. You can see how the layers have been upturned."

The evidence is undeniable. The natural stratification of the soil is disrupted, with deeper layers of earth now exposed to the surface.

I step back, lifting my camera to capture this new evidence. The viewfinder frames the disturbed earth, each photograph recording the violation inflicted upon this land. With every click of the shutter, a growing sense of responsibility to tell this story builds within me to show the world the hidden scars of this landscape.

We stand side by side, looking at the disrupted earth. The tranquil beauty of the river now feels bittersweet, its purity marred by the greed that lurks beneath its surface.

This isn't a case of casual prospecting; it's a systematic exploitation of the land. We follow the trail of destruction, documenting everything.

Ava's expertise as a guide is invaluable; she navigates us through the terrain with a surefootedness that speaks of years of experience, but even she can't mask the growing concern in her eyes.

"We need to report this to the authorities," she says, her voice firm.

"We need more proof than this. For all we know, they could be long gone."

"True," she breathes out in frustration. "But not tonight. It's late, and I'm tired. Let's find a place to set camp away from here. We'll explore in the morning."

We walk in silence, each lost in our thoughts. The river continues its journey, oblivious to the human intrigues that now touch its banks. But for us, the revelations of the day change everything.

What started as a journey to document the untouched beauty of Alaska has become a mission to uncover and report the exploitation hidden within its heart.

As the shadows lengthen and the sky paints itself in the warm hues of sunset, Ava and I find ourselves a suitable spot to set up camp for the night. The events of the day weigh heavily on our minds, the disturbing discoveries we've made refusing to be left behind with the setting sun.

We work in tandem, the routine of setting up camp a familiar dance between us. Yet, there's a new tension in the air, an unspoken shift in our dynamic. The bear encounter and the subsequent discovery of the illegal mining operation have left us raw and on edge.

I can't help but steal glances at Ava as she efficiently sets up her tent, her movements precise and purposeful.

The attraction between us, the slow-burning ember that's been growing with each shared experience, each moment of vulnerability and trust, feels like a physical presence.

As if sensing my thoughts, Ava looks up, her eyes meeting mine across the small clearing we've chosen for our campsite. There's a flicker of something there, a heat that mirrors my own, but it's tempered by a resolve I've come to admire and respect.

"I think it's best if we sleep in separate tents." Her voice is steady despite the undercurrent of emotion. "We need to focus on what we need to do next. I don't want any—distractions."

"You're right," I agree, my own voice sounding rougher than I intend. "We can't afford any distractions." I understand her concerns even as a part of me aches to close the distance between us.

She nods, a small, grateful smile touching her lips before returning to her task. I do the same, focusing on setting up my own tent.

As night falls, we forgo a fire, not willing to risk the miners discovering our presence. We huddle over a cold meal and keep our voices low as we discuss our next steps.

As the fatigue of the day catches up with us, we bid each other good night. The space between our tents feels like a chasm, a necessary boundary, but we share a connection we can't quite sever.

Lying in my sleeping bag, listening to the soft sounds of the night and the gentle rustling of Ava settling into her own tent, I'm struck by the duality of our situation.

Out here, in the vast, untamed wilderness of Alaska, we've found a connection, a bond forged through shared adversity and mutual respect. Yet, at the same time, we're forced to maintain a distance to prioritize the mission over our own desires.

NINETEEN

Cage

___

The next morning, we decide not to break camp. Instead, we travel light, moving quickly and silently, following a faint trail marked by subtle signs of human activity. Small pieces of discarded equipment, a glove lying forgotten among the undergrowth, and the faint, out-of-place smell of diesel hanging in the air.

It's all wrong—a blight on this remote, pristine wilderness.

What we find sends a cold shiver down my spine. A rudimentary gold mining operation—a couple of rough tents, mining tools scattered around, a makeshift sluice box set up by the river, and clear signs of recent excavation.

It's a small setup, but the impact on the surrounding environment is unmistakable—and significant.

Ava gestures emphatically for my silence as she stops by a tree, eyes calculating. We crouch behind the vegetation, hearts pounding, as we peer through the dense foliage.

Hiding.

This is what I was meant to capture: the stark reality of human greed clashing with nature's beauty. I carefully take out my camera, adjusting the settings for the perfect shot.

My lens is now a weapon in a different kind of battle. The camera clicks, each sound a quiet condemnation of the destruction before us. I move as close as I dare, hanging tight to the vegetation, documenting everything with a click of my camera.

As I focus on capturing every detail, Ava keeps watch, her keen eyes scanning the perimeter for any signs of movement. The tension is palpable, a tightness in the air that has nothing to do with the chill of the Alaskan wilderness.

A sudden eruption of raucous male voices disrupts the tranquil silence. Emerging from one of the tents are two men, their appearances rough, ragged, almost savage. Grubby and unkempt, their beards are wild, and their faces etched with lines that speak of hard, unforgiving lives. They move with a brutish lack of grace, swilling amber liquid from a bottle and passing it back and forth with aggression.

The clothes they wear are worn and weather-beaten, chosen for utility and camouflage. Yet, even at this distance, it's clear they belong more to a world of back alleys and hidden agendas than to this pristine wilderness.

The harsh timbre of their voices carries, their words indistinct, but their tone unmistakably menacing. Exuding an air of brash cockiness, there's a dangerous edge to their laughter and gestures.

They have the look of criminals, men who have crossed lines and who view the world, and perhaps other people, as resources to be exploited.

Or eliminated.

A cold prickle of unease slithers down my spine.

Ava's hand tightens subtly on her gun, and her body tenses like a bowstring.

"What are you thinking?" I lean closer to Ava, whispering.

"Report them to the authorities." Her eyes never leave the men. Her voice is a low murmur, barely audible.

We watch in silence as the men move around their campsite. They're rough.

Their movements lack the experience of someone accustomed to the wilderness.

Retreating from the campsite, Ava leads with a quiet urgency. "We need to circle around. The mining operation won't be at their camp. It's likely in the river. That's where we'll find the proof you need to photograph. If they see us…"

"They won't." The determination in my voice surprises even me.

I swap out the memory card with a fresh, new one to capture more of the ecological disaster this operation inflicts on the pristine Alaskan wilderness.

The evidence is damning—the scarred earth, the muddied water, the remnants of chemicals and refuse littering the once-pristine landscape. It's a testament to the callous disregard for the delicate balance of nature, all in the pursuit of profit.

"Do you have what you need?" Ava whispers.

"I do." My jaw tightens with determination.

We begin a cautious retreat, our steps measured and silent, our ears straining for any hint of discovery. But our exit isn't as smooth as our approach. A twig snaps under my foot, loud in the forest's silence.

Shouts echo from the campsite.

"Who's there?"

"What was that?"

"Go check it out!"

My heart leaps into my throat, adrenaline surging through my veins. We've been spotted.

"Run!" Ava grabs my arm, pulling me back into the dense forest.

We plunge into the underbrush, thorns and branches tearing at our clothes and skin. Behind us, the sounds of pursuit grow louder —the thud of heavy boots, the crash of bodies through the foliage. Angry voices call out, demanding we stop and threatening violence if we don't.

But we don't stop. We can't. The stakes are too high, and the evidence we carry is too vital.

The shouts grow louder and angrier. We weave through the

trees, our breaths ragged, our hearts pounding, our only thought to put as much distance between us and the miners as possible.

My lungs burn, and my legs ache as we race through the forest, dodging trees and leaping over fallen logs. Ava is a blur of motion ahead of me, her mastery of the terrain evident in every sure-footed step.

A glance over my shoulder reveals our pursuers, rough-looking men with hard eyes and grim expressions. They're gaining on us, their determination fueled by desperation and the knowledge of what we've uncovered.

Suddenly, a shot rings out, the sound cracking through the forest like thunder. A bullet whizzes past my ear, close enough to feel the heat of its passage.

"Keep going!" Ava shouts, her voice ragged with exertion. "We can't let them catch us."

We redouble our efforts, pushing ourselves to the limit. The forest becomes a blur, a green maze we navigate on instinct and adrenaline. The men fall behind, their shouts and curses growing fainter.

Suddenly, Ava veers sharply to the left, pulling me with her. We burst through a wall of foliage and find ourselves at the base of a steep, nearly vertical incline. The ground is slick and treacherous, full of rock, roots, and dirt, which is precarious at best. The slope is thirty feet high.

Ava's breaths come in ragged gasps. My legs burn with exertion.

We're trapped.

The realization we've stumbled into something far more dangerous than we anticipated sets in. Our very lives may be at stake.

Ava glances back at me, searching.

"We need to climb." There is no other option.

Ava nods, and without hesitation, she scales the slope, grabbing rocks and roots. Her movements are sure and swift. I follow with our pursuers' shouts echoing in my ears.

The incline is steep, the ascent grueling. Above me, Ava's foot slips, and for a heart-stopping moment, she teeters on the edge of losing her balance. Her hand shoots out, seizing a sturdy root protruding from the dirt.

Her gun tumbles from its holster.

"Ava!" Alarmed, I increase my pace, desperate to get to her before she falls.

TWENTY

Cage

Ava grunts as she tries to hold on, her feet scrabbling for purchase. Her grip on the root is fair at best. A shower of dirt pelts my face as she desperately tries to find purchase with her boots.

"I'm okay," she tries to reassure me, but her voice betrays a hint of uncertainty and very real fear.

A fall from this height…

I don't want to think about her tumbling to the ground.

I scramble up the slope, my heart pounding. Reaching for her, I extend my hand.

"Grab on!"

She glances down, assessing the distance between us. "I can't reach without letting go." Her voice is strained and full of fear. The root she holds gives, pulling out from the steep slope. She drops a few inches and gasps.

"Then I'll come closer." But there are no easy handholds between me and where she clings to the steep slope.

Determination surges through me. I edge down a fraction, my feet seeking purchase. I aim to place myself directly below her rather than to the side like I am.

"Careful." Her gaze fixes on me.

I inch closer until I can almost reach her, but her boots are a few inches out of my grasp.

But I can catch her.

"When I say *three*, I want you to let go and try to put your feet on my shoulders."

"Okay…" She doesn't sound convinced, but there's no other way.

"One… two…"

She hesitates, the tension visible in her frame.

"THREE!" I steady my base on the rocks that hold me.

Her grip fails, and she slides down the steep incline, fingers scrabbling for purchase. Her left foot connects with my shoulder, but her right one tangles in the strap of my camera. Her slide accelerates, turning into a fall, and my camera falls with it.

In a split-second decision, I grab at her belt. My other hand finds a solid root, anchoring us both.

"I've got you." A surge of adrenaline rushes through me. "Find your footing."

"I'm trying." She grunts from the strain, but there are no good handholds.

My muscles strain from holding her. "There… To the right… An outcropping of rock. I'm going to swing you."

"Okay." She sees the rocky outcropping.

I swing her toward the outcropping, but it's too far. I need more momentum. Ava swings back. My muscles scream in protest, but I build the momentum I need. On the second swing, Ava soars toward the rocky ledge.

I've done this before—on a mountain—scaling Everest. Then, I was strapped into a harness and had solid anchoring with my rope and gear. I have none of that now.

Her feet find purchase, and her hand grabs at a rock jutting over her head.

"I've got it." She pants, her breathing heavy.

I lean against the steep slope and press my forehead to the cool dirt, giving thanks.

That was too close.

Slowly, cautiously, we resume our ascent. The sound of the men's voices echo all around us.

They lost us, but they're circling back, closing in.

The near-miss leaves a lingering tremor in Ava's limbs.

"Take it slow," I try to caution her.

"But the men…"

"Won't mean a thing if you slip and fall." I climb beside her now and a little below so that I can catch her again if she falls. "Test each footing. We'll make it."

She may be an expert wilderness guide, but I'm the expert when it comes to climbing challenging slopes. I fall back on my mountaineering skills, climbing with a partner on an uncertain rock face.

Speed kills.

When we reach the top, Ava collapses, her breaths coming in ragged gasps. I give her a moment to catch her breath. She's exhausted.

"Thanks for the save." Ava turns to me, a soft smile touching her lips, but then the miners reach the base of the slope.

"Where'd they go?" one of them shouts.

They debate it for a moment, and then another man cries out to his fellows.

"They fucking climbed the slope."

Unwilling to wait for them to join us, I grab Ava and place a finger over my lips, cautioning her to silence. Slowly, I scoot back, gesturing for her to do the same. Once we're a safe distance from the edge, I climb to my feet and then help Ava to hers. Together, we back away from the edge as quietly as we can.

We set off again, hoping the miners give up the chase. The forest swallows us into the vast expanse of its untamed wilderness, but there's no time to admire the view.

Ava's fall cost us, and we need to keep moving.

We plunge deeper into the forest, the canopy above providing scant cover. The shouts of the men fade, but we know they're still on our trail.

Every snapped twig, and rustling leaf sends a jolt of fear through me. I can only hope their tracking skills are non-existent.

Ava keeps pace with me. When I catch glimpses of her, her focus is unwavering. I admire her strength and her resilience, but she has her limits.

"I-I need to—Rest." Ava finally stops. Propping her hands on her thighs, she bends forward to catch her breath.

I use the stop to listen for the men. Ava stands and takes a few more deep breaths.

"I don't hear them, but that doesn't mean they're not on our trail."

"We need to get them off our trail." She glances around, trying to orientate herself.

"What do you suggest?"

The ground is still damp from the previous rain. We can do nothing to prevent leaving a trail of footprints or bootprints behind us, leading them straight toward us.

But Ava knows this.

"Come." She gestures for us to continue. "Talk and walk."

We slow our pace, letting Ava recover her breath.

"I'm all ears."

"We have to head back to the river." Her expression twists into a grimace.

"What about our gear?" We left our gear at our campsite. Ava lost her gun during that climb, and I lost my camera with most of the damning photos on it. I have the other SIM card, but the photos we need are still in my camera.

"We can't risk it. Hopefully, they're too stupid to look for it, but we must assume they found our camp. We head to the river and use it to lose them."

"Won't they just cross behind us? Pick up our trail on the far bank?"

"Not if we head downriver."

"Downriver?" I stop, mouth gaping. "Did you miss those rapids? Or how cold that river is? We'll die smashed against the rocks. If not that, then hypothermia will take us. We have minutes at best before immersion in that water kills."

"If we continue here, they'll follow our trail. If we circle around, we'll most likely find them waiting at our camp. If we cross the river, it won't take but a simple search to find our footprints on the other side." She gestures overhead. "And the trees offer nothing."

Trees? Never occurred to me to think about the trees, but I see what she means.

Ava takes in a deep breath. "I don't see another way."

"Fine." I don't like it, but we're out of options.

We alter course and race toward the river. Before long, the roar of rushing water is unmistakable. The dense forest around us blurs into a green streak as we push through the underbrush and try not to twist an ankle on exposed roots.

Finally, we come to the edge of a steep embankment. Below, the riverbank comes into view with churning water and roaring rapids. White froth crashes against the rocks.

This part of the river is narrower and steeper than what we've seen so far. Instead of a lazy flow, it's an untamed, raging beast.

My heart sinks at the sight because those waters are beyond treacherous.

Ava surveys the scene, her expression grim.

"We have to jump," Ava yells over the din of the river and our pursuers.

I look at her, seeing the determination in her eyes, the unwavering courage that has brought us this far. I nod, gripping her hand tightly.

"You can't be serious about jumping into that?" I turn to her, sure the sight of these rapids will force her to find an alternate escape.

"We don't have much choice. We either risk the rapids or get caught."

"We head into that water, and we'll both drown."

"I know how it looks, and it's going to be cold, but I know this river. The terrain here squeezes its banks, and the rapids form in this stretch, but they don't last long."

She turns to me, but my expression must tell her what I think of her idea.

She places a hand on my shoulder. "You've been white-water rafting before." She points to the scar I showed her, which seems ages ago.

"And?"

"Didn't they tell you what to do if you got tossed out of the raft? Just point your feet downstream. We'll keep our boots on. It'll make it clunky to swim but easier to kick off the rocks. You hit the center flow, kick off the rocks as you come to them."

"You know you're crazy, right?"

"Kick off the rocks…" Ava ignores my sarcasm and continues. "Hit the middle bead of the river. That's where it's the fastest and deepest. It'll be bad for a few hundred yards, but I know this river. It opens up not too far from here. There, it slows, and that will be our exit point."

"The cold will be brutal."

"We'll deal with that on the other end." She scans the river, looking for the safest entry point.

I glance at the turbulent water, the reality of our situation settling in.

"Downriver it is then." My agreement comes reluctantly, but we have no other options. The idea of braving the rapids and their chilling grip is daunting, but the alternative is far worse.

We find a spot where the river seems marginally calmer, although *calm* hardly seems appropriate. The water rushes past with a ferocity that sends shivers down my spine, but there's one deep pool where we can jump.

Ava steps forward. "Keep your head. Let the current work for you."

The icy water looks uninviting, but it's our best chance.

With a deep breath, Ava looks at me.

I nod, and together we leap.

For a moment, we're suspended in the air, caught between the dangers behind us and the unknown ahead. Then, we're engulfed by the icy water, the shock of it driving the breath from our lungs.

The current grabs us, pulling us downstream with terrifying speed. We cling to each other, fighting to keep our heads above water to navigate the treacherous rapids and jagged rocks, but it soon becomes clear we must separate if we're to survive.

I release Ava and pray.

From the way her arms windmill, the current immediately tugs at Ava. She braces against the force of the rushing water and moves steadily toward the center of the rapids. I follow, and the cold bites through my clothes.

Behind us, our pursuers skid to a halt. They shout and gesticulate wildly. One of them pops off a few shots. The bullets whiz through the air but come nowhere close to hitting us.

Fortunately, none of the miners follow. The river, it seems, is a barrier even they won't cross.

As we're swept around a bend, out of sight, a surge of relief mingles with the adrenaline still pumping through my veins. The current sweeps us downriver.

We've escaped.

But the real battle is just beginning.

The evidence we found is a powder keg waiting to ignite. It's a story that needs to be told, a wrong that needs to be righted.

And most of that proof is on my camera.

The water is numbingly cold; its icy grip claws at my muscles and saps my strength. Together, Ava and I battle the current. I scull the water at my hips to keep my head above water while my boots point downstream, pushing off the rocks in my path.

The river seizes control, pulling us into its raging current and tossing us violently like ragdolls. I do my best to control my descent down the rapids, but I'm at the mercy of the water. My heart pounds in my chest, and I catch only glimpses of Ava far ahead of me.

Her form is barely visible through the spray and churn of the rapids. Unlike me, she rides the current like a seasoned navigator. Her body bobs and weaves with the rhythm of the river.

Not to be outdone, I realize the difference between our two

approaches. While I battle the river, trying to control it, she surrenders to the current and lets it carry her where it will.

That might be better than my approach. I let go of my need to control everything around me and let the river take me where it will.

The cold stabs at me with a thousand icy needles. My breath comes in sharp gasps, not from effort but rather from bracing against the biting chill.

The icy water numbs my limbs and saps my strength. I fight a losing battle against lethargy trying to overcome me.

I focus on Ava's advice—things I know and have taught others —feet pointed downstream, hands sculling at the hips. Water crashes all around me, a deafening roar that drowns out all other sounds.

My vision blurs as the rapids pummel me, but then I use my feet to bounce up and over the rocks.

Now, it's a game—a game to see if I can master the river.

A particularly vicious set of rapids catches me off guard. My boot sticks in a crack, and I get twisted and sucked under the flow, where I tumble underwater.

Panic claws at my mind, but I swallow that beast—along with a lungful of water—and kick hard to resurface. When I break through, gasping for air, I catch sight of Ava and something far better.

There's a slowing of the rapids.

Just as she promised, the river opens. The rapids ease into a more gentle flow. My frantic ride ends, and I follow Ava as she steers toward the opposite riverbank.

"Almost there," Ava shouts over the roar of the river.

My exit from the river is as ungraceful as my ride through it. It's more of a collapse onto the bank than a climb out of the river.

"Are you okay?" Ava lies on her back, breathing heavily, arms wrapped around her trembling form.

"I'm not dead." But we're not out of the woods.

I take her hand, pulling her to her feet. Our situation is far from safe. For now, we've evaded the miners. The river, with all its fury, granted that respite, but there's no time to rest. We need to keep moving.

Hypothermia is a real threat now.

"Come." I pull her close. "We need to find shelter and get warm."

I take her hand, and we set off, wet clothes clinging uncomfortably to our skin. Each step is a battle, and fatigue sets in fast.

TWENTY-ONE

Cage

Exhausted and shivering, we trudge through the dense Alaskan forest, our clothes heavy with river water and our boots drenched.

Each step feels laborious. The cold seeps into our bones, sapping our strength and clouding our minds. Hypothermia is a silent and insidious enemy, one that can kill as surely as any predator.

Ava leads the way, her steps determined despite the fatigue that weighs on both of us. I follow close behind, gathering as much dry firewood as possible. It's a challenge; the moisture from the river seems to have permeated everything, leaving even the deadwood damp and resistant to burning.

But I persist, driven by the knowledge that our survival depends on it. Ava and I work in tandem, a team forged in the crucible of adversity.

She focuses on finding kindling, the small, dry bits of vegetation that will be crucial in starting a fire. I handle the heavier branches, breaking them into manageable pieces as I go.

It's grueling work, made harder by the constant shivering wracking our bodies.

My fingers feel numb and clumsy, and my coordination suffers as the cold takes its toll. But I push through, knowing that every piece of wood I gather brings us one step closer to warmth and safety.

Ava periodically pauses to check our surroundings, her survival instincts finely honed from years in the wilderness. I watch her, marveling at the strength and resilience she embodies. Even in the face of such dire circumstances, she remains focused and determined.

It's one of the many things I admire about her.

As we move deeper into the forest, the terrain becomes more challenging. The ground is uneven, littered with hidden roots, and slick with moisture from the recent rain.

We navigate it carefully, mindful of the risks. A twisted ankle or broken bone out here could be a death sentence, and we're already in a precarious position.

Despite the physical demands, we maintain a steady pace. Ava's instincts guide us, leading us to areas where the vegetation is denser, where we're more likely to find the resources we need. I trust her implicitly, knowing that her knowledge of the land is our greatest asset.

Finally, after what feels like an eternity of cold and exhaustion, Ava spots it—a natural shelter formed by a clustering of massive boulders shielded by dense trees overhead. It's not much, but it's a start, a place where we can take shelter and begin the process of rewarming ourselves.

"We can use this." She points to the gap between the boulders, her voice strained with fatigue and cold.

I nod, too tired to speak. We stumble toward the alcove, our legs leaden and uncooperative. As we draw closer, the ground beneath the boulders turns from wet to dry, protected from the damp by the natural overhang. It's a small mercy but one that could make all the difference.

We crawl into the space, the rock walls providing an immediate respite from the biting wind. I set my bundle of firewood to the side, taking a moment to catch my breath. Ava does the same with her kindling, her hands trembling from the cold.

My collection of wood is less than we need. The fire will have to be built carefully and maintained constantly to ensure it doesn't burn out. I steel myself for another foray into the forest, knowing every trip depletes my dwindling energy reserves.

Ava seems to read my mind, her eyes meeting mine in silent understanding. Without a word, she joins me as I venture back out, and together, we make several more trips, each one a herculean effort in our weakened state.

On my final excursion, I gather several large rocks, an idea forming in my chilled mind. Once we get the fire going, we can use the stones to store and radiate heat, hopefully keeping the alcove warm through the long, cold night ahead.

"Now comes the hardest part." Returning to our rocky abode, I find Ava preparing to start the fire. She looks at me, her lips blue and trembling as she speaks.

I nod, understanding the challenge she faces. Starting a fire without tools is a skill that requires not just knowledge but also physical strength and endurance, both of which are rapidly fading in the grip of hypothermia.

I watch as she improvises a fire bow, her movements meticulous despite the cold's debilitating effects. She places a stick vertically on a flat piece of wood and wraps a shoestring from her boot around it. Then, she begins to move the bow back and forth, the string twisting the stick rapidly.

Friction.

Heat.

Hope.

It's a painstaking process, one that demands patience and persistence. She works diligently, her brow furrowed in concentration as she tries to generate enough friction to create a spark. But the cold has sapped her strength, and despite her best efforts, the bow slips and stutters in her grasp.

"Here, let me do that." Seeing her struggle, I step forward.

Ava hands me the bow without argument, a testament to her trust in me and our partnership. I take over, my own hands shaking as I begin the arduous task of coaxing a flame to life.

Time seems to stretch and warp as I work, each movement of the bow a monumental effort. The muscles in my arms burn, protesting the unfamiliar exertion. But I don't stop, can't stop. Our lives depend on this fire, on the warmth and safety it promises.

Minutes crawl by, marked only by the steady rhythm of the bow and the ragged sound of our breathing. Ava hovers nearby, ready to assist at a moment's notice. Her presence is a comfort, a reminder that I'm not alone in this fight.

Just when I think my strength will give out, when despair begins to creep in at the edges of my mind, the faintest wisp of smoke rises from the fireboard.

It's a tiny thing, fragile and ephemeral, but it's enough to send a surge of hope through my chilled body.

Ava sees it too, and she springs into action. Gently, she feeds the nascent ember with pieces of dried moss and lichen, nurturing it with the same care and attention one might give a newborn. She leans in close, blowing softly to provide the oxygen it needs to grow.

I continue working the bow, my movements fueled by a renewed sense of purpose. Slowly, painfully, the ember glows brighter. Ava adds progressively larger pieces of tinder, then small branches, each one placed with deliberate precision.

Before long, we have a respectable fire crackling in the center of our shelter. The warmth is immediate and all-encompassing, a balm to our chilled bodies and weary spirits. I place the rocks I gathered around the flames, allowing them to absorb the heat that will sustain us through the night.

As the fire grows, chasing away the worst of the cold, a wave of exhaustion slams into me. The adrenaline that had kept me going, that had fueled my efforts, ebbs, leaving behind a bone-deep weariness.

I glance at Ava and see the same fatigue etched into her features, but there's something else there too, a softness in her eyes as she watches the flames dance.

Despite the dirt and grime, the tangles in her hair, and the pallor of her skin, she is beautiful.

The fire's warmth slowly seeps into my clothes, thawing the icy grip of hypothermia, but it's not enough, not yet. We're still in wet clothes, the fabric clinging to our skin and sapping what little heat we've managed to generate.

"We need to get out of these wet clothes."

I meet Ava's gaze, seeing the understanding there before I even speak.

"We do, but first…" Ava scoots forward and climbs slowly to her feet.

"Where're you going?" I shift beside her, concern lacing my voice.

"It'll be dark soon, and while these boulders will spread out the smoke, the light of the fire is like a beacon."

"Okay, but what are you doing?" I crouch and follow Ava, crab-walking out from under the protection of the overhand.

"I'm going to build a screen—something that'll hide the light of the fire and protect us from the wind." She wraps her arms around her body, shivering visibly.

"It's not windy." I peer at the dark sky overhead. "We've got shelter and fire. We need to get warm, not head back out."

"Last I looked, the clouds were heavy. It looks like another storm's brewing. Storms bring wind, and wind puts out fires."

"Ah, I get it." I join her outside our tiny shelter and peer into the darkness. "Tell me what we need, and I'll help."

"Honestly, if you could make another run for firewood." She pulls a multitool out of one of her pants pocket, showing it to me. "It's the only thing I have left of my gear."

"Better than what I have." All my gear, including my camera, is either back at our camp or lost during our escape.

"I'm going to find something that'll work to make a screen." A deep sigh escapes her.

My girl's running on empty.

As am I.

But she's right.

"I don't think we should separate." I refuse to leave her side. It's nonnegotiable.

"Okay, we stay together. I don't want to get too far from our fire."

"What are you looking for? I can help. It's getting pretty dark."

I glance back at our refuge beneath the boulder pile and see the bright light of our fire dancing in the growing twilight.

"We passed a small grouping of pines; the boughs heavy with needles. They're young and supple. I'll weave them into a screen."

"I can help with that." I see a piece of deadwood and toss it under the boulder's protection.

With barely enough light left to find the small grove, I'm not surprised when Ava heads directly to where she says the pines are.

Ava hacks several long branches off each tree, never taking too much from one. These, I drag back to our impromptu shelter. While Ava works, I head out, making several more trips to fortify our firewood supply through the night.

From the musty scent in the air, I'm glad we went to the extra effort.

Ava expects rain, which means there will be no dry firewood in the morning except for what we collect tonight. Hopefully, it won't be the deluge we experienced before, but maybe it'll be enough to keep the miners from continuing the chase.

A guy can hope.

I drop the final load of firewood and squat next to where Ava interlaces the pine boughs into a tight weave that will not only cut the light from the fire, hiding our position but provide shelter against the coming rain and winds that precede it.

"Nice job." I help her lace together the last few boughs.

We prop them up as best we can and close off our tiny cave.

"What's up, love? I see the gears behind your eyes whirling."

I feed the fire another branch. With that screen in place, the temperature in our little shelter is getting warm.

"I'm thinking about our next steps," she says. "We need a plan."

"Talk to me."

TWENTY-TWO

Cage

I shift positions to sit cross-legged in front of the fire. My fingers and toes tingle as heat rushes to them. My body temperature is slowly normalizing.

The crackling of the flames punctuates the silence, a silence filled with my concerns about what those next steps should be.

"It's definitely going to rain." Ava settles for something benign, obviously needing time to think about the real topic at hand.

"I smell it in the air." I grab a smaller branch and feed the fire. "We've got a nice setup here."

"True, but we can't stay here."

"Agreed. We get warm. Allow our clothes to dry. Our boots will be another matter. It's going to take a long time for those to dry."

"We can use the stones." She gestures to the ring of rocks I built around the fire.

"That was my plan." It seems we're more and more in sync with each other, thinking the same things. "I'll let them warm up a little more, then tuck them inside our boots. Let the fire heat them from the outside, and the stones steam them from the inside. I love the way your mind works."

"Hopefully, our clothes and boots will be dry enough by tomorrow. The next question is, what do we do next?"

"Speaking about our clothes…" I remove my shirt and lay it beside the fire. Next come my boots, and then I strip out of my pants and shuck my briefs.

Ava nods, the motion slow and weighted with weariness. There's no hesitation, no modesty in the face of survival. We've been through too much together, seen each other at our most vulnerable, to let something like nudity come between us now.

Ava strips out of her sodden garments and lays them out near the fire to dry. The air is cool, raising goosebumps and sending a fresh shiver through me, but it's a temporary discomfort, one that fades as I settle closer to the flames.

Beside me, Ava does the same. In the firelight, her skin is golden, the shadows playing across the contours of her body. I try not to stare, to give her the privacy and respect she deserves, but it's a challenge. She's a vision, a goddess of the wilderness, and I'm but a mortal man.

We sit in silence for a time, watching as steam rises from our drying clothes. The crackle and pop of the fire is a soothing backdrop, a reminder of the life we've breathed into this small space.

"I figure we head back." Her voice is soft.

Troubled.

"Agreed. We cut our losses and head home."

"No." She makes a vague gesture outside. "Those clouds are bringing rain—probably sleet if not snow. All our heavy weather gear is back with our packs. This time of year—this late in the season—storms can be brutal. Without proper gear and shelter… Well, it could be catastrophic."

"Agreed, but what other choice do we have?"

I understand the dangers. I'm as accomplished as Ava when it comes to survival, but our strengths are different. Fortunately, we complement each other well.

She shifts again, drawing her knees to her chest. "I'm worried about our boots. They're a wet, soggy mess. Even with the stones, it'll take a couple of days for them to dry out. With one pair of socks and wet boots, we're looking at blisters best case and trench foot—worst case."

"I definitely don't want that." I shift close to her until our bodies press together. Lifting one arm, I pull her against my solid frame.

"It'll slow us down, and that makes us vulnerable. We also can't ignore the fact that we're low on food…"

"As in, we have none, but I love the way your mind works."

"I'm an obsessive planner, if you recall…"

"Yes." I huff a laugh. "Definitely obsessive, but I recognize it for the strength it is. Please, continue planning our doom and gloom."

"Well, foraging is possible. I can keep us from starving, but it's a temporary solution and requires we stay in one place, either to fish or bait traps for smaller animals. We need high-calorie food if we're going to make the week-long trek out of here."

"Week long? It didn't take that many days to get here, and we dawdled."

"But we're slower now. Weaker. Fighting exhaustion, hypothermia, and having to forage for food. It's going to take longer to get back. Also, if we get wet again, we're back to hypothermia. We barely managed to get warm tonight."

"I don't disagree. You make valid points, but what choice do we have?" I look at her, sensing what she's about to suggest.

"Physical exhaustion brings its own host of worries. In addition to proper rest and nutrition to stay both physically and mentally sharp, if we push ourselves, which we will, the risk of injury skyrockets."

"Agreed." I like the way she talks things through.

"We're experts out here, but we're not immune to a twisted ankle or other injury. A minor injury can escalate quickly and further hamper our ability to hike out."

"You don't paint a very good picture."

"In addition to our gear, we lost my sat phone. If something goes wrong, we have no way to call for help." I stare at the fire, absorbing its heat.

"But that might be a good thing."

"How's that?"

"What about your check-ins with Justin? How long will he wait before he comes out here to check on you?"

"I'm so exhausted. I didn't even consider that." Her eyes brighten with hope, then cloud over, troubled. "He'll wait three days."

"Three days?"

"That's what we agreed on."

My body no longer shivers uncontrollably. It's a win I need right now. The gravity of our situation sinks in.

"I don't know if we can wait three days."

"That's what I'm afraid of."

Our plan, as it's shaping up, sounds like a disaster.

Ava stares into the fire.

"We need a better plan." I reach for her hand and give it a light, comforting squeeze. "If you want to try and retrieve our gear, we can't walk back blindly."

"Agree. Observation first. Know what we're walking into."

"From a safe distance. We can't risk them finding us again."

Our conversation shifts from the risks of continuing on without our gear to the dangers of going back to retrieve it.

"We don't have to go back." I gesture to the boulder, which provides us protection from the elements. "We can stay here and wait."

"But we're nowhere near the satellite phone," she shakes her head. "That's where Justin will search. We have to go back, if only for that reason. Not to mention they have your camera. Otherwise, we have no proof of what they're doing."

"Maybe not all of it." The corners of my mouth lift in a grin.

"What does that mean?"

"I had to swap out a memory chip. Zipped it into the pocket of my pants. There's enough proof on that chip. They don't have that."

"But the water had to have ruined it."

"You'd be surprised." I lean back and blink heavily. Fatigue pulls at us both. "Flash memory SD cards are very robust, and water isn't likely to damage the plastic housing or the electronics inside."

"I thought they'd be ruined."

"Most people think that, but if the contact strips are plated in gold, which mine are, I can find someone who can read their contents. I'm not worried about my camera. I can always replace it, but I can't replace you." I give her a serious look. "I'm not excited by the idea of going back there, especially after what we went through to get away from them."

"We weren't prepared, and we didn't know what we were facing. Besides, we can't survive long without our gear. It's risky, but it's worth a shot. If I can get my sat phone, we can tell Justin exactly where to find us."

The idea of heading back toward the danger we escaped, rather than away from it, sends my heart into palpitations. I half-hoped Ava would talk herself out of it, but from the look in her eyes, she's not giving up.

"It's dangerous, and we have to be cautious." I pull at my chin. "Approach the camp from a different angle? They're looking for us along the river. I guess they'll trudge upstream for a mile or two, and the same goes for downstream. They'll think we went downriver, as it's the easier of the two choices, which means…"

Ava holds up a hand, interrupting me. "We circle around and approach from the far side. Upriver." She blows out a breath. "It'll take a day at least, maybe more, depending on how wide of a berth we want to give ourselves."

"If we do this…" I turn and cup her cheek, gently holding her face in my hand. "We have to think things through. Manage every contingency, but if you say it will take a day, maybe we should wait for reinforcements."

"The miners will be gone. If they're not already packing up, they will be soon. I know it sounds bad, but if they get away, they're just going to keep doing it. I can't live with that."

"If it means that much to you…" I like nothing about this plan, but I trust Ava, and this is important to her.

The best I can do is stand with her and protect her if things go horribly wrong.

"Good thing, I'm an excessive over-planner." The first smile graces her face since our ordeal began.

I laugh and can't help but lean in to kiss her.

The heat of her lips sears my skin, and I wish we were somewhere else besides trapped beneath the overhang of a boulder miles from civilization.

Our situation is not good. Going back is a calculated risk, but without our supplies, we're as good as dead.

As the minutes tick by, I become increasingly aware of Ava beside me. The heat from her body mingles with that of the fire, creating a cocoon of warmth that feels intimate, almost sacred. I want to reach out, to pull her close and share in that warmth, but I hesitate.

She's someone I've grown to care for deeply.

I'm torn between the desire for intimacy and the fear of overstepping—of jeopardizing the trust we've built—but as Ava shivers, I realize that none of that matters.

Not here, not now.

"We need to share our body heat." I keep my voice gentle, my gaze steady as I watch for her reaction.

To my surprise, there's no hesitation, no withdrawal. Instead, Ava dives into my embrace, her cold skin presses against mine as she seeks the warmth and comfort of human contact.

I hold her in my arms, positioning her closest to the fire. Her head rests against my chest, her breath warm and soft against my skin. It's a moment of pure, unadulterated bliss, a connection that transcends the physical and touches something deeper.

We don't speak; both of us are lost in our own thoughts as we bask in the simple pleasure of shared warmth.

The fire crackles and pops, casting dancing shadows on the rock walls of our shelter. Beyond, the wilderness stretches out in an endless expanse of darkness.

But none of that matters.

The world beyond our small circle of light and heat feels distant and unreal. All that exists is the two of us, intertwined and alive, drawing strength from each other in the face of adversity.

As the night wears on, Ava relaxes against me, her breathing slowing into the even rhythm of sleep. I hold her close, marveling at the trust she's placing in me, at the depth of the bond we've forged.

Tomorrow will bring new challenges and new dangers. We'll have to face the consequences of what we've discovered and try to collect our lost gear.

But for now, in the quiet of the Alaskan night, I allow myself to revel in the warmth and companionship of the remarkable woman in my arms.

I feed the fire over the next few hours and check on the progress of our clothes, but exhaustion pulls at me.

When I feel it's safe enough to sleep, that hypothermia failed to claim us, I toss a few large branches over the fire and allow myself to drift off.

Sleep claims me slowly, a gentle tide that carries me off to a place of rest and respite. My last conscious thought is of Ava, of the strength and beauty she embodies, and of the unshakable conviction that together, we can weather any storm.

My dreams are filled with contentment because I hold Ava in my arms, but tomorrow, Ava's plan will test me.

TWENTY-THREE

Ava

Our tiny shelter is warmer than the ambient temperature. With nothing but dirt beneath us and stone all around us, it's far from pleasant. The one thing I'm grateful for is the distinct lack of insects. After the first frost, most of the biting, stinging bugs go into hibernation or do whatever it is bugs do to survive the brutal Alaskan winters.

Which means they leave us alone.

I'd be remiss in saying I'm not also thankful for the warmth of Cage's body as he wraps me tight in his arms. We keep the fire fed and the flames tall. The smoke rises and spreads along the rock overhead, defusing as it goes.

Morning comes with blissful heat that warms my bones. As I stir from an uneasy sleep, my breath forms misty clouds in the cold air.

The heat from the fire welcomes me, and Cage hands me my clothes.

"Held them over the fire to heat them up for you. They're warm and crunchy."

"Crunchy?" I extend my hand and take my clothes.

My shirt and pants are both dry and warm after he held them over the fire, but the grit and sand from the river formed a thin crust over them. They're rough and scratchy, not good to put next to my skin.

They're uncomfortable, but all I have.

With a grimace, I scrunch my clothes, squeezing and bunching them to break apart the worst of the scratchy crust, doing the best I can to make them 'less' crunchy.

Less like putting sandpaper over my skin.

Cage watches silently, then copies my movements. He grabs my boots and shakes out the hot rocks we placed to help dry them from the inside out. After the rocks tumble from my boots, he extends them to me.

"Not totally dry inside, but not sopping wet."

"It'll do." I place my hand inside one of my boots to check how wet they are. "Hey, it's not that bad."

When I head outside to relieve myself, thick frost covers the ground. By the time I return, uncontrollable shivering wracks my body. We need to move if we're going to stay warm.

Cage grabs his boots and shoves his feet inside. Then he kicks apart our fire, spreading the remains out as far as possible. There's no vegetation under the boulder, so there's nothing to catch fire, but still, I don't like leaving embers burning.

We do our best to contain the fire while it burns itself out. Then I realize what I'm doing.

Procrastinating.

Avoiding the inevitable.

There are choices to be made, and I'm stalling. Finally, I take a deep breath and blow it out in a huff.

"We have to make a decision." My voice sounds hollow in the stillness of the early morning.

"I thought we decided last night..." Cage glances at me and arches a brow.

"I was hoping you'd try to talk me out of it." My gut churns with fear. It's not an easy choice and fraught with danger. Even if we do nothing with the miners, we desperately need our gear for the hike back to civilization.

"I have to tell you something." I dip my head, embarrassed by what I need to say.

"What's that?"

"I told you Justin would come in, guns blazing, but I made a fatal error."

"What do you mean?"

"I let the satellite phone's battery drop to dangerous levels. I have a replacement in my gear, but that gear is... Well, it's with everything else. There may be no signal for Justin to hone in on, which means I can't be sure he will help."

"First off..." He extends his hand and waits for me to take it. When I do, he pulls me into his embrace. He kisses the crown of my head and tucks my head to his chest. "We all make mistakes, but won't he have our last known location?"

"He will." We talked about this last night.

"And heading back as we are now, with no provisions and no gear, comes in as a distant second to circling back to our camp and trying to retrieve our things."

"Yes."

We can make it back to town, with our gear or without it. One of those options carries significant risk. I trust myself, and I trust Cage. With him by my side, the chances of making it back are much higher, but that gives the miners at least a week, probably much more, to pack things up and leave.

Then what?

They'll resume operations in a few months when spring returns.

I want to stop them.

Make them pay.

Not to mention, if Justin mobilizes the troops and mounts a search party, we won't be anywhere near the search grid.

"Look..." Cage puts his hand on my shoulder, snapping me out of my thoughts. "I think we talked things through pretty well last night. Neither option is a good one. I see doubt in your eyes, but this is the best decision."

"Are you sure? Because we can always change our minds."

"If you were anyone else, I wouldn't risk heading back, but

you're fucking amazing, and if anyone can lead us back to our camp and our gear, it's you."

It's him too.

I wouldn't be able to do any of this with one of my regular clients. Cage has extensive experience and a string of summits to his name. The man is fearless. He rubs at the back of his neck, then pulls me into a tight bear hug. Kissing the crown of my head, he's my rock.

"Thanks." My arms wrap around his waist, and I lay my cheek against the broad expanse of his chest.

"We need to move," he says. "I figure we'll want to get back close to dusk and use the night to hide our return."

"We do." I bury myself against his chest. My nostrils flare as I breathe in his rich, warm scent.

"Can I admit something?" A soft chuckle vibrates in his chest.

"Sure?" I pull back and tip my head to take in his amazingly handsome face.

"I have no idea where we are, or where our camp is, or even how to get back to town. I can survive out here with what I have on my back, but that river twisted and turned everything around in my head."

"Well, you're wrong about how long it'll take."

"What do you mean? I figure we've got several hours of aggressive hiking." He arches a brow, looking for confirmation.

"More like two days."

"Two days?" His lids pull back in surprise.

"Those rapids are faster than you thought. We're a solid two-day hike away from where we started. Not to mention, we'll be taking a circuitous route back."

"Well, shit." He releases me and then looks around our primitive camp. "Let me put some dirt on those embers, and we'll head out."

We work well together, each grabbing fists full of dirt to cover the remains of the fire. Satisfied it holds no risk of starting a wildfire, Cage and I say goodbye to our shelter of dirt and stone.

My sense of direction is like a sixth sense. I wasn't lying when I told Cage no one knows this land better than I do. I know every mountain, hill, valley, river, and stream. I know the game paths traveled by elk, moose, and caribou. I know where the bears hibernate and where they like to gorge on fish during the salmon runs.

This place was my backyard growing up, and I don't need to find a trail to trace our footsteps back.

I just know.

Just like I know, it will take two full days rather than a one-day hike.

The whole time, I tell myself that it's worth the risk. We need our gear, especially the satellite phone and Cage's camera gear. Fortunately, after the rain last night, the skies overhead are as blue as blue can be. Not a cloud in sight.

It's actually too clear.

That worries me.

The absence of clouds indicates a high-pressure front moving in, sweeping everything in front of it away.

On the heels of a high-pressure front like that, cold fronts generally storm through. We're not talking about rain. We're talking about the first blizzard of the season—the kind of storm where appropriate gear and clothing are barely adequate.

It's the kind of storm that kills—the kind of weather no one wants to get caught in.

I'm a bundle of fear and steely resolve as I get my bearings and head north. Setting a demanding pace, the hike is strenuous. We're both in peak physical condition and move surprisingly fast without the weight of our packs to slow us down.

Two days might turn into less than a day and a half. I'll take the win because that cold front will be here before we know it.

Unspoken fear clogs the air between us. The enormity of our task and its inherent risks weigh heavily on us both.

"We'll keep a wide berth and come at them from a direction they won't expect," I explain my thoughts while cueing Cage into our general direction of travel.

He nods, though there's tension in his jaw. We share a brief but charged look, understanding and accepting the danger ahead.

With a deep breath, we head out.

We make a great team.

Although I can't shake off the dread clinging to me like a second skin, every snapped twig and every rustling of the leaves sets my heart racing.

Cage remains silent beside me; his presence is a steady and reassuring force.

I lead us through familiar terrain—not that this particular patch of forest is known to me. Instead, I live and breathe the rhythms of the land all around me. All of this is familiar to me, but for the first time, it *feels* different.

This land feels hostile, treacherous, and dangerous. I find myself second-guessing every decision. This land used to be a place of solace for me, but now it feels like a dangerous expanse filled with potential threats.

"What are your thoughts about when we get there?" Cage keeps his voice low as he asks his question.

"Scout the area before we go in. It might be worthwhile to watch for a day and learn their patterns. Make sure they're not watching our camp when we get there."

It also gives Justin one more day.

"You think they're really waiting for us to return?"

"I don't think they have the manpower to keep watch on our camp and continue their mining operation. The kind of mining they're doing in the river is incredibly labor-intensive. To be honest, I'm hoping they've written us off."

"I agree with you there." Cage pulls at his ear, thinking hard. "And I think you're right. We should watch for a day and figure out their patterns. I doubt they care enough about our camp to waste manpower on watching it. As for the rest of it, I bet they're physically exhausted by the end of the day. They'll cook dinner, sit around the fire, and then retreat to their tents for bed. We check out our camp but don't move unless it's night."

"Sounds good."

"We need to know how many men are in their operation," Cage continues. "Once we know that, we can do a head count. When we see them all taking to their bunks, that should be our best opportunity to approach."

"Agreed."

I continue to push, increasing the pace. We move cautiously, avoiding major game trails. I look for signs of human presence but find none.

Cage is right about the miners being complacent. Their work is strenuous. From what little we saw of their camp, they appear well-supplied, which means there's little reason for them to forage for food. That implies they're relatively confined to a small area around their camp. It shouldn't be hard for us to approach without being noticed.

The underbrush thickens the closer we get to the miners' camp. It grabs at our clothes and scratches our skin, but it provides the cover we desperately need.

I take us on a circuitous route, avoiding the camp by all means necessary until we're finally in a position to approach directly.

"How are you holding up?" Cage puts a hand on my shoulder.

"Tense. Scared." I glance at him and immediately relax. Something about his commanding presence calms me. "My heart's taken up residence in my throat."

It's not a lie.

Every sense is heightened, every noise amplified in the relative quiet of the forest. The pounding of my heart feels like it's in my throat rather than my chest.

It's an odd, uncomfortable sensation.

We crouch low, moving with a stealth I didn't know I possessed. I locate an outcropping of rock that gives us a great vantage point to observe the men.

Their camp is set in a clearing about a hundred yards from the river, which is somewhat far when it comes to daily operations. But the camp is flat and the ground clear. It's perfect, really, for the canvas tents that make up their primitive camp.

There are four tents in all. Not the kind of tents adventurous hikers would buy. These are expedition canvas tents with solid floors, interior supports, and iron stoves with chimneys poking through the tops of the tents.

They're rugged enough to survive the strongest storms, and the presence of those chimneys says they're prepared to hunker down throughout the winter.

Outside each tent, stacks of firewood show their determination to occupy this land for quite some time. There's a central firepit for casual gatherings during the long nights and two other firepits clearly designated for cooking.

One holds a massive steel pot—a stew pot, perhaps—a staple for places like this. Another holds four kettles of steaming water.

Water quality is generally high out here, but depending on what happened upstream, there can still be impurities in the water. Therefore, all water needs to be filtered or boiled to prevent the transmission of disease.

This camp is impeccably set up, which surprises me if I'm honest with myself. One of the things I harp on with the teens I take out into the wilderness is to focus on the things that can kill them.

Most think it's the bears and wolves—predators. Few realize it's the microbes thriving in the water that kills the unprepared.

As we crawl to the edge of a vantage point fifty feet above the camp, my heart pounds in my chest. I can't believe we're doing this.

But here we are.

TWENTY-FOUR

Cage

———

As dusk bleeds into night, Ava and I inch closer to the edge of our vantage point. The miner's camp, a haphazard collection of tents and equipment, sits below us.

"What's the plan?" I twist around to catch Ava's eye. My voice is a soft whisper, barely carrying over the wind rushing through the trees.

With her eyebrows knitted, her eyes lock with mine. The tip of her tongue peeks out from between her pursed lips in silent testament to her focus. Every muscle in her face tenses, sculpting a portrait of unwavering determination.

"I'm not sure." Her brows pinch tighter.

My eyes squint as I try to resolve details of the miner's camp in the fading light. "We got lucky last time. I don't want to push it. I say we wait and watch."

"How long?"

"At least until they lay down for the night. We can slip away and backtrack to our camp, get our things, and decide what to do from there."

Something in the semi-darkness catches my eye, and I suppress a groan.

"Ava…" My voice trails off as I point toward the edge of the camp.

On one of the rickety tables, crudely fashioned from logs and planks, stands something that's virtually a part of me.

"What?" Her voice is sharp, laced with a tension that mirrors my own.

"See that table?" My gaze fixes on the objects laid out with obsessive precision.

My camera, with proof of their illegal mining operation, and Ava's phone, our only link to the outside world, sit mockingly on the miner's table, proof they discovered our camp.

Yes, I have the first SIM card, but it could be severely damaged. Most of the photos on that card are from our trek to this place. There may be one or two images of the miners' operation, but most of the evidence we took still sits within my camera.

They hold what could be our only leverage against them. The sight of our belongings in their camp changes everything.

We returned to recover our gear for the long trek back to town. There was never any thought of actually going into the miners' camp itself.

It's too dangerous, but without proof of the miners' activity, we can't stop them.

Unless we recover our things.

Ava's hand tightens on mine, her grip firm but shaky. Her ragged breath churns the air.

"We need to get them back." Her fiery gaze is resolute, clearly set on immediate action.

I grab her arm gently but firmly, the weight of my next words heavy on my heart.

"I know what you're thinking, but we must be smart about this."

Her eyes flash with defiance. She knows what I'm going to say but values my opinion.

"Those men…" The weight of my next words presses down on me like a physical force. "If they catch us, especially you…" The words choke in my throat and trail off into the chilling silence of the wilderness. The unspoken horrors of what these rough men might do to her if they get their hands on her hang heavy in the air between us.

There's no need to finish my thought. The dawning realization on her face tells me she understands the gravity of the situation far more profoundly than words can express.

Her eyes widen, not just with fear but with comprehension. The fierce determination that so defines her indomitable spirit falters, if only for a heartbeat, and shakes her to her core. Her body visibly tenses, a subtle but telling reaction. For a moment, she looks vulnerable, a stark contrast from the fearless woman I've come to know.

But even that tiny bit of weakness is quickly masked by the resilience that is as much a part of her as her shadow. Ava swallows hard, the movement in her throat visible in the twilight. She shifts slightly as if to steel herself against the fear seeking to drown her.

The set of her jaw tightens, the only outward manifestation of the battle she wages within herself to maintain control in the face of fear.

"Okay," she finally whispers. Her voice remains steady despite the clear effort it costs her. "What do you suggest?"

"We keep to the plan. Grab our gear first, then we can discuss what to do about that." I make a vague gesture toward the miner's camp. "If we take them now and get caught, we'll be left with nothing again."

"Makes sense."

Her agreement is more than just acceptance of our plan. It's a testament to her strength and her ability to face fear head-on.

She's a smart woman, not driven by emotion. She knows this is the path that offers the best chance of survival, even when her every instinct screams to act immediately.

"I sense a storm coming." I sniff at the air.

"I know." Ava's weather sense is better than mine, but we both know what follows a high-pressure front, especially as the temperature drops.

Together, we turn back and execute a strategic withdrawal. It's a necessary step in our fight to survive this. We'll return, but we'll do it prepared to take back what's ours.

Only then will we bring down holy hell on these miners who rape the land.

Relief floods through me, but it's tempered by the knowledge of the daunting task ahead of us. Ava and I inch away from our concealed vantage point. Night's fallen, and darkness envelops us like a shroud.

We navigate the treacherous terrain that separates us from our goal. When we made camp, which seems eons ago but has only been a matter of days, we didn't know about the miners. It's about a klick or two from their camp, but the darkness makes it feel so much farther.

The forest around us comes alive in the darkness with a nocturnal symphony of crickets and the distant hoot of a lone owl. The sound is eerie yet familiar.

Calming.

We move in silence, each step deliberate, avoiding the dry twigs underfoot and the crunching of leaves and pine needles that litter the forest floor. We're mindful of making any noise that could betray our presence, which slows us down to an agonizing creep through the night.

The moon, the tiniest sliver of silver in the ink-black sky, offers scant light, deepening the darkness and making our trek that much harder.

Our progress is slow but measured.

Determined.

The tension we carry is a palpable force. Ahead of me, Ava's silhouette is barely visible; her movements are lithe and graceful. Assured despite it being nearly pitch black. I follow closely, admiring her resilience and the graceful way her body sways with each step.

The distance to our camp, a mere click or two, feels like miles. Every rustle in the underbrush sets my heart racing, making me think the miners found us. I keep to the rear, following Ava. Because if there's an attack, I'll be the one to defend her.

She sets a determined pace. It's slow at first, but as we gain distance from the miners' camp, she picks up the pace. There's definitely a change in the air. A musty scent. The chill turns decidedly crisp. There is a steeper temperature drop than what a normal night should bring.

A storm's brewing.

Remnants of the earlier rain remain. The scent of wet earth and pine is sharp and invigorating. The undergrowth, still damp, provides a slippery surface, catching us here and there. It adds to the challenge of our nocturnal journey.

Despite the obstacles, we press on, driven by the need to recover our things. The thought of the miners going through our stuff makes me worry about what we might find.

Or what we won't find.

We need our gear if we're to survive.

Finally, after what feels like an eternity, the familiar outline of the meadow where we made camp comes into view. Ava pauses at the edge of the clearing, her posture tense as she surveys the damage.

I join her, my gaze sweeping over the destruction.

"Shit." Ava places a hand over her abdomen. "They destroyed everything." Her breaths come rapid and shallow as she battles her fear. A storm brews in her eyes, intense anger and a burning need for revenge.

"Hold on." I take her hand in mine. "Let's give it a moment and ensure no one's been placed as a lookout."

Too much anger fills her gaze, but she gives a tight nod.

Our camp stands ransacked and deserted. Perhaps they believe they chased us off for good, but I'm not ready to bet our lives on maybes. We wait, hidden by darkness, seeking any sign of a miner left to guard against our return.

I whisper into Ava's ear to stay where she is, then make a slow circuit of the perimeter, keeping to the trees and out of sight. Finally, after I'm certain we're the only ones here, I circle back around to where Ava waits.

"All clear."

This time, she grabs my hand, and we step into the ruins of our camp together.

The meadow, once a serene and orderly campsite nestled within the embrace of towering pines, now resembles a scene of carnage, as if a tempest swept through, leaving a trail of destruction in its wake.

Our tents are shredded, their tattered remains flung across the clearing. The ground is littered with our belongings, gear strewn haphazardly as the intruders rifled through our things. Our sleeping bags are unrolled and tossed aside, their insulation spilling out like the guts of a raw, open wound. Our rations, what little we had, are scattered, packages torn open, and their contents spilled onto the forest floor.

It's a shock that bears haven't found the place.

I place my hand on her shoulder. "I don't think it's as bad as it looks."

"They shredded our sleeping bags and destroyed our tents."

I take her hand in mine, and together, we step into the ruins of our camp. Our task is daunting, made all the more challenging by a crescent moon that provides barely any light.

The miners' destruction of our camp is complete, down to the fire pit, once the heart of our campsite. The stones ringing it are scattered, kicked aside as men trampled through our camp. Our water filters, crucial for our survival, lie in pieces; the filters are ripped apart and their innards exposed.

It's a deliberate act of sabotage.

I stumble across my knife tossed in the grass. A few steps away lies my multitool. Our clothes are strewn everywhere, but the miners didn't rip and shred them like they did our sleeping bags and tent.

The miners took or destroyed most of what we had, yet we scrape together what little remains. I grab a few packs of food that survived and find an empty water flask. I salvage the cording from the ripped tent and gather as much of the ruined fabric as possible to fashion a makeshift pack.

The night presses in on us, a tangible force breathing down our necks.

"We need to go." I feel incredibly exposed and in the open.

Ava and I gather what we can until a sudden crack pierces the silence of the night, freezing us in our tracks. Our eyes meet, a flash of fear passing between us, the unspoken question hanging heavy in the air. Ava's hand tightens around mine, and her body tenses for the threat we both anticipate.

Is it the miners?

Did they discover we're alive? Did they circle back? Track us through the forest?

We stand motionless, barely daring to breathe, as seconds stretch into eternity. Each beat of my heart is heavy in the silence.

But as we stand motionless, the intruder reveals itself—not a miner fueled by greed and malice, but a creature far more formidable. From the edge of the trees, a massive shape emerges, its form silhouetted by the moonlight.

A bear steps into the clearing with a presence that commands the night. Its fur is a matted tapestry of browns and blacks, moonlight glinting off its hulking frame.

A grizzly, its raw, feral power is evident in every muscle that ripples beneath its thick coat. The bear huffs and snorts, its breath visible in the cold night air. It surveys the meadow, drawn by the scent of food. Its eyes, twin pools of the deepest black, lock onto us, assessing, calculating. The bear moves with a grace that belies its size.

Ava and I freeze, our breaths caught in our throats as the bear snorts, nose twitching as it scents the air. Ava lost her pistol during our escape, and the canister of bear spray, along with much of our gear, is lost in the debris of our ransacked camp.

We have no defense.

We can't run, and we can't fight off a grizzly.

A spike of panic shoots through me. My mind races, searching for options, any solution that offers a chance of escape without provoking the bear.

Ava's gaze meets mine, and silent communication flows between us. Our only hope lies in remaining calm and appearing as nonthreatening as possible.

The bear takes a few steps forward, its movements deliberate and powerful. It sniffs the air, its massive head turning from side to side as it picks up our scent.

We stand still, knowing any sudden movement could provoke a charge. Despite their bulk, grizzlies can move with surprising speed, and we are painfully aware of our vulnerability. The bear sizes us up, its interest piqued by our presence.

Then, without warning, the bear's attention shifts. A rustle of underbrush to our right draws its attention away from us. From the trees behind it, two smaller shapes dart into the clearing—cubs. Their coats are a lighter, softer brown as they chase and play with each other. Their innocent antics are a stark contrast to the interaction between us and their mother.

A mama with her babies.

The realization brings a new wave of fear. Grizzlies are fierce creatures, but a mama bear with cubs is truly terrifying. We're a threat to her cubs. Her entire existence is to protect and feed her young. I can only hope feeding her young takes precedence over eliminating us as a threat.

The cubs, curious and unaware of the danger humans pose, tumble over each other, making their way toward the ripped and scattered remains of our provisions. The mother bear watches us closely, gauging the threat we pose. A low growl rumbles in the back of her throat, a warning that's loud and clear.

The grizzly's demeanor shifts instantly, its maternal instincts taking precedence as it turns to corral its young. It huffs again, a clear warning for us to keep our distance, but its focus is now divided, giving us a precious opportunity.

Ava's hand finds mine, her grip tight.

"Back away slowly. If she doesn't see us as a threat, she'll ignore us in favor of her cubs."

Capturing the raw beauty of a mother with her cubs is one of the shots I've always dreamed about. Sadly, I have no camera to capture this incredible moment.

Step by step, we retreat, our movements cautious, our eyes never leaving the mother bear. She watches us warily for several long moments, then seemingly satisfied we're moving away from her cubs and pose no threat, she turns her attention back to her cubs.

We continue our retreat until the meadow and its family of grizzly bears are nothing but a memory I will keep with me forever.

Once we're a safe distance away, Ava and I pause and catch our breath. It feels as if I've just run a marathon.

That encounter with the mother bear, while terrifying, serves as a stark reminder of the inherent danger of the wilderness. It's a world where humans have never been apex predators, a world that demands respect and caution. Our mission, to expose the miners' illegal activities, takes on a deeper significance. We're not just fighting for ourselves. We're fighting for the land and for all the creatures that call it home.

As we resume our journey, a new fear fills my heart because I'm taking Ava into danger.

I don't know how I feel about that.

TWENTY-FIVE

Ava

———

THE FOREST EMBRACES US AS WE SLIP THROUGH ITS DEPTHS. OUR trek to our camp, salvaging as much of our gear as possible, and the hike back used up most of the night. We've been on the go for what feels like forever. Exhaustion pulls at me, but so does determination.

There's no moon, leaving us only the dim light of the stars to guide us. Their cold glow does nothing to light our way or push back the shadows. Despite the lack of light, my sense of direction remains true. I know instinctively where to go.

I navigate more by instinct than sight, trusting in the familiarity of the path that leads back to the miners' camp. The thought of what awaits us there sends a shiver of anticipation down my spine.

And so we trudge until night slowly gives way to day.

Predawn twilight wraps the forest in a shroud of ethereal beauty, casting each detail in a soft, otherworldly glow. As the first light filters through the dense canopy, it transforms the ordinary into something almost magical, something spiritual.

The trees, these ancient guardians of the woods, stand tall and silent around us. Their branches sway in a slow, graceful dance with the early morning breeze. It feels as if they're whispering secrets in those hushed tones, secrets that only they understand.

Secrets they've held for centuries.

Those first rays of sunlight carve shafts of light that reach all the way down to kiss the forest floor. Its heat awakens tiny insects caught in their path. In these beams, a silent ballet unfolds, a dance of life that swirls and twirls, each mote and tiny insect moving with a purpose known only to them.

The air around us is thick with the scent of loam and pine, a rich, earthy aroma that seeps into my soul. It's a fragrance that speaks of life, decay, and the unbreakable cycle that binds every creature, plant, and particle in this forest.

Breathing it in, I'm filled with an overwhelming sense of belonging, a deep, visceral reminder that we are but a small part of a much larger, more ancient tapestry.

This moment is a rare gift.

The forest, with its towering trees, dappled light, whispering winds, and the earthy scent of pine, is a sanctuary. It embodies the simple, profound beauty of the world—a beauty that demands nothing but our respect, reverence, and protection.

In this moment, standing on the precipice between night and day, I feel a rare connection not just to the world around me but to Cage, who stands beside me, sharing in the awe and the silence.

"It's beautiful, isn't it?" I turn to Cage, loving that we can experience this together.

"Absolutely gorgeous." His gaze settles on me with the warmth of unspoken promises and hints of forever.

Without a word, he steps closer, the gap between us disappearing as if it were never there to begin with. His arms encircle me, pulling me into the warmth of his embrace,

And then, he leans down, his lips meeting mine in a kiss that is gentle yet filled with an intensity that turns my legs to jelly and makes me swoon.

It's a kiss that speaks of the growing intimacy between us, of this shared experience that has bound our lives together in ways I never could have imagined.

It's tender and profound, a promise of protection, intimacy, and something blossoming beautifully between us amidst the chaos of our survival.

The towering trees witness the birth of something new between two souls who have found each other in the wild—a reminder that even in the darkest times, beauty, love, and connection can flourish.

Our steps are cautious and deliberate as we navigate the underbrush, mindful of every sound that punctuates the silence of the forest. My heart beats a rapid tattoo against my ribs. Each rustle of leaves and snap of a twig underfoot sends spikes of anxiety shooting through me.

It feels as though the forest holds its breath, waiting for what comes next.

We have arrived.

As we approach the edge of the clearing, the outline of the camp emerges as a haphazard collection of tents and rusty equipment. Eerily quiet in the early morning, my gaze is immediately drawn to a table next to one of the tents. Even from this distance, the familiar shape of Cage's camera and my sat phone are unmistakable, glinting faintly in the first light.

My entire body tenses.

"Maybe this isn't a good idea." Doubt fills me, and I second-guess this decision I've made.

Anger and desperation drive me. What these men are doing to that river and to the land is criminal.

It has to stop.

"We need that phone to call for help, and we need my camera for the proof it holds." Cage stands beside me, strong and supportive.

We're in the wilderness, cut off from the world, and those items are our lifeline. What we plan carries great risk, but we don't have a choice.

They're unpredictable, and their potential for violence is a risk we can't ignore.

"We need to be strategic about this." Cage wraps his hand around my waist, pulling me back against him.

"What does that mean?"

"Those guys aren't going to let us waltz in there and take it."

A sudden urge to dash forward, to grab our belongings before the miners wake, seizes me, but rustling from one of the tents halts me in my tracks.

A figure stumbles out from one of the tents, his movements sluggish with the remnants of sleep. His hair is a tousled mess, sticking out at odd angles, a testament to his recent battle with his pillow. The miner, barely awake, scratches his belly as he ambles forward. He heads right toward our hiding spot.

Cage and I instinctively hunker down, our breaths held tight in our chests. Cage places a hand on my shoulder, a firm grip holding me back.

A protective gesture.

The miner, oblivious to the world around him, stops just a few feet from us. He spins around, faces the camp, takes a leak, then yanks his pants down. He squats and takes a dump with a carelessness that speaks volumes to his disregard for his surroundings.

We're forced to watch, silent and unmoving, as he completes his morning ritual, the sound of his actions disturbingly loud in the quiet of the forest. Once he's done, he gives a satisfied grunt and zips his pants. We huddle together, barely daring to breathe as the miner saunters back toward the camp.

Cage and I share a look, a blend of relief at remaining undetected and silent laughter at the indignity of what we've just witnessed.

"We wait until they sleep." Suddenly, Cage's grip tightens around my wrist, a silent command that pulls me deeper into the underbrush where we can watch the camp without risk of discovery.

Our 'close encounter' is a stark reminder of the peril we're in.

As dawn paints the sky with strokes of pink and orange, the camp stirs to life. From our hidden vantage point, we watch the miners emerge from their tents, stretching and yawning, their movements slow and uncoordinated in the early morning light.

The camp comes alive in a way that belies the rough nature of its inhabitants.

It's almost civilized.

The aroma of brewing coffee cuts through the morning chill, its familiar comfort clashing starkly with the tension that tightens around my heart. Around the fire, the miners congregate, a motley crew united by their rugged lifestyles and the day's hard work that awaits them.

They're a rough-looking lot, each face telling a story of hard living and harder choices. Their gruff morning greetings and cacophony of coarse voices are interspersed with the crackle of the flames, adding to the raw atmosphere of the camp.

Beards thick and unkempt, clothes bearing the stains of yesterday's toil, and perhaps many days before, they embody the untamed wilderness that surrounds us.

One miner, more burly than the rest, with a beard as thick as a thicket and hands that have known nothing but labor, assumes the role of cook. He lords over the fire, flipping strips of bacon with practiced ease.

The sizzle and pop of fat hitting the flames rends the air, intertwining with the scent of coffee to create a bubble of normalcy that sits oddly with me, a stark reminder of the life we're temporarily estranged from. A stew pot sitting over a second cook fire bubbles and spits what looks to be oatmeal.

My stomach grumbles, reminding me how long it's been since we've had a meal.

Cage nudges me gently. We count the men, a necessary step in gauging the size of the threat they pose.

One, two, three...

We count them quietly, our whispers blending with the forest's natural sounds. By the time we reach seven, the weight of our task settles heavily on my shoulders.

Seven men, each likely as crass and rough as the setting they've made their own.

Their harsh laughter seems to be the currency of their camaraderie. However, it's a laughter devoid of warmth, a sound that grates on my nerves, reinforcing the divide between us and them.

As they eat, their conversations are a mesh of shouts and grumbles, lacking any semblance of civility. It's a stark reminder of a world where the law of the land is dictated by those who shout the loudest, fight the hardest, and care the least about the consequences of their actions.

Cage meets my gaze.

We're up against the embodiment of human ruthlessness. While unsettling, the morning's observation has given us valuable insight.

We share a look, and the same thought is unspoken between us. The sat phone and his camera lie tantalizingly close, just on the edge of the camp. I feel their pull, a magnetic draw that tempts me to throw caution to the wind and reclaim them without regard for stealth or safety.

But daylight is our enemy, a danger we can't afford to ignore.

"We could try now." My whisper is barely audible above the sound of the miners' laughter. "They're leaving to work."

To rape the land.

"It'll take only one pair of eyes to spot us." Cage shakes his head, his eyes scanning the camp strategically. "We've been pushing ourselves hard. We retreat, sleep if we can, and wait for night to come." His voice is laced with a firm resolve that brooks no argument. In this, Cage takes the lead in our unique partnership.

I nod, the logic of his words cutting through the impulsive desire that threatens my judgment. The risk of being caught in broad daylight, of finding ourselves at the mercy of these men, is a gamble with stakes too high to contemplate.

So, we wait, our bodies pressed close, as the miners finish their breakfast and gather their tools. One by one, they head off toward the river, their mining operation calling them away from the camp.

The sounds of their departure, the clanking of metal, and the low murmur of their voices fade into the distance, leaving behind a silence that's ominous.

Cage and I make a strategic retreat.

He finds a secluded spot, a haven hidden from prying eyes, where the only observers are the ancient trees standing like sentinels around us.

Here, he says, we can rest.

TWENTY-SIX

Ava

———

The luxury of sleep, so often taken for granted, now feels like a sweet indulgence.

Our resting spot is a natural alcove, cradled by towering pines whose branches form a canopy that filters the sunlight into soft, dappled light. Pine needles carpet the ground, offering a bed far softer than the hard earth we've grown accustomed to.

The air hums with the quiet energy of life all around us. A gentle brook borders the alcove, its waters murmuring soothing melodies as it flows and tumbles over stones and roots. The sound is a lullaby, natural and pure, inviting us to rest.

Cage is right beside me, his body radiating a warmth that cuts through the chill of the forest air. His presence is a constant I've come to rely on, grounding me in a way that the earth beneath us cannot match.

As we settle down, I'm keenly aware of his presence beside me. His hand finds mine, a gesture that speaks volumes. His touch is comforting and invigorating, a reminder of the strength we draw from each other.

The dynamic between us has shifted subtly over the course of our ordeal. Once, I was the guide, the one with the knowledge and the plan. Now, Cage steps into the role of leader and protector. It's a change that feels as natural as the forest around us, and it stirs something deep within me.

As Cage scans the perimeter of our little haven, he turns to me, his gaze softening. "You should get some sleep. I've got the first watch."

"We should both rest." I shake my head, ready to argue for fairness, for equality. "I can take—"

"No, Ava," he cuts me off gently but firmly. "You've been navigating and planning, and you're exhausted. Let me do this for you."

A tenderness in his voice catches me off guard, a depth of care that goes beyond mere survival. It's in how he looks at me as if seeing right through to where my fatigue is the deepest.

"But what about you?" My concern for him is as palpable as his concern is for me. "You need rest, too. We can't afford for both of us to be worn out."

Cage smiles, a soft, reassuring curve of his lips that does strange things to my heart.

"I'll rest later. Right now, I need you to sleep. It's going to be a long night."

I want to protest, to insist that we share the burden equally, but the weariness dragging at my bones is a persuasive argument in itself. And there's a part of me, perhaps selfishly, that revels in the feeling of being cared for, of being cherished in a way that's as protective as it is gentle.

The warmth of his gaze stops me from arguing further. This is more than a strategic decision for him; it's an act of caring, of protection.

"Okay, but only because you're stubborn," I relent, finally, with a soft sigh.

"And you're not?" His chuckle is low, warm like the dappled sunlight that filters through the trees.

I settle down, finding a comfortable spot against the earth. The forest floor is surprisingly accommodating. Cage settles close. His warmth is a reassuring reminder that I'm not alone.

Even as I drift toward the edge of sleep, I'm acutely aware of the soft sounds he makes as he shifts, ensuring I'm shielded from the elements and any potential threats that might venture too close.

"Just—wake me for the second watch, okay?" My eyelids are already heavy and bouncing with impending sleep.

"I promise." He pulls me close, letting me use his lap as my pillow. The soft weight of his arm folds over me. "Sleep well, Ava. I've got you."

At that moment, with his words wrapping around me like a blanket, I realize how much Cage has become an important part of my life.

I'm filled with a profound sense of gratitude and affection for this man. Our relationship, forged in the crucible of survival, has blossomed into something far deeper than mere client and guide, far more meaningful than either of us could have anticipated.

It's a bond of mutual respect and burgeoning love, strengthened by every challenge we face together.

As my eyes grow heavy, the last thing I see is Cage's steady gaze and a promise of safety in his arms. As sleep pulls me into its restorative depths, I do so with a heart overflowing with emotion. Cage's willingness to stand guard while I rest, to place my well-being above his own, is a gesture that encapsulates the essence of who he is.

And as I succumb to my fatigue, I do so with the knowledge that, in Cage, I've found not just a partner in survival but a companion in life, someone who values me as much as I value him.

My sleep is fitful, and my mind a whirlwind of plans and possibilities, fears and what-ifs that chase each other in endless circles.

But the physical need for rest is undeniable, and eventually, I succumb to exhaustion, slipping into a fitful slumber that offers little in the way of peace.

When I wake, the forest is bathed in the soft light of late afternoon, the shadows long and stretching. Cage watches the forest around us, ever vigilant.

"We wait for night." His quiet affirmation of our plan remains steady and resolute.

"You need sleep."

We've both pushed our bodies through and past exhaustion. These past few days, from the moment we stumbled across the miners to the chase through the woods, that crazy climb up the cliff, the plunge into icy waters, and sheltering beneath the boulders have taxed our reserves.

We're sleep-deprived, physically exhausted, and running on empty.

After tonight, after we reclaim our gear, we have to make a decision. Do we stay and hope Justin brings help? Or do we decide to head back ourselves?

Cage settles down with his back against a log. He dozes off while I watch over him, loving how his features soften in sleep.

Hours pass while I watch over Cage. Tonight, we will make our move, and I'm terrified. I pace back and forth, waiting for dusk to fall and night to claim the sky.

I don't realize Cage is awake until his hand finds mine in the darkness. His fingers wrap around mine with a gentle firmness. Without a word, he pulls me into his arms.

"We should get going." I brace myself, half-expecting him to argue, to suggest we abandon this reckless quest.

To my surprise, he simply nods. His concern is palpable, but he's not going to try and talk me out of this. He understands how important this is to me and is willing to stand beside me, no matter the risk.

"Wait a few more hours. Make sure they're all asleep." He keeps his voice low and measured.

I don't want to wait, but my impulse to act—to rush—is tempered by his wisdom.

I value his opinion.

He's not wrong.

I'm merely eager to get this over with, and that unchecked eagerness could lead us into danger. His caution and ability to balance my impulsiveness with quiet deliberation grounds me.

As darkness falls, the forest around us comes alive with the sound of nocturnal creatures. Cage and I begin a cautious trek back to the miners' camp. The temperature drops as the warmth of the day recedes, and that chill sharpens our senses and heightens our awareness.

This time, Cage leads the way.

The camp gradually comes into view, a dim outline of tents and equipment. We pause again at the edge of the clearing, hidden by the dense underbrush.

A fire crackles at the center of the camp; its glow casts dancing shadows on the rough faces of the men gathered around it. They're not asleep like we hoped, and it's almost midnight.

Bottles pass from hand to hand, the liquid within catching the firelight and sparkling briefly before disappearing into eager mouths. Their laughter is loud, raucous, filled with the edge of inebriation.

The alcohol fuels not just their laughter but their tempers as well.

Voices rise.

Voices fall.

With each swig from their bottles, a cacophony of subtle slights and vague disagreements escalates. It's a volatile mix, and Cage squeezes my hand, silently reminding me of the danger these men represent.

Suddenly, a shout cuts through the laughter, sharp and angry. Two of the miners stand, their faces flushed with drink and rage. Their dispute turns physical with a swiftness that's startling.

Fists fly, a brutal battle illuminated by the flickering firelight. The others shout encouragement or jeers, their voices blending into a discordant chorus that fills the night.

The fight is brief but intense, ending only when the others intervene, pulling the combatants apart with grunts and curses. The men back down, nursing bruises and wounded pride, the atmosphere sullen. The big, hulking one sends the men to separate tents to 'sleep things off.'

There's a rawness to their interactions, a primal quality that's terrifying. These men live in a world where disputes are settled with fists rather than words.

"It won't be long now." Cage's eyes meet mine, a storm of emotions swirling within their emerald depths.

We remain hidden, our bodies pressed close, as the fire dies down and the camp settles into an uneasy silence.

It takes another two hours before the men retreat to their tents. The camp slowly falls into deep slumber while Cage's hand in mine grounds me in the present.

"This is it." His voice is barely audible.

I nod, unable to find words that encompass the storm of emotions raging within me. Fear, determination, hope—they all swirl together.

This is our only chance. And I'm going to take it. We skirt the edge of the camp. Our approach is careful.

Measured.

Every sense is attuned to the slightest sound.

TWENTY-SEVEN

Cage

Ava and I move stealthily toward the miners' camp. Shadows become our accomplices. Every hushed breath of the wind aids our clandestine advance, like a conspirator in our silent mission.

Ava takes the lead; her steps are ghostly silent, a testament to her skill and agility. I follow, every sense sharpened, every instinct honed for protection and defense.

The camp looks different now—more vulnerable, less imposing—but I know better. The table where our goal lies, the sat phone and camera, sits tantalizingly close, yet lies across a minefield of peril.

As Ava slips forward, I'm right there, watching over her, ready to intervene at the slightest hint of danger.

Without warning, a twig snaps underfoot—a sound so incongruously loud in the quiet that it feels like a gunshot.

Ava freezes, her body tensed for action.

For a heartbeat, time stands still.

My heart races, every muscle coiled, ready to spring to her defense, to protect and shield her from whatever threat might emerge.

Every conceivable scenario plays out in my mind, but then a

seven-point buck, its coat dark brown in the starlight, steps into the clearing.

Ava dodges behind the tent in front of her. I retreat back to the tent we just passed. In the stillness of the night, each sound is amplified. The deer steps with the wary grace of a creature attuned to the wilderness.

Yet, even the most careful creature can be caught unaware. The buck's hooves catch an aluminum can and send it rattling through the camp. The deer's ears prick at the sudden noise, and sensing it's no longer safe, it bounds, disappearing into the dense thicket of the forest.

The sound invades the miners' sleep, sharp and urgent. It cuts through dreams and pulls them into half-awakened confusion. They emerge from their tents, searching for the source of the disturbance that shattered the peace of their rest.

They squint into the darkness. One of them sees the buck. It spooks at the movement of humans and races out of the clearing, seeking shelter within the trees.

Guns point in the general direction of the retreating buck. Shots fire, more of a reaction than an intent to kill.

The miners' excitement quickly dissipates, and they retreat back to their tents, still unaware of Ava's and my presence.

My protective instincts surge. We tread a razor-thin margin between success and catastrophe.

Ava blends with the shadows, a part of the night itself, and moves toward the rough-hewn table where our gear sits. She retrieves our belongings with a delicacy calculated to avoid the slightest whisper of sound that might betray her presence.

Lifting our things gingerly from the table, she cradles them close to her chest as if they're fragile relics. Her eyes scan the camp one last time, ensuring the miners remain none the wiser to our theft.

I stand guard, every sense alert to the slightest sound. My role is clear—protector, defender, the one who will stand between her and any man who dares to harm her.

I expect her to join me, but she places her index finger over her lips. My gut clenches in apprehension.

She takes a step back, and then another, until she disappears into the trees behind her, away from me.

Where I can't see her.

Can't protect her.

Fuuuuck.

For a moment, my heart races. We didn't plan on getting separated, and it's pitch black in the trees. I have no idea where she is. If I move, we could pass each other in the night. The only way I can find her is to wait for her to find me.

By venturing deeper into the woods, she seeks to throw off any pursuit before it can begin. It's a bold move that speaks to her intimate knowledge of these woods and her unwavering determination to protect us both.

As she vanishes from sight, a part of me wants to call out, but I trust her, just as she trusts me. I wait, my eyes fixed on the spot where she disappeared, knowing that our reunion will come when she deems it safe.

And she does find me.

"Cage…" Her urgent whisper comes from behind me, the best sound in the world.

Our retreat from the camp mirrors our approach, a silent navigation of shadows and silence.

Once we're a good distance away, Ava fiddles with the satellite phone, her fingers stiff from the cold. The screen flickers to life, only to reveal a dangerously low battery.

She punches a series of buttons, fingers flying too fast to follow, and then her forehead bunches with concern.

"No signal. We need higher ground," she whispers, hoping the elevation will give us a better chance at a signal.

We pick our way carefully through the underbrush, seeking a vantage point that might offer a better signal.

Just then, distant voices shatter the silence of the night.

"Shit!" Ava curses as she clutches the phone, fingers tapping a mile a minute.

Chaos erupts as the miners discover the theft. Their violent curses split the night, sending Ava and I sprinting through the forest.

Our breaths come in ragged gasps as we push our bodies to their limits.

The miners give chase, and we run faster.

The air around us feels electric. Every rustle of leaves, every snap of a twig, amplifies our fear. Time stretches, each second an eternity. The voices rise and fall, coming dangerously close to our position. I grab Ava's hand, pulling her through the underbrush.

"We need to move." Urgency laces my voice. "Higher ground, now."

The forest around us is alive with nocturnal sounds, each snap of a twig, each rustle of leaves heightening our senses. Our feet pound against the forest floor, propelling us deeper into the concealing darkness.

Cold air whips past us, filling my lungs as we navigate a labyrinth of trees, raised roots, and underbrush, desperate to trip us and twist our ankles.

Suddenly, a loud crack pierces the night. We freeze. My heart races, the sound too close for comfort. Images of the miners catching us race through my mind. Ava exchanges a tense glance with me, her body rigid with anticipation.

Seconds tick by, each one stretching into eternity. Then, a shadow moves. A deer, its form ghostly in the dim moonlight. It steps onto a game trail and continues its journey, unaware of the drama unfolding around it.

"Should we keep running or find a place to hide?" Ava asks, her voice strained with the effort of our escape.

I dart a glance over my shoulder, half-expecting the glow of torches or the sound of pursuit.

"Running's too loud. It'll draw them to us," I reply, my voice laced with urgency. Each snapped twig underfoot might as well be a flare in the night. "But hiding gives them the chance to find us."

Hiding is the greater risk, a gamble on the miners' laziness or lack of interest. I weigh our options in the span of a heartbeat, the decision heavy on my shoulders.

"Let's slow down. Move quietly. It's our best shot."

Agreement passes between us without another word. We slow

our pace, each movement deliberate, calculated to make as little sound as possible.

The forest around us feels alive, and every shadow and sound is a potential threat. We move stealthily, using the dense foliage as cover.

Suddenly, the sharp crack of a gunshot pierces the air. Birds scatter into the sky, their cries mixing with the sound of bullets whizzing past us. One grazes a tree near Ava, splinters flying. She stumbles, catches herself, and keeps running, her eyes full of fear and steely resolve.

A bullet hits the ground near my foot. The miners are closing in. Ava creates a diversion, knocking over a dead tree. Its crash echoes through the forest, hopefully misleading our pursuers.

Just when we think we're gaining ground, a figure bursts from the shadows directly into our path. It's one of the miners, his face twisted in rage, and a pick axe clutched in his hand. He attacks Ava.

Time slows as he lunges toward her. Instinctively, I step in front of Ava, positioning myself between her and the threat. My heart hammers in my chest as I brace for the impact.

TWENTY-EIGHT

Cage

THE MINER SWINGS, HIS MOVEMENTS FUELED BY ANGER. I DODGE, feeling the rush of air as the weapon whizzes past my head. Counterattacking, I drive my fist forward, connecting with his jaw in a satisfying crunch. Pain explodes in my knuckles, but the thrill of the fight overshadows it.

He staggers back, more surprised than hurt, giving us the opening we need.

"Run!" I shout to Ava, grabbing her hand and pulling her along.

The forest becomes a blur as we navigate its treacherous terrain. As we run, protecting Ava is my singular focus. The fear of what might have happened if I hadn't been there to intercept the miner fuels my determination.

"We'll lose them," I assure Ava, though my voice betrays the edge of my own uncertainty. "Just keep moving."

The night presses in around us, a silent witness to our desperate flight.

Our breaths come in ragged gasps, the sound of our flight echoing through the dense forest. We push our bodies to their limits, the fear of capture a constant specter at our backs.

But then, two figures emerge from the shadows, blocking our path.

Their silhouettes are sharp and angular, like knives slicing through the darkness. One is tall and imposing, with broad shoulders and a square jaw. The other is shorter and wiry, but his movements are quick and calculated.

My heart races as I try to make out their faces, but the dim light makes it impossible.

Without hesitation, I position myself between Ava and the miners, a primal instinct to protect surging through me.

The look in the miners' eyes is one of grim determination; they're not here to negotiate. They're here to reclaim what we've taken and punish us for our transgression.

Their attention shifts between Ava and me and then dips to my camera slung around my neck. They're calculating their next move.

"Run, Ava. Run."

I refuse to let my fear over Ava's safety paralyze me, but I need her out of the equation so I can focus on the fight. The miners take a step forward, with wildness in their eyes.

She shakes her head, unwilling to leave me. It's a decision made in a heartbeat, born of desperation and the deep bond we've shared since our paths first crossed.

The first miner lunges toward me. I meet him head-on, throwing every bit of skill and strength I possess into the fight.

My fist connects with his jaw, a solid blow that sends a jolt of pain up my arm. For a moment, I dare to hope it might be enough.

But the second miner is on me before I capitalize on the moment; his attack is a brutal reminder of the odds stacked against us.

They move as one, their attacks relentless and calculated. Every punch, every block, is driven by desperation. I manage to land a few solid hits, but they're bigger, and there are more of them. Ava struggles beside me, her movements swift and calculated, but we're outnumbered.

I dodge and weave, trying to keep them at bay, but it's like fighting a two-headed beast. They fight with ruthless efficiency—like one—their familiarity with violence is evident in every punch and grapple.

I fight back with everything I've got, spurred by adrenaline and the desperate need to protect Ava. My body is bruised and bloodied from their blows, but I refuse to give up. With renewed ferocity, I unleash a barrage of punches on my attackers.

But my victory is short-lived.

The noise alerts the other miners.

Shouts echo through the forest.

Closing in.

A right hook to the jaw snaps my head and rings my ears. I stumble but come back fighting.

One of them staggers back, his nose broken from my fist, but the other one comes at me with wild abandon. I land a solid kick to his chest, sending him crashing to the ground, but before I can catch my breath, he reaches into his pocket and pulls out a knife.

The glint of steel sends a chill down my spine as he springs to his feet and lunges at me. Dodging his attack, I disarm him, sending the knife clattering to the forest floor.

There's no time for celebration or relief because they're relentless.

The miners attack again, their blows sending me to the ground. I struggle against them, but their combined strength is too much.

As they rain down, punches, and kicks, my vision blurs. The world spins, swallowed by a chaotic blur of noise and pain.

I try to rally, but it's not enough. A heavy blow lands on the back of my head. Stars burst across my vision, and I stumble, disoriented. More hands grab me, dragging me down.

I try to fight back, but my limbs feel heavy and unresponsive. The world spins, and darkness edges my vision. I hear more shouts, the sound of struggle, but it's all fading.

Ava screams. Her cry cuts through the fog in my mind. She fights with the ferocity of a cornered animal, but another miner joins in, and the situation quickly turns dire.

I call out and tell her to run, but my body refuses to respond; the fight drains from me with every brutal blow.

The miners continue their assault; one of them kicks my gut, while the other lands blows to my head. Something snaps inside of me.

A primal rage takes over, and I fight back with renewed ferocity. Adrenaline courses through my veins, numbing the pain and giving me the strength to push back against my attackers.

I break free from their grasp and get back on my feet. The miners are caught off guard by my sudden surge of energy, giving me a momentary advantage.

But it's short-lived.

They regroup and launch another coordinated attack. I dodge and block as best I can, but they're relentless.

They're playing with me, taunting and teasing with each strike.

Ava swings a jagged branch, which crashes against one of the miners' heads. The loud crack reverberates through the air.

I look to Ava. Raw fear fills her face.

We're in serious trouble.

Shouts of reinforcements turn my blood cold.

More miners arrive.

Two turns to three.

Three to four.

They send me crashing to the ground, where boots replace fists, kicking me.

Ava fights beside me, but it's not enough. A fifth miner arrives. He grabs Ava, pinning her arms as he pulls her back to his chest and off her feet.

She kicks and screams.

Struggles to free herself.

But the miner is too strong.

A feral grin slides across his face.

Fucker looks damn pleased with himself.

I try to crawl to her, to protect her in any way I can, but a heavy boot lands on my back and pins me against the loamy ground.

"Stay down," one of the miners growls at me.

I struggle against his hold, but he's too strong. Ava looks back at me with terror in her eyes. A swift kick to my ribs has me huffing in pain.

Rough hands drag me to my feet.

"Let her go!" I scream, struggling against my captors.

"Shut your mouth," one of them growls in my ear.

With a swift, brutal motion, he grabs my camera from around my neck and yanks. The strap snaps under his strength.

He tosses it to one of the other men, a silent order that's quickly obeyed. Then, cold steel flashes in the dim light as he draws a knife and places its blade chillingly against my skin.

The miners drag us through the woods, their grip unrelenting. Ava's panicked glances twist my guts in knots.

My heart races as I try to come up with a plan. We can't take on all the miners, especially when they have weapons, but I can't let them harm Ava.

The return to the camp is a blur, the details lost in a haze of pain and regret. We stumble through the dark for what seems like hours and yet arrive far too soon.

I'm dimly aware of the jeers and taunts from the other miners as we're thrust into the center of their camp. I struggle against my captors, driven by a surge of anger and the unbearable thought of any harm coming to Ava.

But it's futile.

Ropes appear, and I'm trussed up in no time flat.

The ropes that bind me are too tight.

The miners too many.

For the first time since this nightmare began, I feel truly helpless.

There's an eerie glow cast by the flickering flames of the campfire that's been relit. Its light dances devilishly across the sharp angles of the miners' faces as they loom over us.

A palpable sense of lawlessness hangs in the air, thicker even than the mist that creeps like tendrils amongst the trees that encircle us. The miners' features are as rugged and harsh as the landscape surrounding us. Their eyes hold a glint of something feral, a wildness not tamed by the presence of authority.

We're forced to our knees.

I turn to Ava. Our eyes lock.

We've faced challenges before.

Survived against the odds.

This is not the end.

Not for us.

Even bound and bruised, there's something the miners haven't taken from us—our resolve.

It's a flame that burns bright in the darkness, a promise to each other that we will find a way out of this.

Together.

The leader of this group, the heavily built man with a wild beard, steps forward. His gaze rakes over Ava hungrily.

"Looks like we've caught ourselves some spies." His craggy face splits into a wicked grin. "What do you think, boys?"

The other miners whoop in response.

I feel sick to my stomach.

"Take them to the tent. Let them stew until I figure out what to do to them."

He wants to hurt us.

Hurt Ava.

With a grunt, he turns away.

Ava lets out a small whimper as our captors drag us toward a tent.

We're shoved inside, the fabric walls flimsy against the assault of the cold. The ground beneath is hard and unforgiving, the scent of pine and earth mingling with a less welcome smell of diesel and stale sweat that seems to permeate from the miners' very skin.

We're thrown inside and left alone.

"I'm scared," Ava whispers, her eyes wide with fear.

"It's going to be okay," I reassure her, though I'm unsure if I believe it myself.

Suddenly, the tent flap opens, and the miners' leader enters. He leers at Ava before turning his attention to me.

"You two are a pain in my ass." His lip curls, and he spits on the ground. With a swing of his boot, he clocks me in the head.

The last thing I remember is Ava's voice, filled with fear and fury, calling out my name.

Then everything goes black.

TWENTY-NINE

Cage

I wake to the sounds of an argument. My hands are bound, and the coppery taste of blood and dirt fills my mouth. The miners loom over us, their faces twisted in triumphant sneers.

"You won't get away with this." Ava glares at them, her spirit unbroken despite our dire situation.

The leader, a burly man with cold, calculating eyes, leans in. "Oh, we already have. No one knows you're here, and no one's coming for you."

Fear coils in my stomach, but I refuse to let it show.

"People will start looking for us when we don't return." Ava tries to keep her voice steady, but it trembles with fear.

The miner laughs, a harsh, grating sound. "By then, we'll be long gone. And you? Well, you'll be part of the Alaskan wilderness."

I test the ropes binding my wrists, but they're tight and secure. Ava does the same, her jaw set in determination.

"Looks like your friend's awake." He scratches an unkempt beard, eyeing us both head to toe. "Now, you don't look like the usual day-tripper crowd. What's your deal?"

I bristle at the heckling, but before I can reply, Ava lifts placating palms. "We're just hikers. That's it."

"I think it's more than that." He reaches out to one of the others, hand outstretched. One of the other men slaps my camera into our interrogator's massive hand. "Got some interesting pictures here. Photos of my operation."

He and the others exchange an uneasy look.

"Look, it's the truth," Ava says. "We're just hik…"

"Listen, missy, dial it down a notch."

"We're not here to cause harm or stir up any trouble," Ava continues trying to appeal to their base humanity. Only these men lost that a long time ago. "We're just minding our business, enjoying backcountry camping."

The tension inside the tent amplifies. I shift closer to Ava, needing to show solidarity.

Needing to be close.

Before things escalate further, I clear my throat. "Look, guys. Clearly, you don't want company, so we'll be moving on. We didn't mean to intrude."

The lead miner, a giant man with a face carved from granite, steps forward. His beard is a tangled mass of dark hair peppered with gray, and his hands are like slabs of stone, stained with the earth they have ravaged.

When he speaks, his voice is deep and guttural, each word a rumbling from the depths of his barrel chest.

"You were spying on us." He grabs me by the collar of my shirt, pulling me forward. "Don't lie to me." His fetid breath is foul against my face. "I saw the shots you took. Thought you could play spy and not get caught?"

"That's not…"

The leader, clearly frustrated, fixes us with a glare that promises more pain. "You're making this harder on yourselves." His gaze lingers on Ava in a way that makes my blood run cold.

"Cooperate, and maybe you walk out of here. Keep stonewalling me, and something else will happen." Once again, he turns his lecherous gaze on Ava.

The implied threat to Ava hangs in the air, a noxious miasma of violence and danger. I fight to keep my expression neutral and not let my fear and anger show.

My only concern is for Ava's safety.

It's the only thing that matters.

"We're telling you the truth."

"You think you're tough?" A smirk plays at the corner of his mouth. It's a cruel imitation of hospitality, sending a shiver through me that has nothing to do with the night's cold.

His harsh laughter rings out behind him, a grating sound that cuts through the silence, leaving us alone to face the grim reality of our situation.

I examine the damage done to Ava by the miners. Each bruise on her skin ignites a rage within me, a promise of retribution that I silently vow to fulfill.

My physical pain is nothing compared to the helplessness of not being able to protect her from both very real veiled threats and lecherous stares.

Ava is silent beside me, her jaw set in a firm line, her tiny hands balled into fists at her sides. Tension rolls off her in waves, her entire being coiled like a spring, ready to react at the first sign of danger.

The ropes bite into my wrists, and the fibers abrade my skin, but I barely register the pain.

"Time for questions." His guttural voice drips menace as his cronies haul me to my knees. I don't dare resist, playing docile and disoriented for now, buying time to assess the situation.

The leader grabs Ava, wrenching her up to kneel beside me. I sear him with unconcealed loathing, which he returns tauntingly before addressing us both.

"Here's how it is. We keep knocking your heads together until you tell us who you told you about our operation and what they know." He emphasizes this with another rough shove to me. "And if you still hold out, well…" His lewd gaze roams Ava, his vile meaning clear.

Revulsion and volcanic fury roar inside me, but I betray nothing, projecting limp exhaustion instead.

Choose the moment.

The odds aren't in my favor.

Not yet.

But when they are, this savage will regret threatening Ava. For now, though, we're his captives.

I focus on steadying my breathing. Killing the leader with my bare hands, however satisfying, won't save Ava from the other grubby-handed miners who are ready to take their turn with her.

The brutal questioning begins, each miner taking their turn like a grotesque parody of an interrogation. Their questions are sharp, probing for weaknesses they can exploit.

I do my best to shield Ava, to answer with just enough truth to keep their suspicion at bay without revealing anything important.

"Who knows you're here?" The leader leans close. His eyes gleam with malice.

I keep my gaze steady, offering only silence, my mind racing for a way out of this.

Another man steps forward, his fist clenched. The blow comes without warning, a sharp pain across my cheek that sends stars dancing through my vision.

Beside me, Ava flinches, her fear a tangible thing that fills the tent. I want to tell her it'll be okay, but I won't lie.

The interrogation turns brutal, each miner taking their turn to intimidate and threaten. Amidst the harsh glare of their flashlights and the cold, unforgiving ground beneath us, Ava and I endure their relentless questions.

One of the miners, a bulky figure with a sneer that seems permanently etched onto his face, leans in too close for comfort.

"Who did you tell about Ronin's operation?" His voice is a harsh whisper that slices through the tense air.

The name drops like a stone, Ronin.

It doesn't mean anything, but now we know this is the man who leads this lawless crew. It's a small victory, and I file away the information.

My eyes flicker to Ava, signaling her to stay silent. The miner who slipped up glances nervously toward their leader, a clear mistake made.

"They're not going to talk." Ronin, the apparent kingpin of this grim assembly, fixes his gaze on us, his eyes cold and calculating. He turns his attention back to me, his hand gripping my chin, forcing me to meet his gaze.

Ronin watches us for a moment longer, his expression unreadable. Then, with a dismissive grunt, he signals for his men to back off.

"Keep them here," he orders, his voice carrying the weight of a threat that's as explicit as it is unspoken. "We'll decide what to do with them in the morning."

As the miners retreat, leaving us in a silence heavy with unspoken fears, Ava and I glance at each other. Ronin's name is a piece of knowledge that could prove valuable. It's a small victory in the face of our defeat.

But it's a victory nonetheless.

As soon as we're alone, I scoot to Ava's side. My movements are awkward, with my hands and feet tightly bound. Up close, I examine her face critically, noting a swollen bottom lip and a purpling bruise along her jawline. Impotent rage wars with tender concern inside me at the sight.

"Are you okay?" I keep my voice low, barely above a whisper. We have no guarantee of actual privacy here.

I flop onto my back with a frustrated sigh, my mind racing. Ava lies next to me, wrists tightly bound. Her eyes closed as she concentrates on steadying her breathing, but faint tremors ripple through her slender frame.

However brave a front she puts up, imagining her at the mercy of these ruthless men fills me with dread.

Shimmying closer, I whisper. "Ava—Ava, look at me. We need to get you out of here."

Her eyes flash open, strikingly blue even in the dimness. "I'm not leaving you."

Her face is a mess of bruises and swelling that speaks to the brutality of the miners when they took us. Anger courses through me, hot and fierce, a storm raging within.

I jostle my body nearer until we're elbow to elbow.

"We have to be smart about this. We don't stand a chance outnumbered like we are. But if I create a distraction…" I let the thought trail off, appealing to her logical side.

She knows I'm right.

Frustrated anger wars with fearful prudence on her dirt-smudged face.

"Cage, I won't… I can't. Don't ask me to leave you."

Her tone wavers slightly. She turns her face aside, avoiding my gaze, though we both feel the intensity crackling between us, this bond forged through days of reliance on each other.

"If I can free your hands, you need to go." Although she's extraordinarily capable, the thought of sending her out there, alone, without me, feels like a kick in the gut.

But it's her only chance…

"I might never see you again." Her words fade away, the dire possibilities too awful to voice. "It's been three days."

"Has it?"

I know what she's referring to, but I refuse to say it aloud. We don't know if the miners are listening, hoping we reveal something because we think we're alone.

"I need you to promise me."

"Cage, please don't ask that of me."

"You know what they're going to do to you. I can't have that on my conscience. We're going to free you, and you have to run."

Ava nods, her eyes filled with emotion and lingering pain as she surveys my own fresh injuries. Her unflinching bravery constantly astounds me. Beneath the warrior exterior, though, I sense her terror.

My need to shield and protect this remarkable woman wells up powerfully.

"We'll get out of this, I swear it." I inject absolute conviction in my tone. "I just need you to be ready to run at the first opportunity."

Ava's eyes flash with rebuttal before she visibly swallows it back. Wrong-headed noble instincts war across her face.

"Cage, I told you. I won't leave you behind with these animals." Her heated whisper denies arguments.

I shift closer still; our shoulders now pressed together. My eyes bore intensely into hers, willing her to accept reason.

"I'll find a way out. I promise. But I need to know you're safe."

I hold her defiant gaze, neither of us backing down. The stakes are too high, but she finally dips her chin a fraction of an inch.

Relief gusts through me. Our chances diminish by the hour, yet I cling fiercely to the faith that opportunity will present itself.

"Ava…" My entreating whisper is cut off by approaching footsteps outside.

Voices sound, footsteps scuffing closer. We spring apart, feigning unconsciousness as the tent flap parts.

The hulking leader enters, along with the wiry, broad-nosed miner who busted my rib last session. My muscles coil instinctively, but instead of hauling me upright, Ronin moves for Ava.

"You two think you're smart, huh?" His voice grates like gravel tumbling down a mountain. "Separating you will make you sing a little easier."

"No." My mind screams denial, even as they drag Ava out without a glance my way.

"We'll see if a little alone time loosens her tongue…" Ronin's parting taunt has me seeing red.

Icy horror douses my veins.

"If you touch her…" I roar after them.

"Oh, I plan on doing a lot of touching." He spits at the ground by my knees.

"You won't get away with this."

"Who's going to stop us? You?" His laugh is a harsh bark that cuts through the silence.

He gestures to his man, who grabs Ava, then turns his back on me as if I'm nothing. The tent flap closes, leaving me alone and Ava in their hands.

THIRTY

Cage

___

I LUNGE AGAINST MY BONDS UNTIL MY SKIN SPLITS AND BLOOD FLOWS, snarling desperate threats. My hysteria goes unacknowledged; their footsteps are already fading.

Alone, panic threatens to choke me. Ava faces unspeakable danger, and I'm trapped here.

Goddamn useless.

Frantically, I squirm and writhe, trying to rupture my restraints through strength alone.

But the knots and cords hold fast.

My wrists are on fire, slick with blood from my efforts to free myself. I scarcely notice the wounds and keep straining with animalistic intensity, every fiber of me enraged.

Their strategy is to break us, to divide and conquer, but the thought of Ava alone with them tightens my throat.

How long I battle against my restraints, I don't know.

Time loses meaning.

The minutes stretch to hours, and the cold seeps deeper into my bones with each passing minute.

Ava's absence is a void that scares me more than the miners' threats.

A shuffling outside the tent has me on alert, every muscle tensed. The flap bursts open, and the lead miner looms in the entrance, a dark silhouette against the bright light of day.

"Where's Ava?" I grind my molars and glare at him.

"Ready to talk?" He arches a brow, the threat implicit in his tone.

"I've got nothing to say to you." Despite my bonds, I rise to my feet, refusing to let him see any sign of weakness.

"We'll see about that." He steps closer, the stench of tobacco and sweat preceding him.

Ronin leans in, close enough that I can see the flecks of silver in his dark beard, a stark contrast to the icy hostility in his eyes.

His breath reeks of stale coffee and cigarettes—a noxious cloud in the tent's already stifling air. With each exhale, it wraps around me like a vice, a palpable reminder of the danger that hovers over us.

"Who sent you?" His eyes glint menacingly under the tent's dim light.

The question is a bullet aimed not to kill but to probe for a weakness he can exploit.

I meet his gaze, every instinct screaming at me to protect Ava. If he's questioning me, he's not hurting her.

I hope.

"No one sent me." My voice remains even, betraying none of the adrenaline that courses through my veins.

He grunts, unimpressed by my defiance.

"You expect me to believe that? That you're out this far just to take shots of nature?"

His sneer is a grotesque mask, one that speaks of a life spent in the shadows, away from the warmth of human kindness.

"That's exactly what I'm doing."

"Nobody comes this deep into the bush for pictures."

"I don't care what you believe. I'm a nature photographer. I take pictures of—nature." This truth costs me nothing and causes no harm.

"No way you're out here for pretty pictures. Your little photo session has a purpose." The accusation is a whip, each word lashing against my resolve. "Did you send copies to anyone?"

"They're just pictures."

I swallow the fear that threatens to choke me. The more he speaks, the more I realize that Ava's safety hangs by the same precarious thread that holds my own life.

His laugh is a low rumble, a sound devoid of humor.

"Just photos?" He mocks me using a falsetto voice. "How long have you been spying on us?"

"We weren't spying. Your men chased us. We ran for our lives."

"But you came back. Why? To take more pictures?"

"We came back to retrieve our gear." I keep to the truth as much as possible. "We needed it to make the hike back. We don't care what you're doing here and want no part of it. If you want the pictures, take the SIM card. Let us go, and we'll walk out of your life."

I try to negotiate a way out of this nightmare, but my words, rather than defusing the situation, only ignite Ronin's fury.

Without warning, his hand clenches into a fist, and in a flash of movement too quick to anticipate, he strikes.

The blow lands with brutal precision, a sharp crack against the side of my face that sends white-hot pain searing through my skull. It's a calculated display of his power, a clear message that words or pleas do not sway him.

The force of his punch knocks me sideways. Makes my ears ring. Spots dance in my vision. The ground tilts beneath me, and for a moment, I'm disoriented, struggling to maintain my balance.

Ronin stands over me, his breath heavy, his expression of cold satisfaction. The message is clear: he's in control, and he'll mete out punishment as he sees fit. My attempt to beg for our freedom, to offer a solution that could benefit us both, is brushed aside with violence that leaves no room for negotiation.

His steps, measured and deliberate before, now seem menacing in their stillness. He watches me, waiting to see if I'll rise, challenge him, or crumble.

But even as pain throbs through my face, a defiant spark ignites within me.

He's shown his hand, revealed the depth of his cruelty, and though he may have knocked me down, he hasn't broken me.

I meet his gaze, the unspoken challenge clear in my eyes. Ronin may have won this round, but the fight for our freedom, for our survival, is far from over.

"You're a tough nut to crack. I'll give you that, but everybody breaks eventually. And you will break." The cold glint in his eyes speaks of danger, a warning of the violence he's capable of.

"I've told you everything."

Ronin steps closer, his presence imposing, a tangible force that sucks the air from the tent.

"Why are you here?" A low, rumbling growl reverberates in the back of his throat.

Here we go with the questions again.

"Like I said…" I work my jaw back and forth, still processing the pain of his attack. "I'm a nature photographer. That's what I do."

"This is more than a little stroll in the woods."

"I'm an *adventure* wildlife photographer. Everything I do is extreme."

One of the other miners enters the tent, carrying my camera. Ronin snatches it out of the man's hands.

"Did you think you could spy on my operations and not face consequences?" He turns on the camera, waving it mockingly in front of me. "If you're some great adventure photographer, where are those pictures?"

"Lost with my gear you destroyed." I don't mention the SIM card I carry. It doesn't have the bulk of the photos on it, but there's enough to implicate Ronin and shut down his crew for good.

His questions are rapid-fire, designed to disorient and weaken. With each word, he leans closer, his breath foul and hot against my face.

"You think you're smart, huh?" he continues, his tone laced with venom. "Think you can just waltz in here, take some pretty pictures, and expose what we're doing?" The camera dangles from his hand, an unspoken threat of what he's willing to do to protect his secrets.

My muscles are coiled springs, every nerve ending alight with the urge to fight, flee, and do anything but kneel here helplessly.

But I give him nothing.

Not a word.

Not a twitch.

Not a sign of the turmoil that rages like a tempest inside of me. My silence is my armor, a defiant shield against his attempts to break me.

Ronin's sneer deepens, a predator frustrated by its prey's resilience. "You will tell me what I want to know." The cold glint in his eyes speaks of danger, a warning of the violence he's capable of.

His boot connects with my side. An explosion of pain sends me sprawling to the ground. I taste blood, and it's a sharp reminder that this is no game. This is survival, and I am far from safe.

"I've already told you everything."

"You'll talk," he says with chilling certainty, stepping over me as he exits the tent. "They always do."

And then I'm alone, left to the mercy of my own racing thoughts and the cold, unforgiving ground beneath me. I must hold on, for Ava, for justice, for the truth that lies captured on my camera —a truth that must be brought to light.

I slump from exhaustion, the taste of iron sharp in my mouth. My side throbs in time with my pulse.

The lead miner hovers, a looming specter ready to unleash more questions, each one loaded with the threat of further violence and powered by his fists and boots.

The intensity in his eyes doesn't waver, and I brace for another onslaught. The silence stretches, filled only by my labored breathing and the distant howl of a lone wolf.

Abruptly, he leans in, his face so close I can count the droplets of sweat beading on his brow.

"Last chance."

I teeter on a knife edge, torn between the primal will to survive and the protective shield I've become for Ava.

But even as I open my mouth to weave a tale that might buy her safety, the tent flap is thrown aside.

A miner bursts in, his face ghostly pale under a smear of dirt. He leans in, whispering urgently into the leader's ear. The words are lost to me, but their effect is not.

The lead miner's face blanches. His eyes widen—an animal caught in headlights.

"What?" The word is a gunshot in the silence.

He turns on his heel, barking orders as he exits, leaving me forgotten for the moment, a reprieve from the storm.

In the lull, I strain against my restraints, but it's a futile gesture. I'm spent, pain filling every breath. I close my eyes, summoning strength from some well deep within me. Then I hear it—the faintest rustle of canvas behind me.

Impossibly, Ava crawls under the canvas.

"Thank God! Are you…?"

Clearly, she escaped. Is that what pulled away my interrogator?

Wild-eyed, her hair's a tangled halo around her dirt-streaked face. The fire in her eyes is as tangible as the cold ground beneath me.

She moves quickly and efficiently, but as she reaches for the knots binding me, I shake my head.

"We have to go." Ava scrambles behind me; her fingers work at the bindings on my wrists.

"How did you escape?"

"I stabbed one in the crotch when he got too handsy, then ran." Her words punch through my stupor. "Can you stand? We have maybe a minute before they sound the alarm."

"They already have," I whisper fiercely. "You have to go. Get help."

Tears glimmer in her eyes, but she shakes her head, a silent warrior refusing to leave her comrade. "I won't leave you like this."

"You must." I yell at her, regretting it immediately. "I can handle this. Your escape is the only hope we have. I'll stall them."

Her hands linger on mine, a fleeting touch that says more than words ever could. With a nod, more felt than seen, she slips away, back into the shadows from which she emerged.

Moments later, the lead miner returns, his face a thundercloud of rage.

"Where is she?" He yanks me to my feet, his grip iron on my bruised flesh.

"How the hell would I know." I meet his fury with rage.

He snarls, dragging me outside and into the camp's heart.

The men gather in a loose circle, their faces eager for the spectacle. Rough hands hoist me up. Ropes bite into my flesh as I'm strung up like some macabre marionette. The leader steps back, a malicious glee in his eyes as he signals his men.

The first blow hits me directly in my solar plexus, knocking the wind out of me. I gasp, but the pain is a distant thing compared to the dread of what Ava might be walking into.

The leader's voice cuts through the grunts and jeers of his men.

"This is for you, little bird," he yells into the forest. "We'll keep going until you come back to us."

Each punch and kick is a message, a brutal telegraph to Ava that they will continue until she returns.

My vision blurs. My head lolls. Through the haze, I cling to one thought—Ava is free, and with her lies our chance for survival.

As for me, I'll do my best to—endure.

THIRTY-ONE

Ava

———

THE MEN DEPOSIT ME IN ANOTHER TENT, LEAVING ME ALONE WITH MY racing pulse.

The miners make a fatal mistake. They underestimate me, thinking I'm nothing but a helpless female.

They don't know Ava Livingston.

I'm not weak or defenseless.

I'm the storm they never saw coming.

When they separated me from Cage and threw me into another tent, I had no illusions about what they planned.

Once they leave me alone, I pull out my multitool. Bastards didn't even consider searching me for weapons.

I work the ropes against the serrated edge of my multitool, sawing back and forth. The fibers give way, little by little, but they do give way.

Once I free my hands, my muscles scream in protest, but that's a small price to pay for freedom.

My hands are my own again, and I use my multitool to cut a slit in the canvas at the back of the tent. I don't waste a moment except to pause and take in my bearings.

The guards celebrate, clearly not expecting anyone to break free, especially not the woman they so foolishly underestimated.

I move with the shadows, a whisper on the wind, and make my way back to the tent where Cage is being held.

I crouch and crawl under the canvas fabric.

My heart hammers against my ribs, a frantic beat that echoes my thoughts. The sight that greets me wrenches a gasp from my lips, stifled quickly behind my hand.

Cage, beaten and bound. They worked on him after separating me, and it shows in the purplish bruising all over his body.

He turns at the sound, eyes widening.

Then speaks the words I never wanted to hear. *"You have to go."*

I try arguing, telling him I won't leave him, but he's insistent and most likely right.

Those words break me.

The thought of leaving him, of abandoning Cage, is unbearable, but he is unyielding.

Our hands touch—a fleeting connection.

A promise.

A goodbye.

I lean in, my lips brushing against his forehead—a kiss laden with all the things I cannot say, a vow that I will return for him.

Then, I'm gone, slipping back into the night. The forest envelops me again, but this time, I carry the weight of Cage's safety, the urgency of our plight propelling me forward.

I'll bring back help.

No matter what it takes.

Just a second before I'm hidden by the foliage, the leader drags Cage out of the tent and strings him up in the center of the camp.

Tears stream down my face as the miners jeer and strike Cage. The leader, Ronin, looks to the edge of the clearing.

I will never forget his words. *"We'll keep going until you come back to us."*

I'm ripped to shreds inside, leaving a piece of my heart behind with every step I take away from Cage.

I move with a purpose fueled by desperation and fear. My mind is a tumult of images—Cage, bound and beaten; the miners, cruel and taunting.

I race through the woods, sprinting to where Cage and I so unwittingly set our camp.

The miners underestimated me, thinking a few ropes could hold the wild spirit of Ava Livingston.

They thought wrong, and I'm betting on them being rather dumb. It takes time to race back to the site of our camp, but I make it there in record time.

Finally, I burst into the clearing, my lungs burning, my heart pounding a frantic rhythm against my ribs. Sunlight shines down on the small clearing, its harsh rays illuminating the devastation.

The sight hits me like a physical blow, stealing the breath from my lungs. Shredded tent fabric flutters in the breeze, a mocking reminder of the violence that tore through this place. The ground is littered with the detritus of our ransacked belongings—broken tools, torn clothing, shattered containers.

But I don't have time to dwell on the carnage. Every second counts; every heartbeat reminds me that Cage is suffering and that his life hangs in the balance. I force my feet forward, my boots crunching on the debris-strewn ground.

The air is thick with pine and the metallic tang of fear. I can taste it on my tongue, bitter and sharp. My gaze darts around the campsite, searching for a glint of metal, a hint of where I packed the spare battery.

I try to recall the last time I saw it, my mind racing through a haze of adrenaline and desperation.

Where did I pack it?

My memory, usually a steel trap, falters under the weight of my task.

Frustration knots in my chest, tight and suffocating. But surrender isn't in my nature. Cage's face, bruised and resolute, flashes behind my eyelids, stoking the fire in my veins.

I dig deeper, fingers scraping against fabric and earth, refusing to let despair cloud my focus.

Was it in my backpack?

The side pocket of the tent?

My hands shake as I claw through the wreckage, tossing useless items aside. My movements grow more frantic with each passing moment.

I barely notice the sting of cuts on my palms, the splinters embedding themselves in my skin. All that matters is finding that battery.

I barely notice my discomfort or fatigue; my focus is narrowed to a single, all-consuming goal: find the battery and save Cage.

Without it, the satellite phone is nothing more than a useless hunk of plastic and circuitry. Cage's chance of rescue slips further away with each passing second. The weight of that knowledge presses down on me, a physical burden that makes each movement feel like I'm wading through quicksand.

A cracked water filter lies in pieces, a cruel reminder of how ill-prepared we are for what lies ahead.

But still, no battery.

Frustration claws at my throat, hot and bitter. I want to scream, to rage against the injustice of it all. How can something so vital be so elusive?

I dig deeper, tossing aside mangled tent poles and shredded sleeping bags. Sweat drips into my eyes, blurring my vision. I blink it away, refusing to let a moment's distraction slow me down.

Our gear mocks me, a jumbled mess of broken promises and shattered hopes.

Each empty container I toss aside, each fruitless search through a pile of debris, feels like a personal failure.

And yet, I can't give up. Giving up means condemning Cage to death. Giving up means letting those bastards win. I grit my teeth, tasting blood where I've bitten my lip raw.

I turn to the remains of one of the tents, now little more than a twisted heap of fabric and poles. I drop to my knees, ignoring the bite of gravel through my pants. My fingers scrabble through the wreckage, searching, praying for a miracle.

My heart lurches as my fingers brush against something hard and unyielding amidst the chaos. I freeze, hardly daring to breathe.

Could it be…?

I tentatively brush aside a tattered remnant, my pulse pounding in my ears. There, nestled in the debris, is a glint of metal. The midday sun reflects off its surface, a beacon of hope in this nightmare.

And then, there it is.

I inch closer, my movements slow and cautious, as if any sudden motion might make this tantalizing promise disappear. The metal object is partially obscured, covered in a layer of grime and dust. I hold my breath, reaching out with trembling fingers.

As I make contact, a jolt runs through me, electric and overwhelming. The shape, the size—it's achingly familiar. I grasp the object, feeling the contours of the battery casing beneath my fingertips.

For a moment, I'm afraid to hope, terrified that this might be some cruel trick of the mind. But as I pull it free from the wreckage, there's no denying the truth.

The spare battery.

A sob catches in my throat, relief and disbelief warring in my chest. I snatch it up, cradling it to my chest like the precious lifeline it is.

It's scuffed and dirty but appears intact. A hysterical laugh bubbles in my throat, filled with relief and disbelief. Against all odds, I've found it.

But there's no time to savor this small victory.

The battery is just the first step, a means to an end. My elation is short-lived, quickly replaced by a renewed sense of urgency.

Having the battery is only half the battle. I still need to retrieve the satellite phone and pray that it's in working order.

I allow myself one brief moment to catch my breath and let the magnitude of this small victory sink in. Then I'm on my feet again, the battery clutched tightly in my sweat-slicked palm.

I orient myself, scanning the tree line for the path that will lead me back to where Cage and I were captured. Back to where I hid the phone in a last, desperate act before they took us.

I still need to find the satellite phone, make the call that will save the man I've grown to care for more than I ever thought possible, and get help.

The forest calls to me, a maze of shadow and light. I know what awaits me—the journey back to where Cage and I were taken, the satellite phone our only chance for help.

Every instinct screams at me to run, to fly through the forest as fast as my legs will carry me, but I force myself to be cautious, to place each foot carefully. I can't afford a twisted ankle or a careless mistake—not now, when everything hangs in the balance.

I tuck the battery into my pocket, its weight a comforting presence against my thigh.

I melt into the shadows of the trees, my senses heightened, my nerves thrumming with adrenaline. The forest seems to hold its breath, an eerie stillness broken only by the pounding of my own heart.

Then I'm running again, tearing through the underbrush, retracing the steps that led us to this nightmare. The forest blurs around me as I sprint, my heart pounding frantically in my chest.

I stumble over a root, catching myself before I fall. The memory of where I tossed the sat phone is vivid in my mind.

Branches whip at my face, leaving stinging cuts in their wake, but I barely feel them. All I can focus on is the path ahead and my desperate need to reach the spot where everything went so horribly wrong.

Each step is a battle against the terror that claws at my throat, the sickening knowledge that every second I'm away is another second Cage spends in agony.

The thought of what those bastards might be doing to him makes my stomach churn, fueling the fire that propels me forward.

I dodge around a fallen log, my boots skidding on the damp leaves. The air is thick and heavy, the scent of pine and earth mingling with the acrid tang of my own fear. I suck in lungfuls of it, using the burn in my chest as a focus, a reminder of what's at stake.

As I near the spot where Cage and I were captured, a new kind of dread settles in my gut. The miners could be scouring the woods, hungry for retribution. The thought makes my skin crawl, but I force it aside. I can't afford to be paralyzed by fear, not when Cage's life hangs in the balance.

I slow my pace as I approach the place where they captured us, my senses stretched to their limits. Every rustle of leaves, every snap of a twig, sends a jolt of adrenaline surging through my veins. I scan the underbrush, looking for any hint that our captors are out here.

But the forest is quiet.

Almost too quiet.

The log comes into view, a hulking silhouette against the lighter background of the forest floor. I creep forward, my breath coming in shallow gasps. The satellite phone is here, hidden in a last desperate act before we were dragged away. If I can just reach it.

Send out a call for help…

There.

A glint of metal catches my eye, nearly obscured by a tangle of vegetation. My heart leaps into my throat as I lunge forward, my fingers scrabbling at the earth. I brush aside the foliage, and there it is—the satellite phone, nestled in the hollow of a tree root.

My hands shake as I snatch it up, and I hardly dare believe this is real. The phone feels solid in my grip, a lifeline to the outside world. For a moment, I'm dizzy with relief, and my knees threaten to buckle beneath me.

But I can't afford to fall apart, not yet. I take a steadying breath, forcing my fingers to still their trembling. I turn the phone over in my hands, praying that it's still intact.

The screen flickers to life, and I nearly sob with relief. But the battery indicator blinks red, a warning that time is running out in more ways than one. I fumble in my pocket for the spare battery, my heart in my throat.

The battery swap feels like delicate surgery, and my fingers are clumsy with anticipation and dread. I nearly drop the phone, catching it at the last moment with a gasp.

The compartment clicks open, the dead battery sliding out with a finality that echoes in the hollow space of my chest. I replace it with the spare, the symbol of all our hopes, and press the power button. The device remains dark for a heartbeat too long, and my breath catches, a silent plea in the stillness.

For an agonizing moment, nothing happens. Then, the screen lights up, and the startup logo blinks into existence. Giddy relief rushes through me, tempered immediately by the knowledge that I'm not safe yet.

None of us are.

I need to call for help before it's too late. But as I stand there in the clearing, clutching the satellite phone to my chest, a sudden, terrible thought hits me.

What if I'm already too late? What if in the time it's taken me to find the phone and locate the battery, the miners have already exacted their revenge on Cage?

The thought is like a punch to the gut, leaving me breathless and reeling. But I force it aside, clinging to the desperate hope that Cage is still alive, still fighting. He has to be.

Because the alternative is too horrific to contemplate.

With shaking fingers, I dial a number I know by heart. As the phone rings, I send up a silent, desperate prayer.

Please let Justin answer. Let him hear me. Let him bring the help we so desperately need.

Please, don't let me be too late…

Hang on, Cage.

Just hang on…

"Come on, Justin. Pick up. Please." The words are a whisper, a mantra.

Then, a click, and a voice breaks through the static.

"Ava? Ava, is that you?"

Tears of relief well up in my eyes, and for a moment, I can't speak. I'm overwhelmed by the sound of a friendly voice, a lifeline in the vast wilderness.

"Justin. Help. They have Cage. They're…" Sobs choke my words, the horror of the situation crashing down on me anew.

"We're coming for you."

Without hearing him, I relay the coordinates with painstaking accuracy, each number a step toward rescue. "Please, hurry," I add, the plea a whisper carried away by the wind.

"We're already on our way. Lost the beacon to the phone, but we've got it now. Hold tight. I'm bringing reinforcements." Justin's assurance is a balm to my frayed nerves.

THIRTY-TWO

Ava

———

"Justin, please, you have to hurry." My voice cracks, desperation clawing at my throat. The satellite phone feels slick in my sweat-drenched palm, a lifeline that could be cut at any moment.

"Talk to me." Justin's voice is steady, but I can hear the undercurrent of concern.

I take a shuddering breath, trying to force my thoughts into coherence. "It's Cage. They have him."

"Who has him?"

"Miners, they…" A sob chokes off my words, the memory of Cage's battered face searing behind my eyelids.

As quickly as possible, I tell Justin about the miners and their illegal operation, how they chased and then captured us.

"Please. I don't know how long he has." The unspoken hangs heavy in the air—Cage's life might be measured in heartbeats now.

"We're already on the way." Justin's tone sharpens, urgency bleeding through the static.

For a moment, I'm sure I mishear what he says. The rush of blood in my ears drowns out everything else.

"What?"

"When you failed to check in, I started tracking your sat phone. We're en route to your location." There's a rustling on the other end, voices in the background.

Relief and confusion war within me. How could they already be coming? But there's no time for questions, not when every second brings Cage closer to the unthinkable.

"Hurry, please." It's all I can manage, all I can force past the lump in my throat.

"ETA 10 minutes. Find a clear spot, Ava. We're coming in hot. Keep this line open."

I'm left staring at the phone, my heart pounding a staccato rhythm against my ribs.

Help is coming.

But will it be enough?

Will it be in time?

I squeeze my eyes shut, trying to banish the images of Cage at the miners' mercy. The thought of what they could be doing to him, even now, sends a wave of nausea rolling through me.

No. I can't think like that. I have to believe he's alive. I have to believe we'll save him.

I force my feet to move and find a place where they can land.

The forest is a blur of green and brown as I race through the underbrush, my heart pounding in my ears. Branches whip at my face, leaving stinging trails across my skin, but I barely feel them. All I can focus on is the need to find a clearing, a space for the rescue team to land.

Justin is already on his way, and he's bringing a team with him, but without a place to land, they might as well be a world away.

I vault over a fallen log, my muscles screaming with the effort. The ground beneath my feet is treacherous, a tangle of roots and rocks threatening to send me sprawling with each step. But I can't slow down, can't afford to be cautious. Every second I lose is a second that Cage doesn't have.

The trees press in around me, a suffocating wall of foliage that seems to stretch forever. I scan the canopy desperately, searching for a break, a gap, or anything that might offer a glimmer of hope.

But there's nothing. Just an endless sea of green, broken only by the shafts of sunlight that pierce the gloom.

Desperation claws at my throat, a bitter taste on my tongue. How can there be no clearing, no space in this vast wilderness? It's as if the forest itself is conspiring against us, a silent ally to the men who hold Cage captive.

I stumble, my foot catching on a gnarled root, and nearly go down. I catch myself at the last moment, my palms slamming into the damp earth. The impact jolts through my bones, but I barely register the pain.

I push myself up, my breath coming in ragged gasps. The humidity is oppressive, clinging to my skin like a second layer of clothing. Sweat trickles down my back, mingling with the grime and blood that already stain my shirt.

But I keep moving, driven by a fierce determination that borders on madness.

I will find a clearing.

I will bring help to Cage.

There is no other option.

And then, as if in answer to my silent prayers, the trees thin. The change is subtle at first, gradually lessening the press of trunks and branches, but as I push forward, it becomes more pronounced, the forest giving way to a small glade.

I burst into the clearing, my lungs burning, my legs trembling with exhaustion. The sun hits me like a physical force, bright and blinding after the gloom of the forest. I blink, my eyes watering as I take in my surroundings.

It's not much—just a small patch of grass ringed by towering pines—but it's enough. It has to be.

The distant thrum of rotor blades cuts through the forest's silence. At first, it is a whisper, then grows louder with each passing second. The sound is unmistakable, a rhythmic beating that sends a jolt of adrenaline surging through my veins.

He really was already on his way.

My heart leaps, hope and fear intertwined in a dizzying spiral. I spin around, scanning the sky, searching for a sign.

There, in the distance, a shape emerges.

It's a speck at first, a dark smudge against the brilliant blue sky. But as I watch, it grows larger, taking on the distinctive outline of a helicopter. The thrum of the blades intensifies, vibrating in my chest and bones.

Tears blur my vision, relief a tangible force pressing against my chest.

He came.

He's here.

I clutch the satellite phone tighter, my knuckles turning white.

But even as I stand there, watching salvation approach, a cold tendril of dread curls in my gut.

What if we're too late? What if, even now, Cage is…

No. I refuse to finish that thought. I cling to hope, to the belief that he's fighting, that he's holding on.

He has to be.

Because the alternative is unthinkable.

The helicopter draws closer, the downdraft from its rotors whipping the trees into a frenzy. Leaves and debris swirl around me, stinging my skin, but I barely feel it. All my focus is on the approaching aircraft, on the promise and the threat it represents.

I squint against the wind, trying to make out any identifying marks, any sign that this is friend and not foe. But the glare of the sun reflects off the helicopter's body, blinding me.

My heart pounds a frantic rhythm; each beat a countdown to an unknown fate. I lick my lips, tasting salt and fear. The satellite phone feels slick in my grip, my lifeline to the outside world.

I raise it to my ear, praying that Justin is still there. "Justin?"

"It's us, Ava." His voice crackles through the static.

For a moment, I can't breathe. The knot in my chest loosens, just a fraction, as the realization sinks in. Help is here. They came.

But even as relief floods through me, it's tempered by the knowledge of what still lies ahead. Cage is out there, in the hands of those monsters. And until he's safe, until I see him with my own eyes, I won't be able to fully believe that this nightmare is over.

The helicopter is directly overhead now, the roar of its engines deafening. For a moment, my heart sinks. The clearing is too small for it to land, and the trees are too close.

But then ropes snake down. They're not going to land. They're going to rappel down.

I raise a hand to shield my eyes, squinting against the maelstrom of wind and debris.

And then I see them—figures clad in black, leaning out of the chopper's open door. For a heart-stopping moment, I'm back in the camp, surrounded by the miners, their leering faces and rough hands.

But then one of the figures raises a hand, a signal. And I see the flash of a familiar face.

Justin.

Tears prick at my eyes, relief and gratitude welling up like a tidal wave. I raise my hand, waving it, a beacon in the chaos.

The helicopter hovers, the downdraft flattening the grass around me. I shield my face, my hair whipping around me in a wild dance.

Several figures, clad head to toe in black tactical gear, their faces obscured by helmets and goggles, move with a fluidity that speaks of countless hours of training,

And then they're descending, sliding down the lines like spiders on a web, moving with a grace and precision that speaks of years of training.

I step back, my pulse racing as I watch the figures descend, black against the brilliant blue of the sky.

And then they're on the ground, unhooking from their lines, their faces grim with determination. They fan out in a protective circle. At the center is Justin.

He strides toward me, his eyes searching my face, looking for answers to questions he hasn't yet asked. I open my mouth, ready to spill everything, to beg him to hurry.

I'm moving before I realize it, my legs carrying me forward. And then I'm in his arms, the solidness of him, the realness, a balm to my battered soul.

"You came." It's all I can manage, my voice muffled against his chest.

"Always." His arms tighten around me, a promise and a vow.

And with those words, the fear that's been my constant companion begins to recede, replaced by a steely determination.

And anger. Hot, bright anger.

The moment Justin's arms wrap around me, the dam inside me breaks. A thousand questions pour out, tumbling over each other in a rush of desperate confusion.

"How did you get here so fast? And who are they?"

Justin pulls back, his hands gripping my shoulders, his gaze intense. "Cage has some powerful friends. The moment his brothers heard he was in trouble, they mobilized a rapid response team. These men," he gestures to the armed figures surrounding us, "are the best of the best: hostage rescue specialists. They'll stop at nothing to bring Cage home."

I nod, trying to absorb the information through the haze of adrenaline and exhaustion. It's almost too much to process, the idea that help had already been on the way, that we weren't as alone as I'd feared.

I turn toward the men, my voice steady despite the tremor in my hands. "The miners' camp is about two klicks north of here. It's set up in a clearing, with tents and equipment scattered around the perimeter."

I close my eyes, visualize the layout, and recall every detail that might be crucial.

"We counted seven men. They're armed, and they're ruthless. They won't hesitate to kill."

The words taste bitter on my tongue, a reminder of the brutality I witnessed, of the cruelty that Cage is enduring even now.

"The leader, Ronin, is the worst of them. He's sadistic and enjoys inflicting pain. He'll be the one to watch out for."

My voice wavers and the image of Ronin's leering face and hands on Cage threatens to shatter my composure.

The team listens intently, their expressions grim. I can see them processing the information, their minds working to formulate a plan.

A tall, broad-shouldered man with piercing blue eyes steps forward, his presence commanding attention.

"I'm Ethan Blackwood, ma'am. I lead Charlie team with the Guardian Hostage Rescue Specialists." His voice is low and urgent as he addresses me directly. "What's the terrain around the camp like? Are there any potential hazards or advantages?"

I think back, trying to recall the details that had been lost in the haze of fear.

"The forest is dense, with heavy underbrush. It could provide cover for an approach, but there's a deep, fast-moving river to the east, which could cut off escape routes."

The rescue team gathers around, their faces etched with grim determination.

"Here's the plan," Ethan says in a low and intense voice, devising a plan that excludes me.

"I know the terrain," I say, my voice growing stronger. "I can guide you in and help you avoid any potential hazards."

Ethan hesitates, his brow furrowing. "I know you want to help, but this is a dangerous operation. It's no place for a civilian."

"I know this area." I shake my head, my resolve hardening. "You need me."

Justin steps forward, his hand resting on my shoulder. "She's right, Ethan. We can't do this without her."

Ethan sighs, his shoulders slumping slightly. "Alright. But you stay close, and you follow my orders to the letter. Understood?"

"Understood." My heart swells with gratitude and determination.

"Then please..." He makes a sweeping gesture with his hand. "Lead on."

The team springs into action, their movements precise and efficient. They check their weapons, their fingers moving over the metal with practiced ease. They synchronize their watches, the soft beeps echoing in the stillness of the clearing.

The weight of what we're about to do settles over me like a shroud, the reality of the danger we're facing sinking in.

Ethan gives the signal, and the team moves out, melting into the shadows of the forest like wraiths. I lead, my senses heightened, my nerves thrumming with adrenaline.

The forest is a different place now, no longer a sanctuary but a battlefield. Every rustle of leaves, every snap of a twig, sets my heart racing. I can feel the tension in the air, the weight of the impending confrontation.

We move swiftly and silently, our footsteps muffled by the soft earth. The scent of pine and damp moss fills my nostrils, mingling with the acrid tang of fear and determination.

Ahead, the miners' camp looms, a place of cruelty amidst the beauty of the wilderness.

And they have Cage.

THIRTY-THREE

Ava

The forest blurs around me as we move, a silent force cutting through the underbrush. The scent of pine and damp earth fills my nostrils, mixing with the tang of adrenaline on my tongue. My heart pounds in a staccato rhythm, each beat a countdown to the moment of truth.

I lead the way, my senses heightened to a razor's edge. Behind me, the Guardian Hostage Rescue Specialists, Charlie team, and Justin move with the precision of a well-oiled machine. Their footsteps are whispers, their breaths controlled and even.

Tension hangs thick in the air, a palpable force that presses against my skin. It's in the set of my jaw and the coiled readiness of each team member, their eyes scanning the shadows for any hint of danger.

I'm glad these men are with me because they're a formidable fighting force. Armed to the teeth. Highly skilled.

Deadly.

Those miners won't know what hit them.

Thoughts of Cage drive me forward and fuel the fire in my veins.

I can almost feel his presence like a tether pulling me toward him. The memory of his bruised and battered face, the desperation in his eyes as he told me to run, is seared into my mind.

I push onward, my legs burning with the effort. The team matches my pace, moving as one.

We're getting close.

Sounds from the camp filter through the trees—harsh laughter, the clink of metal on metal.

And beneath it all, a sound that makes my blood run cold.

A solid thud of skin on skin.

A muffled cry of pain.

Cage.

My heart clenches, and my breath catches in my throat. I force myself to keep moving and focus on the mission at hand. We're here to save him, to bring him back.

As we approach the edge of the camp, Ethan raises a fist, signaling for us to halt. We drop to a crouch, our bodies blending into the foliage.

I find myself beside Justin; his presence a solid comfort at my side. He gives me a nod, his eyes reflecting the same determination that burns in me. My brother from another mother; we're in this together. I don't know what I would do without Justin's support.

My heart is a drumbeat in my ears, my palms slick with sweat. Every fiber of my being is coiled tight, ready to spring into action. The seconds stretch into eternity as we wait, the stillness broken only by the distant murmur of voices from the camp.

And then, there's a flicker of movement.

A figure emerges from one of the tents, his silhouette backlit by the glow of a campfire. He's followed by another and then another. I count six, seven, eight...

The numbers keep growing, a knot forming in the pit of my stomach.

There were only seven before.

My eyes dart to Ethan, seeing the flicker of surprise cross his features. I mouth the word '*Sorry*' and shrug my shoulders.

I told him there were only seven.

He puts out a hand, telling me it's fine, then adjusts his grip on his weapon, his posture shifting subtly.

I breathe in deeply, trying to calm my heart's rapid flutter. More miners mean more danger.

More risk.

But it also means we can't afford to wait any longer.

Cage needs us.

"Charlie team, Plan B." Ethan's plan adapts and evolves to meet this new challenge.

Charlie's team truly is formidable. Kitted out in black tactical gear, helmets, and crazy tech. They reach for their belts, pulling out smoke grenades and flashbangs.

Ethan makes a series of hand gestures—his commands clear and concise. Two team members peel off, melting into the shadows to the right. Two more head left, their movements quick and silent.

Ethan, Justin, and I stay put, our gazes fixed on the camp ahead.

I meet Ethan's gaze, a silent question in my eyes. He gives a sharp nod, the signal to move, but he tells Justin and me to stay put.

It's time.

With a synchronized motion, his men lob the devices into the midst of the miners.

The effect is immediate and devastating.

Smoke grenades explode, releasing a thick, billowing cloud of acrid smoke. It's disorienting, blinding.

But it's nothing compared to the flashbangs.

They detonate with a searing white light, brighter than a thousand suns. The concussive blast is like a physical force, slamming into my chest and knocking the breath from my lungs.

My ears ring, and the world becomes muffled and distant.

Through the haze of smoke and the afterimages burnt into my retinas, the miners stagger, disoriented. Their hands press to their ears. Some are on their knees, retching and gasping.

Ethan's team moves like a well-oiled machine of speed and precision. They're a blur of motion, striking with ruthless efficiency. Rubber bullets fly, and beanbag rounds slam into flesh. Tasers crackle and spark, dropping miners like puppets with their strings cut.

I hate having to sit on the sidelines, but this is their area of expertise. Even knowing I'd be a liability out there, it's still hard to let the experts do their thing when all I can think about is rescuing Cage.

Ethan melts into the shadows as Justin and I crouch low near the ground.

The team works with ruthless efficiency, their movements a blur.

Pressure points, choking techniques, swift and silent takedowns. It's a deadly dance, and Charlie team are the masters.

My heart is a jackhammer in my chest, my palms slick with sweat. I battle against the urge to run, to scream Cage's name.

But I force it down, lock it away.

Stealth is our ally, our only chance.

Shots fire, followed by another, then another. Voices raise in alarm—in anger—as the miners fight back.

My heart stops, then kicks into overdrive.

Miners pour from the tents like angry hornets from a kicked nest. There are easily a dozen or more.

They're armed, some with guns, others with knives and clubs. And there are more of them, far more than we anticipated.

Ronin must have called in reinforcements.

I watch in awe as Charlie team adapts on the fly. Tasers crackle to life, the air humming with electricity.

Nonlethal is the word of the day, although I wouldn't mind if Ronin didn't make it out of this alive.

The miners are far more organized than I would ever believe. They're a tide of anger and aggression crashing into Ethan and his team. They close in, their faces twisted with rage.

Weapons are exchanged for fists, feet, and knives.

Justin grabs my arm, holding me. The urge to reach Cage overwhelms me. Men fight all around him, and with how he's tied up, he's powerless and vulnerable.

"Stay," Justin hisses at me, placing his body like a shield between me and the fighting.

I shake off Justin's grip, my eyes scanning the camp desperately.

And then I see him.

Tied to a post in the center of the camp. Even from here, I can see the damage they've done to him. Cage's head lolls against his chest.

His face is a mass of bruises, his shirt torn and stained with blood. His chest rises and falls in shallow, labored breaths.

A sob catches in my throat, a sound of pure anguish. My heart clenches—a physical pain that steals the breath from my lungs.

Cage.

A red haze descends over my vision, fury that burns through my veins like wildfire. I'm up and moving before I realize it, my feet carrying me forward.

Justin shouts my name, his voice lost in the roar of blood in my ears.

I dodge past a miner, my elbow slamming into his face. Bones crunch, blood sprays.

I don't stop, don't slow.

Another miner lunges for me, his knife glinting in the firelight. I twist, and the blade misses me by a hair's breadth.

Ethan appears at my side, his face grim. "Get the hell out of here."

A miner plows into Ethan like a raging bull, pushing Ethan away from me. All around me, men fight.

Tasers crackle.

Bullets fly.

Bodies hit the ground, groaning and twitching.

The miners are relentless. They're a sea of snarling faces and grappling hands—a nightmare made of flesh.

And at the center of it all, Cage.

Battered, broken, but still breathing.

Still alive.

I clench my fists, nails biting into my palms. I'm going to get him out, no matter what it takes.

No matter who stands in my way.

The sharp crack of bullets rips through the air, the acrid scent of gunpowder burning my nostrils. I flinch as a round whizzes past my ear, close enough to feel the heat of its passage.

"Get down!" Ethan roars, his voice barely audible over the din.

He's not happy with me.

I drop to a crouch, my heart slamming against my ribs. All around me, Charlie team returns fire, their weapons barking in short, controlled bursts. The miners fire wildly, their shots going wide. It's only a matter of time before a bullet finds its mark.

"Ava, you need to get back," Justin shouts in my ear, his face inches from mine. His eyes are wide, the pupils dilated with adrenaline. I didn't even realize he was with me.

I nod, my throat too tight for words, but there's no way I'm leaving.

Not now.

I sprint forward, zigzagging to avoid the hail of bullets. My lungs burn, my legs pump. I feel the heat of the rounds as they whip past me, the rush of displaced air against my skin.

The camp is a blur of motion, a whirlwind of bodies and muzzle flashes.

"We have to get to him." I point toward Cage.

Ethan grits his teeth, his jaw set. Like Justin, I don't remember him joining me.

"Charlie team, provide cover."

The team responds instantly, their movements precise and coordinated. They fan out, creating a wall of suppressing fire. The miners duck and scatter, their shots going wild.

My feet pound against the hard-packed earth. Justin is at my side, his weapon raised. We weave through the chaos, dodging bullets and bodies alike.

But the closer we get to Cage, the heavier the resistance becomes. The miners rally, and their suppressive fire intensifies. I hear a cry of pain and see one of the miners stumble and fall, but I can't stop, can't look back.

Cage is all that matters.

I'm twenty feet away, then ten.

His eyelids flutter.

He's alive, but barely.

And then I'm there, my hands scrabbling at his bonds. They're tight, the knots complex. I tug and pull, my fingers slick with sweat and blood. Justin is at my back, his body a shield between me and the raging battle.

"Hang on, Cage," I whisper, my voice cracking. "We're here. We're going to get you out."

His eyes flicker open, glazed with pain. His lips move, forming words I can't hear over the roar of gunfire. But I can read them, and I feel them in my heart.

"Ava."

My name, a prayer, and a plea.

Tears blur my vision, hot and stinging. I blink them away, my fingers working frantically at the ropes.

Then, suddenly, they're loose.

Falling away like cobwebs.

Justin cut through the ropes.

I catch Cage as he slumps forward, his weight heavy. My arms wrap around his battered body.

His blood soaks my shirt, warm and sticky against my skin. Each rasping breath he takes is a knife in my heart, a reminder of how close I came to losing him.

Justin is there in an instant, helping me to support him.

"We've got to move," Ethan shouts, his voice strained. "Charlie team, cover our exit."

Ethan pushes me to the side. He hoists Cage up and over his shoulder.

Cage groans, his head lolling.

My heart is in my throat.

We fall back with Ethan's team.

And that's when I notice the quiet.

The tide of battle turned. The miners fall back. Weapons clatter to the ground. Some turn and flee, disappearing into the smoke and shadows. Others raise their hands in surrender, their faces pale and stunned.

Around us, Charlie team is a well-oiled machine moving with

practiced efficiency. They secure the captured miners, check for wounds, and gather intel.

It's a testament to their skill and training that they can switch from full-on combat to the delicate work of cleanup and control.

But even as I watch them work, a nagging sense of unease tugs at the back of my mind. Something isn't right, something is missing. I scan the faces of the captured miners, searching for the one I know all too well.

Ronin.

He's not there, not among the bound and beaten men that litter the camp. A cold chill runs down my spine, a premonition of dread.

"Ethan." My voice is raw and desperate. "Ronin and some others, they're getting away."

Ethan spins, his eyes narrowing as he takes in the situation. Behind his gaze, I can see the calculations whirring, the rapid-fire assessments and decisions. He's a leader, a tactician, and in this moment, he proves it.

"Charlie team, pursue those runners." His voice cuts through the chaos like a blade.

It's like watching a ballet, a perfectly choreographed dance of precision and power. Charlie team is off before Ethan finishes speaking, their weapons up and ready as they melt into the shadows of the trees.

But I barely register it, my attention focused solely on Cage. Ethan finds a clear spot near the trees. He lowers Cage gently to the ground.

Justin is at my side; his presence a solid comfort in the chaos. He meets my gaze, his eyes shining with fierce pride and determination.

"You did it, Ava," he says, his voice rough with emotion. "You got him back."

"No." I nod, too choked up to speak. "You did that. You and your silly check-ins." I always thought his check-ins were silly, but I humored him because it was so important for him to know I was okay when I took clients out.

The relief is overwhelming, a tidal wave that threatens to sweep me away. But I cling to it, to the knowledge that Cage is safe, that we're going home.

I sit beside him and cradle his head in my lap. His eyes flutter open, glassy and unfocused.

"Ava?" His voice is a ragged croak.

"I'm here." My voice thickens with emotion.

Tears spill down my cheeks, hot and fast. I hardly feel them, lost in the overwhelming rush of relief and love. I press my forehead to his, our breath mingling.

He's alive; he's here in my arms.

Nothing else matters.

Ethan kneels beside me, his face softening as he takes in Cage's condition.

"He needs medical attention, fast. I've called the chopper in." His tone is gentle but urgent.

"Thank you." I swallow hard, my vision blurring with unshed tears. "For everything."

"Don't worry about Ronin or his men. We've got this. You focus on getting Cage to safety and the help he needs. Leave the rest to us." Ethan places his hand on my shoulder.

"You have to find Cage's camera and the SIM card it carries. It has all the proof of what's been happening here."

"Will do." With a final squeeze of my shoulder, Ethan turns to his team, his voice ringing out over the din. "Charlie team, move out! We've got some rats to catch."

My throat is too tight for words.

Cage is fading fast.

His breathing shallow and labored.

His skin cold and clammy.

His pulse weak and thready.

The full extent of what they did to him is written in the bruises and blood that mar his body.

It's a sight that will haunt me forever, a nightmare seared into my memory.

Before I know it, the roar of a helicopter fills my ears, the downdraft from its rotors whipping my hair into a frenzy. I squint against the wind, my arms tightening instinctively around Cage's battered form.

He's so still, so pale, his breath coming in shallow, labored gasps.

Two men jump out of the helicopter and sprint toward us with a stretcher carried between them.

Justin is at my side; his presence is a solid comfort in the chaos. He helps me lift Cage onto the stretcher, his hands gentle but firm.

Justin and I, along with the two men, carry Cage to the waiting helicopter, each step a battle against the exhaustion that threatens to drag me under.

I cradle his head in my lap, my fingers brushing the matted strands of his hair.

"He's going to be okay." Justin places a reassuring hand on my shoulder, a silent gesture of support. His eyes shine with fierce determination.

Cage's eyelids flutter, a glimmer of verdant green beneath the swollen, bruised flesh.

"Ava," he rasps, his voice a barely-there whisper.

"I'm here." I manage a weak smile, my heart too full for words.

We did it. We saved him.

But even as the relief washes over me, I can't shake the memory of those fleeing figures, of Ronin's cold, cruel eyes.

He's still out there, still a threat. And I know, with a certainty that chills me to the bone, that this isn't over.

Not by a long shot.

The medics secure Cage into the helicopter, their movements swift and efficient. I climb in beside him, never letting go of his hand.

As the helicopter lifts off, the ground falls away, swallowed by a blur of dense, green canopy. The beat of the rotors pulses through me, mimicking the frantic rhythm of my heart. Below, the wilderness sprawls vast and unyielding, a reminder of what Cage and I endured.

What we've survived.

The flight to the hospital is a blur of motion and noise. The medics work tirelessly to keep Cage stable. I can only watch my heart in my throat as they monitor his vitals and administer what care they can in the cramped confines of the helicopter.

When we finally land at the closest hospital, a team of doctors and nurses wait for us. They whisk Cage away with a flurry of medical jargon and urgent commands. I try to follow, but a gentle hand on my arm holds me back.

"Let them work," Justin says, his voice soft but firm. "He's in good hands now."

The wait is agonizing, each second stretching into eternity, but finally, a doctor emerges, his face tired but relieved.

"He's stable," he says, and the knot in my chest loosens just a fraction. "He's got some serious injuries--contusions, bruised kidneys, a few cracked ribs--but he's strong. We'll want to observe him for a few days, but I don't see any issue with him going home after that."

Tears of relief sting my eyes, but I blink them back. There will be time for that later. Right now, all that matters is Cage.

When I'm finally allowed to see him, he looks fragile in the hospital bed, his skin almost as pale as the sheets. But he's alive, his chest rising and falling with each steady breath.

I sit by his side, my hand finding his, my thumb brushing gently over his bruised knuckles.

Justin offers to make all the necessary calls to Cage's family, who are likely as frantic as I am for news on Cage's condition.

"You're safe now," I whisper, my voice cracking on the words. "I'm here. I'm not going anywhere."

In the days that follow, as Cage begins the slow, painful process of healing, I rarely leave his side. I help the nurses change his bandages, bring him sips of water when he's thirsty, and hold his hand through the worst of the pain.

One afternoon, when he's resting comfortably, I fill a basin with warm, soapy water and gather some soft cloths.

I dip a soft cloth into the basin, wringing it out gently. With each tender wipe, I cleanse the grime and blood from his skin, revealing the man beneath the wounds. His face, marred with bruises, still carries the rugged determination that drew me to him in the wilderness.

The room is quiet, save for the soft beeping of the heart monitor and the distant sounds of the hospital. I trace the line of his jaw with the sponge, careful over the tender spots, each stroke a silent vow of care and protection.

"Cage," I whisper, my voice thick with emotions held too long at bay. His eyelids flutter, a sign he hears me even in his drug-induced slumber. The corners of his mouth twitch, a ghost of his usual smirk.

Outside, the wind howls softly against the window, a stark contrast to the chaos of the rescue. In here, with the smell of antiseptic mingling with the faint scent of his soap, I allow myself a moment of peace.

We're safe, and we're together. For now, that's enough.

I set the sponge aside, lean over, and press a gentle kiss to his forehead, my heart swelling with intense relief that he's going to be okay. It's an intimate act, a silent promise of comfort and care. As I work, my hands gentle on his battered body, the last of the tension I carry drains away, replaced by a bone-deep weariness.

But it's a good kind of tired, the kind that comes from knowing you've given everything you have to someone you love.

Because that's what this is, I realize with a clarity that steals my breath.

Love.

Pure, fierce, and unshakable.

THIRTY-FOUR

Ava

Days later, Cage is released from the hospital with not much more than cracked ribs, bruised kidneys, and a patchwork of contusion. As the car pulls up to my lodge, a surge of emotions wells up inside of me. Relief, exhaustion, and an overwhelming love for the man beside me.

Cage looks pale and bruised, his eyes shadowed with pain, but he's here, alive and safe.

I reach over and take his hand, feeling the reassuring warmth of his skin against mine. "We're home," I whisper, my voice thick with unshed tears.

Cage squeezes my hand, a small smile tugging at the corner of his mouth.

"Home," he echoes as if savoring the word.

As we step out of the car, the front door of the lodge bursts open, and two identical figures come rushing out. For a moment, I'm struck by the surreal sight of Cage's brothers, who look exactly like the man I love.

It's uncanny.

A little bit weird.

"What the…" Cage gasps as his brothers rush toward us. "How did they get here?"

The first to reach us pulls Cage into a hug while I step away. His brother's face is etched with worry.

"Thank God." Cage's brother pulls him into a fierce hug.

Cage winces, and his brother immediately loosens his grip. His eyes widen as he realizes the extent of Cage's injuries.

"Whoa, little brother," he teases gently. "Looks like you went a few rounds with a grizzly bear."

His other brother is right behind the first.

"Jesus, Cage, you look like hell." The second brother gently clasps Cage's shoulder. "What did you do, try to headbutt a mountain goat?"

"Yes to the bear. No to the goat." Cage manages a weak chuckle. "Feel like shit." He leans heavily on his brother.

"You look like shit."

I step back, feeling out of place amidst this intimate family reunion. These men share a bond beyond words, a connection forged in the womb and strengthened by a lifetime of shared experiences.

But before I retreat too far, Cage pulls me close, his arm wrapping securely around my waist.

"Ava, these are my brothers, Asher and Brody. Guys," he says, his voice rough with emotion. "This is Ava, my guide. She's the reason I'm still alive."

His brothers turn to me, their identical faces breaking into warm smiles. When Cage introduced them, he didn't specifically point to who was who, leaving me confused.

"Thank you," one of them says, reaching out to shake my hand. "For bringing our brother back to us."

"We owe you everything." The other brother shakes my hand as well.

It's all very—weird.

A lump forms in my throat, overwhelmed by their gratitude and suddenly unsure where Cage and I stand.

He introduced me as *his guide*. I thought we were a lot more than that.

"I couldn't have done it without Cage." I squeeze Cage's hand. "Your brother is the strongest, bravest man I know."

Cage smiles at me, his eyes soft and affectionate. Then he sways slightly, his exhaustion catching up with him.

His brothers are there in an instant, supporting his weight between them.

"Whoa, easy there, tiger."

"Let's get you inside before you faceplant in the dirt."

Their voices are as identical as their faces and their bodies. It makes my head spin and my eyes cross.

As Cage leans on his brothers for support, I feel a sudden pang of unease. The easy camaraderie between the identical triplets and their unspoken connection makes me feel like an intruder, an outsider looking in on a private moment.

They guide Cage toward the lodge, their faces etched with concern. They move as one, anticipating each other's actions, leaving no space for me.

I trail behind, unsure, my steps faltering.

When Cage glances back, his eyes fill with love and gratitude; I feel less out of place but not completely at ease.

Inside, the lodge is warm and welcoming; the familiar scent of pine and woodsmoke envelops us like a comforting blanket.

Cage's brothers settle him on the couch closest to the fire and hover anxiously, their faces mirroring each other's worry.

I bustle around, fetching blankets and pillows, trying to make Cage as comfortable as possible.

Trying to feel like less of an outsider.

"Ava, could you grab some water?"

Not sure if it's Asher or Brody who makes the request, I jump at the chance to be useful and hurry to the kitchen.

Returning to the living room, I hand the water to Cage, our fingers brushing. He smiles at me, but his expression is strained, pain and exhaustion clouding his eyes.

Brody, or Asher, can't tell them apart, shifts his attention between me and Cage. His brows furrow, but then he asks a question.

"So, Ava," he says, his tone carefully neutral. "How long have you been in the guiding business?"

"It feels like forever." I swallow, my mouth suddenly dry. "I grew up out there."

"Grew up?" the other brother asks.

"My parents were guides. It was the family business, and they always took me with them."

The first brother raises an eyebrow, exchanging a look with the other one, an unspoken communication that makes my stomach twist. I'm trying to find any distinguishing characteristic that can help me identify these brothers, but I'm at a loss.

"Well, we appreciate you getting him back to us in one piece," Cage's brother's words are sincere, but I feel like I've been dismissed.

My role in Cage's life has been neatly compartmentalized and filed away.

As the brothers tend to Cage, their low voices fill the room, and I find myself edging toward the door. The urge to flee, to escape this feeling of not belonging, is overwhelming.

"Ava." Before I can slip away, Cage's hand shoots out, fingers reaching for me. "Stay. Please?"

I hesitate, torn between the desire to run and the plea in his eyes. Slowly, I allow him to tug me beside him, his arm wrapping around my shoulders.

His brothers exchange another look, surprise flickering across their identical features.

Cage takes a deep breath, wincing slightly at the motion. "Guys…" His tone turns serious. "There's something you should know. Ava… I'm in love with her."

The words hang in the air, a declaration that makes my heart swell and my eyes sting with sudden tears. Asher and Brody stare at us, momentarily speechless. Then, slowly, identical grins spread across their faces.

"Well, damn," Brody chuckles—at least, I think that one's

Brody. "Leave it to Cage to find love in the middle of the Alaskan wilderness."

Asher reaches out, clasping my hand in his. "Ava…" His voice fills with warmth and sincerity. "Welcome to the family."

I blink back tears, overwhelmed by their automatic acceptance and the realization that I'm not just a temporary part of Cage's life but a permanent fixture.

At least, I hope.

He pulls me closer, pressing a kiss to my temple. "I couldn't have made it without her," he murmurs. "She's my everything."

As Asher and Brody nod, their expressions softening with understanding, I feel the last of my doubts melt away.

I'm not an outsider. Not anymore.

"So…" Asher sits on the couch opposite us. "I want to hear all about how my baby brother fell in love."

"Baby?" Cage scoffs. "Just because you slipped out before you were fully cooked."

"Huh?" I look between the brothers and what is obviously an inside joke.

"Asher was born early. Came out six weeks before Brody and I."

"Is that even possible?" I look between the triplets because that doesn't seem possible.

"It is. I came out six weeks before these blokes. They wanted to gestate a bit more, so I'm technically the eldest."

"Yeah, and the shit is always lording that over us." This time, I know it's Brody who's speaking.

Maybe.

The brothers settle around the fireplace, the crackling flames casting a warm glow on their identical faces. Cage sits close to me, his arm draped around my shoulders, a comforting weight.

"So, little brother," Asher leans forward, a mischievous glint in his eye, "tell us how you snagged this lovely lady."

Cage grins, squeezing my hand. "Well, it all started with a swim."

"A swim, huh? In what, a frozen lake?" Brody raises an eyebrow. "What about shrinkage?"

"Shut up and let me tell the story." Cage throws a cushion at his brother. "We found this gorgeous mountain lake, crystal-clear water, and well, one thing led to another…"

"Wait, wait, wait." Asher holds up a hand, a grin spreading across his face. "Are you telling us you went skinny-dipping? In Alaska?"

"When you've got a view like that, you take advantage." Cage shrugs, unabashed.

My cheeks heat, remembering the exhilaration of that moment, the thrill of the icy water and Cage's warm skin against mine.

"But that's not even the best part," Cage continues, his eyes sparkling. "We got out of the water, and there was this massive grizzly bear."

"Damn, bro. Talk about a mood killer." Brody whistles low.

"You have no idea," Cage laughs. "We barely made it out of there with our skin intact. And our dignity."

"What happened with the grizzly?"

"Ava, of course." Cage looks at me and places a big fat grin on his face. "She tossed me a can of mace, well, bear spray. Sprayed that shit into the fucker's face."

"Shit, that's unreal." Brody's eyes widen, perhaps realizing how *real* it got out there. "And it worked?"

"Worked like a charm, but I also maced myself. That was no fun."

The brothers erupt in laughter, the sound echoing off the rafters.

"But that was just the beginning," Cage says, his tone softening. "We got caught in this crazy rainstorm and had to shelter under this ledge. We spent the whole night huddled together, trying to stay warm."

"I bet that was a real *hard*ship for you." Asher smirks and uses air quotes to emphasize '*hard.*'

Cage throws another cushion, hitting his brother square in the face. "Get your mind out of the gutter. It was survival."

"Sure it was," Brody drawls. "Survival snuggles."

I can't help but laugh, remembering the feel of Cage's arms around me and the steady beat of his heart against my ear.

"Then there was the time we jumped into the rapids to escape those miners." Cage's voice turns serious.

"Wait, I thought they caught you?" Asher and Brody exchange a look.

"That was the second time."

"Second?"

"Are you going to shut up and let me tell my story?" Cage glares at his brothers, but it's just for fun.

"We're all ears." His brothers settle onto the couch, getting comfortable.

"I thought we were goners for sure. But Ava… She was incredible. She kept her head and got us to safety."

The brothers get quiet as the gravity of the situation hits home.

"You're fucking serious, aren't you. Like you jumped into a raging river?"

"Yup." Cage takes my hand and kisses my knuckles. Then he pulls me in tight against him, draping his arm over my shoulders. "Jumped right in. Rode the rapids. We had to find shelter and dry our clothes by the fire," Cage continues. "And that's when I knew I never wanted to let her go."

Tears prick at my eyes, my heart swelling with emotion.

"Aww, look at that," Asher teases gently. "Our little Cage, all grown up and in love."

"Shut up," Cage grumbles, but there's no heat in it. "It's not like you're any better, making googly eyes at your wife all day."

Asher clutches his chest in mock offense. "I'll have you know. My googly eyes are a work of art."

The brothers dissolve into bickering, their insults flying fast and furious. But underneath the snark, a deep bond of love and affection ties them together.

And as Cage pulls me closer, pressing a kiss to my forehead, I know I'm part of that bond now—a part of this wild, wonderful, infuriating family.

"Face it, bro," Brody says, grinning at Cage. "You've gone soft on us. You fell in love, and now you're getting all sappy."

"Nah, I'm not soft." Cage flips him off, but he smiles. "I just finally found someone worth fighting for and hanging onto."

He looks at me then, his eyes shining with love and promise. And I know, with a certainty that fills every corner of my heart, that I've found the same.

Our love can weather any storm and survive any rapids. It's the kind of love that lasts a lifetime.

As the evening wears on, we talk softly, filling each other in on the events of the past few days. Cage's brothers listen intently, their faces darkening with anger as they hear about the miners and the horrors Cage endured.

But there are moments of lightness, too, of laughter and love.

As the hours grow late, I insist that Cage get some rest. He's barely able to keep his eyes open, the exhaustion of his ordeal catching up with him.

THIRTY-FIVE

Ava

I help Cage to the bedroom—my bedroom—our bedroom?—my heart clenching at the sight of his battered body in my bed, but as I tuck him in, brushing a stray lock of hair from his forehead, I'm filled with an overwhelming sense of love and protectiveness.

I lean down to press a gentle kiss to his temple. My lips linger against his warm skin. His eyes flutter, heavy with fatigue, and a soft smile spreads across his face at the sight of me hovering over him.

In that moment, a raw vulnerability in his gaze tugs at my heart-strings.

"You need rest." I trace the line of his jaw with my fingertips, but before I can pull away, Cage's hand snakes out and curls around the back of my neck.

"I need you." He pulls me down into a searing kiss, his lips urgent and hungry against mine.

His body may be battered and bruised, but he exudes raw masculinity and strength. Heat coils deep within me, a hunger that continues to grow when I'm with him.

He exudes sex appeal with the air around him supercharged with a scent that is all male, wild, and untamed. Strands of his hair glint in the light, framing a rugged beauty that never fails to catch my breath. A raw allure clings to him, a blend of confidence and magnetism that leaves my senses reeling.

In his touch, I feel the weight of all our shared moments, both joy and pain, and it's like being enveloped in a warm embrace that I never want to leave.

The kiss is fierce and desperate, filled with all the longing and pent-up desire that has been building between us for weeks.

And his mouth… It promises sin and salvation all at once. I crave the taste of him, the feel of him against me.

Cage's lips are warm and soft. His tongue slides over mine in a way that makes my knees weak. To kiss him is to flirt with danger, play with fire, and surrender completely to his masculine need.

"No fucking way are you leaving this bed." His words rumble against my lips, a growl that vibrates deep in his chest, stirring a wild desire that claws at my restraint.

His voice, rough and husky, carries a power, a possessiveness that wraps around me, binding me tighter than any physical restraint could.

"But you're hurt," I whisper against the heat of his mouth, a feeble attempt to anchor myself to reason.

Yet, even as I speak, my body betrays me, responding with a fervent longing to every touch and caress he dares to offer. His calloused and demanding fingers trace fire along my skin, igniting a flame I'm helpless to resist.

"I'm hurt, but I'm not dead." The words are barely a whisper, tinged with humor and a resilience that takes my breath away. His smile, faint yet undeniably present, speaks of battles fought and won, of a spirit unbroken. "Come on, Ava, I've waited long enough. I need you in this bed."

Who am I to resist?

There's no fight left in me, not against this force of nature, this man who demands my surrender with nothing but the strength of his will and the heat of his gaze.

I let go, allowing him to pull me closer, to draw me into his embrace. Our bodies collide in a tangle of limbs that twist the sheets, each caress feeding a spark that fuels the growing blaze between us. Our lips meet in a passionate kiss, a clash of desire and need that leaves no room for thought or hesitation.

With every movement, every caress, the world beyond this bed fades into insignificance. There's only him, only me, and the overwhelming sensation of being utterly consumed by the man whose presence is both a balm and an inferno. In his arms, I find a dangerous, intoxicating freedom, a surrender that feels suspiciously like flying.

I don't fight as he pulls me into bed with him. Our bodies tangle together, our lips still locked in a passionate kiss.

Cage's hands roam over my body, tracing every curve as if trying to memorize every inch. His touch is gentle yet possessive; like a drug, he's addictive and all-consuming.

I can't resist the pull toward him, my body melting into his with each caress. Every worry and fear fades in his arms, replaced only by pure bliss.

My body ignites under his touch, and I surrender completely to the pleasure that he gives me. Cage makes me feel alive. Every nerve ending is on fire as we move together.

I moan softly as his featherlight touch sends shivers down my spine. His mouth leaves mine and travels down my neck, leaving a trail of hot kisses in its wake.

Heady warmth spreads through my body and travels to my core. He's so insanely handsome and brutally sexy, and that warmth turns into a raging fire within me, settling into a delicious ache between my legs.

"Tell me what you want." He places his mouth along my collarbone, soft but heated.

The heat of his words fans out, touching me everywhere at once. My need for him burns, frightening me and doing crazy things to my body.

"You," I speak without hesitation, my voice filled with need. "But your injuries?"

I'm torn between my desire for him and not wanting to aggravate his injuries.

"Not bad enough to miss this." Cage's lips form into a smirk before he captures my lips once again. "Especially if you stay on top."

No problem there.

His mouth moves against mine with a desperation that mirrors the intensity of our emotions. The taste of salt lingers on his skin from his ordeal, but underneath that is the familiar flavor of him that I've come to crave.

I groan as pleasure rushes through me, soaring in the decadence of feeling his mouth on me.

Knowing we're finally going to have sex.

Tension coils in his muscles, and then relaxes against mine as if he finds respite from his injuries in my arms.

My fingers thread through his hair, pulling him closer as the kiss deepens, igniting a fiery passion that has been simmering between us for far too long. His fingers explore my curves, trailing around my waist, sending shivers cascading down my spine.

His touch is gentle but firm as if trying to hold on to me lest I disappear. His heart beats against my chest, matching the rhythm of my own.

As our kiss deepens, his desire grows, lengthening and hardening his cock beneath the sheets. Heat radiates from his body, reminding me of all the times we clung to each other for warmth during our adventure in the wild.

Despite his injuries, he lifts me, surprising me with his strength. I straddle his waist and place my hands on his chest. Our bodies press tight together, and there's no denying he wants me.

I grind my hips against him, feeling the heat of my pussy pressing against his hardened length. Every touch sends sparks of pleasure shooting through my body.

"God, you feel so good," Cage moans as his hands roam over me, teasing every inch of my skin.

I lean down to capture his lips in a searing kiss. Our tongues dance together in perfect harmony.

He runs his hands over my back, tracing the curve of my spine, and his lips travel down my neck, leaving a trail of hot, wet kisses in their wake. His touch is electric, sending sparks of electricity shooting down my nerves. Pleasure rushes through me as he pulls me closer.

Cage's hands are strong and sure as he pulls my shirt over my head. His hands move up my back, tracing every curve until they reach the clasp of my bra. With one swift motion, he unclasps it and throws it aside, exposing my bare breasts to him.

He takes them in his hands, massaging them gently before taking one nipple into his mouth. I gasp at the sensation and run my fingers through his hair as he continues to worship every inch of me. When his thumbs lightly stroke my nipples, a pleasurable moan escapes me.

He leans up to lave my nipples, and I arch into him as waves of pleasure surge through me. My body trembles under his touch and grows wetter by the second.

His hands continue to explore my body. I'm lost in his touch, in the way he looks at me with hunger, desire, and need. Cage lifts his head slightly, gazing into my eyes with an intensity that takes my breath away.

"I need you, Ava." He pulls back slightly, his eyes filled with a raw desire that mirrors mine. "I need to be inside of you."

I respond with a nod, my own hunger matching his. Our eyes lock, and I see the deep yearning in his gaze. It's been too long since we began this dance, and the tension between us has grown unbearable.

Slowly, he removes the rest of my clothes, each item discarded onto the floor like a trophy of our passion. I help him remove his clothing, hating the way he winces in pain as he lifts his hips for me to remove his briefs.

When I stop, he shakes his head.

"The pain is nothing, love. Get me out of these clothes. I have to be inside of you. Now."

His fingers trace the curves of my body, caressing my skin with an urgency that speaks to the depth of his desire for me. His fingers glide down my sides, tracing the path of nerves that will be singing for hours.

He knows what he wants from me, and I want it just as much.

My own hands roam over his body, feeling the muscles that ripple beneath my touch. I kiss him deeply. Our tongues entwine, exploring the hidden corners of each other's mouths.

As our kiss deepens, Cage traces the curve of my waist and the swell of my hips. His fingers leave trails of fire on my skin, making me squirm. I arch my back, seeking more of his touch.

"Ava, I need you," he whispers hoarsely.

As his breath washes over me, I melt into his touch, my soul connecting with his in a way that only true love can create. I run my fingers down his chest, loving the warmth of his skin beneath my fingertips.

Without breaking our gaze, he reaches between us to cup my pussy. Then he runs his fingers along my slit, lighting a line of fire from my slit to my clit. He adds a second digit, teasing my clit, then makes me scream when he sinks his fingers into my wet heat, thrusting them in and out.

I cry out, my entire body coming alive as he commands my body. Cage definitely knows his way around a woman's body.

"I want to fuck you." He takes his time positioning the flare of his cock at my entrance. Hot and ready, he presses against me.

"Please."

"Are you sure about this?" His brows tug together. "I don't have a condom, but I'm clean."

"I'm on the pill."

"You're sure?"

"Yes." I reach down, gripping his cock to show him how much I want this.

Cage glides the plump head of his cock through my folds, tormenting me. My world narrows down to this moment and converges on the inevitable union of our bodies.

He enters me slowly, our bodies melding together in a perfect fit. His hands tremble slightly as he guides me down onto his cock, but I take his hesitation as a sign of his vulnerability, not weakness.

I lower myself onto him, loving the feel of him filling me. Stretching my walls. Sinking all the way down his hard length.

My heart bursts into overdrive. Everything feels amazing. I'm dizzy with pleasure. My nerves spark with electricity. My body hums as wave after wave of pleasure slams into me.

Both of us gasp at the sensation of him penetrating my aching body. Then he's fully seated inside of me. A moan escapes me, trembling through the stunning sensation of him filling me.

"Oh, God, Ava…" His hips jerk, and he groans. "I may not last as long as I want. You feel like heaven and sin all wrapped up in one."

Cage's hands grip my hips tightly as I start to move, slowly rocking back and forth on his cock. The tight, shallow strokes send waves of pleasure through me. He moves with me, thrusting up as I come down, deepening our connection.

The sound of our bodies moving together fills the room, and I can't help but moan as Cage's cock slides in and out of me. Each thrust brings me closer to the edge, and I know he's feeling it too.

I lift my hips, arch my back, and ride his cock as pleasure sweeps through me. The temperature in the room seems to rise, although that might be the heating of my blood.

"Harder, love," he rasps, his eyes dark with desire.

I comply, picking up the pace and riding him harder. His hands grip my hips tightly as I move, his breath coming in short gasps. Our bodies slick with sweat, and the sound of our lovemaking fills the air.

Cage's body tenses beneath me, his breathing becoming more ragged. He reaches between us to rub my clit in tight circles. The added sensation drives me wild.

I lean down to kiss him again, our lips crashing together in a frenzy. My nails dig into his chest as I ride him harder, chasing my own pleasure until it consumes me.

My movements become more urgent as pleasure builds.

More frantic.

His hands roam over my body, gripping my breasts and kneading them gently. I moan as he pinches my nipples, sending even more sparks of pleasure shooting through me.

"You feel so good, Ava," he groans, his voice thick with desire.

I grind down onto him harder, feeling the tension building in my core. His fingers dig into my hips as he thrusts up into me, deepening our connection.

As we move together, our breathing becomes ragged and frantic, and our moans become louder. We're lost in each other, consumed by the passion that has been building between us for so long.

We move in sync, our bodies becoming one. The sheets are a tangled mess beneath us, but we don't care. All that matters is the pleasure we give each other, the pain we share, and the connection we forge.

His hands grip my hips as he thrusts into me, his eyes locked on mine. The heat of his gaze is almost too much to bear, but I love the intensity of it. I love the way he looks at me, the way he touches me, and the way he makes me feel.

My body trembles, the pleasure building within me.

Cage's thrusts become more forceful, his hips thrusting with me with a ferocity that matches my own desire.

"Cage," I murmur, my voice barely audible above the sounds of our lovemaking.

He groans, his eyes fluttering shut briefly before they meet mine once more. "I love you, Ava."

His confession sends me over the edge, the orgasm washing over me like a tidal wave. My body convulses, my nails digging into his chest as I ride him. I arch my back, crying out his name as I lose myself in ecstasy.

Cage's orgasm barrels down on him. The sight of me coming undone pushes him over the edge. He thrusts hard one last time, his cock twitching inside me as he climaxes.

We collapse onto the bed, our bodies still joined as we catch our breath. Cage wraps his arms around me, pulling me close to his chest.

"That was—amazing," he says, pressing a kiss to my forehead.

I smile against his skin, feeling completely satisfied and content in his arms.

"I love you," Cage whispers against my neck as he kisses me tenderly.

Something so sincere and genuine in his tone brings tears to my eyes. I lean forward and press a tender kiss to his lips before snuggling back into his embrace.

Being with Cage feels like home—safe and comfortable yet exhilarating at the same time.

"I love you too."

"Sleep well, my love." I press a soft kiss to his lips.

Cage smiles sleepily, his hand resting on the small of my back as I lay over him.

His eyes drift shut, and I stay with him until his breathing evens out and the lines of pain smooth from his face. My eyes grow heavy, the events of the past few days catching up with me.

In this moment, I reflect on our story: how we met, the obstacles we overcame, the memories we've created, and the dreams we share. Each memory is a thread weaving together the tapestry of our beginning, creating an indestructible bond.

Together, we braved the storm and emerged stronger than ever. I can't help but wonder what the future holds for us—the highs and lows, the laughs and tears.

The bond we created is unbreakable.

As is our fledgling love.

I'm eager to see what happens next.

THIRTY-SIX

Ava

——————

Days and nights blend into one. The weather I predicted hits full force and we're snowed in. The days pass in a blur of healing and quiet moments of intimacy. Asher and Brody are a constant presence. Their boisterous energy and fierce protectiveness comfort both Cage and myself. They welcome me into the fold with open arms, their easy acceptance and unwavering support a testament to the strength of the La Rouge family ties.

In the evenings, Cage and I retire to the sanctuary of our bedroom, the space filled with gentle touches and whispered words of love and reassurance. We map each other's bodies with reverent hands and lips, mindful of his healing wounds but aching with the need to reconnect, to reaffirm the life and love that pulses between us.

As his strength returns, our explorations grow bolder, the heat building slowly until it consumes us both, leaving us sated and entwined, our hearts beating as one. In those moments, the horrors of the past fade away, eclipsed by the sheer joy and passion we find in each other's arms.

The mornings bring a different kind of intimacy, lazy and sweet. We linger in bed, trading soft kisses and teasing caresses, learning each other anew in the gentle light of dawn. I delight in discovering the ticklish spot behind his knee, the sensitive hollow of his throat. He memorizes the constellations of freckles that dance across my skin and the silken feel of my hair sliding through his fingers.

We talk, too, in the sanctuary of tangled sheets. Of hopes and dreams, fears and triumphs. I share stories of my childhood, painting vivid pictures of sun-drenched days and the fierce love of my found family. In turn, Cage opens up about the challenges of growing up a triplet, the unbreakable bond he shares with his brothers, and the weight of expectations that come with the La Rouge name.

I marvel at how far we've come, from those first tension-filled moments the day we met to this soul-deep bond we forged.

Through it all, a deep sense of peace settles over me, born of the knowledge that we weathered the worst storms and emerged stronger and more committed to each other than ever. The future stretches out before us, bright with promise and possibility.

One morning, I wake to birdsong and the gentle rustling of leaves outside the window. For a moment, I'm disoriented, my mind still caught in the hazy space between dreams and waking.

Cage.

Where is Cage?

I turn to look beside me, but the bed is empty, the sheets rumpled and cool to the touch. Panic rises in my throat, and I'm out of bed in an instant, padding barefoot down the hallway.

As I enter the kitchen, I stop short, my breath catching in my throat. There, standing at the stove is a familiar figure. Broad shoulders, tousled dark hair, the strong lines of his back tapering to a narrow waist.

"Cage?" I breathe, relief and love welling up inside me.

He turns, and I'm moving before I realize it. I cross the room in a few quick strides and throw myself into his arms.

"Oh, Cage," I murmur, burying my face in his chest. "I was so worried when I woke up, and you weren't there."

He stiffens slightly, his arms coming around me tentatively. "Uh,

Ava?" he says, and there's something odd in his voice, a note of hesitation that I can't quite place.

I pull back, looking up at him quizzically. My eyes widen, and I stumble back, my cheeks flushing with embarrassment.

"Oh my God," I gasp. "Asher. I'm so sorry. I thought you were Cage."

Asher grins, his eyes twinkling with amusement. "It's okay," he chuckles. "It happens more often than you'd think."

I bury my face in my hands, mortified. "I'm such an idiot," I groan.

Asher laughs, reaching out to pat my shoulder. "Hey, don't worry about it," he says kindly. "We're used to it. I once had a girl-friend who called me by Brody's name for a whole week before she figured it out. My wife felt Brody up in the kitchen and then groped Cage out in our barn. You're not the first to mix us up."

I can't help but giggle at the absurdity of the situation. "I guess it's going to take some getting used to," I admit ruefully.

Asher winks at me, turning back to the stove. "Well, you'd better start practicing," he teases. "Because I have a feeling you're going to see a lot more of us from now on."

I smile, warmth blooming in my chest. The thought of being a part of Cage's life, of having his brothers as my family, fills me with a joy I never knew was possible.

"Oh, by the way," Asher says casually, stirring the eggs in the pan, "Cage went for a walk earlier. Said he needed to stretch his legs and work out some of the soreness from being couped up so long. He should be back soon."

"Thanks." My heart skips a beat at the mention of Cage, a flutter of anticipation in my stomach. "I'll see if I can find him."

After the embarrassing kitchen incident with Asher, I head outside for some fresh air. The morning sun is warm on my face, with a hint of winter snapping at its heels. I take a deep breath, savoring the scent of pine.

As I round the corner of the lodge, I stop short, my eyes widen-ing. There, in the middle of the yard, is a shirtless figure chopping wood. Muscles ripple under tanned skin as Cage swings an axe, his movements powerful and precise.

Beside him is an impressive stack of freshly cut firewood. I'm surprised he feels well enough to work that hard, but that's Cage.

The man is unstoppable.

My heart skips a beat, and a flush of heat spreads through my body as I take in his muscled form, shamelessly ogling the perfection of his body.

I approach quietly, a mischievous smile tugging at my lips. He doesn't seem to hear me; he's too focused on his task.

When I'm close enough, I reach out and run my hands over his bare back, tracing the lines of his muscles. "Hey, handsome," I murmur, pressing a kiss to his shoulder.

He stiffens, the axe faltering in mid-swing. "Ava…" There's a strangled note in his voice that makes me pause.

He turns to face me, and I realize with a jolt of horror that it's not Cage. It's Brody, his eyes wide with a hint of amusement.

"Oh my God," I gasp, snatching my hands back as if burned. "Brody. I'm so sorry. I thought you were Cage."

Brody bursts out laughing, his shoulders shaking with mirth. "Wow, Ava," he teases. "I knew you were into Cage, but I didn't realize you were into all of us."

I bury my face in my hands, mortified. "I can't believe I did that again. I'm such an idiot."

"Again?" Brody reaches out and pats my shoulder, still chuckling. "Hey, don't worry about it," he says kindly. "I'm flattered. It's not every day a beautiful woman mistakes me for my brother and feels me up."

I peek out from between my fingers, my face still burning with embarrassment. "I'm never going to live this down, am I?"

Brody winks, his eyes sparkling with mischief. "Probably not," he admits. "But don't worry, I won't tell Cage. I value my life too much."

I'm about to reply when a familiar voice sounds behind me. "Tell me what?"

I spin around to see Cage standing there, his arms crossed and an amused expression playing on his face.

"Cage!" I yelp, my voice an octave higher than usual. "I was just… I mean, I thought…"

Cage raises an eyebrow, his lips twitching as he tries to suppress a smile. "You thought what, Ava?" he asks innocently. "That Brody was me, and you decided to feel him up?"

"That's not…" I groan, burying my face in my hands again. "I'm sorry," I mumble. "I just saw him chopping wood, and I thought…"

Cage bursts out laughing, the sound warm and rich. "It's okay, Ava," he chuckles. "I understand. My brothers are irresistible."

"Damn right, we are." Brody grins, flexing his muscles.

I swat at them both, trying to hide my smile. "You're both terrible," I inform them. "I hate you."

Cage grabs my hand and pulls me into his arms. "No, you don't," he murmurs, pressing a kiss to my forehead. "You love me—and my brothers, apparently. But for the record, I don't share."

"Share?" Completely mortified, I bury my face in my hands. "That's not…"

"I'm teasing." Cage pulls me in for a bear hug and leans down to whisper in my ear, "Actually, I'm not. You're mine."

"Maybe you should tattoo your names on your foreheads. It would make things easier." I laugh, leaning into his embrace.

"Evidently, it's our ass, backs, and junk that need the tattooing." Brody looks to his brother. "She copped a feel."

"I did not." I totally didn't do that, but my face burns with heat.

Cage grins, his eyes soft with affection. "Maybe," he agrees. "But don't worry. No matter how often you mistake my brothers for me, I'll always know it's me you love."

I smile up at him, my heart full to bursting. "Always," I whisper.

The next morning, I'm in the kitchen preparing breakfast when footsteps pad down the hallway. I turn, expecting to see Cage, but instead, I'm greeted by another identical face.

"Morning, Ava," Brody yawns, rubbing his eyes sleepily.

I blink, my brain struggling to keep up. "Brody?" I venture cautiously.

"The one and only." He grins, his eyes crinkling at the corners in the same way Cage's do. "You might figure us out after all."

"I don't know, it's going to take some getting used to." I shake my head, laughing helplessly.

Brody slings an arm around my shoulders, giving me a brotherly squeeze. "Don't worry, sis," he says cheerfully. "We'll make sure you can always tell us apart. Cage is the ugly one."

I swat at him, giggling. "Watch it, that's my man you're talking about."

"My apologies." Brody holds up his hands in mock surrender, his eyes dancing with mirth. "I meant to say Cage is the slightly less handsome one."

I roll my eyes, turning back to the stove to hide my smile. It feels good to laugh, to feel the warmth of family surrounding me.

I take the bacon off the stove and get ready to start on the eggs when someone else pads down the hallway. I turn, hoping to see Cage, but another identical face greets me.

"Morning, Ava." Asher yawns, rubbing at the sleep in his eyes.

I blink, my brain struggling to keep up. I take in the tousled hair, the sleepy eyes, the slight curl of his lip.

"Morning, Asher?" I venture cautiously.

He grins, his eyes crinkling at the corners in the same way Cage's do.

"Guess again, beautiful."

"Cage?" My eyes widen, realization dawning. I breathe, my heart skipping a beat.

He laughs, closing the distance between us and pulling me into his arms. "The one and only." Cage presses a kiss on my forehead. "Although I'm a little hurt that you can't recognize your own boyfriend."

"In my defense," I mumble, "you and your brothers *are* identical." I bury my face in his chest, inhaling his familiar scent.

Cage chuckles, the sound rumbling through his chest. "Well, I guess we'll just have to remedy that," he murmurs, his voice low and suggestive.

"Oh?" I look up at him, my pulse quickening at the heat in his gaze. I manage, my mouth suddenly dry. "And how do you propose we do that?"

"I think," he says slowly, "that we're going to have a very long and thorough session. Just you and me, no clothes, no distractions. So you can really get to know every inch of me." Cage's grin turns wicked, his hands sliding down to my hips.

"I like the sound of that." My cheeks flush, and my body responds to his words. I stretch up to brush my lips against his.

Cage groans, deepening the kiss, his hands tightening on my hips. For a moment, I forget where we are, lost in the taste and feel of him.

A pointed cough breaks us apart, and we turn to see Asher standing in the doorway, a smirk on his face.

"Well, well, well," he drawls. "Looks like someone's feeling better."

Cage grins, completely unabashed. "What can I say? I've got the best medicine right here."

"Just keep it PG in the kitchen, okay? Some of us want to eat." Asher rolls his eyes, but his gaze is affectionate.

As he saunters to the coffee pot, I lean into Cage's embrace, marveling at the brothers' easy banter. I get to see a side of Cage I've never seen before, a glimpse into the closeness and love that bind these men together.

As Cage holds me close, his laughter mingles with Brody's good-natured ribbing. Warmth spreads through me that has nothing to do with the stove's heat.

I'm home.

And no matter how many identical faces surround me, I know I'll always be able to find my one.

Because he's my heart.

My home.

My forever.

And nothing will ever change that.

~

Enjoyed Cage and Ava's story?
Want to see Cage and Ava face off against Ronin in the courtroom?
Come join us, six months down the road for an exclusive bonus
scene as Cage and Ava fight for justice.
You can read Cage and Ava's bonus scenes here.
elliemasters.com/Cage_BonusScene

Grab the First Book in The Guardian Hostage Rescue Specialists Series for Free

https://elliemasters.com/RescuingMelissa

ELLZ BELLZ

ELLIE'S FACEBOOK READER GROUP

If you are interested in joining the **ELLZ BELLZ**, Ellie's Facebook
reader group, we'd love to have you.

Join Ellie's **ELLZ BELLZ**.
The **ELLZ BELLZ** Facebook Reader Group

Sign up for Ellie's Newsletter.
Elliemasters.com/newslettersignup

Also by Ellie Masters

The LIGHTER SIDE

Ellie Masters is the lighter side of the Jet & Ellie Masters writing duo! You will find Contemporary Romance, Military Romance, Romantic Suspense, Billionaire Romance, and Rock Star Romance in Ellie's Works.

YOU CAN FIND ELLIE'S BOOKS HERE:

ELLIEMASTERS.COM/BOOKS

Military Romance

Guardian Hostage Rescue Specialists

Rescuing Melissa

(Get a FREE copy of Rescuing Melissa

when you join Ellie's Newsletter)

Alpha Team

Rescuing Zoe

Rescuing Moira

Rescuing Eve

Rescuing Lily

Rescuing Jinx

Rescuing Maria

Bravo Team

Rescuing Angie

Rescuing Isabelle

Rescuing Carmen

Rescuing Rosalie

Rescuing Kaye

Cara's Protector

Rescuing Barbi

Charlie Team

Rescuing Rebel

Rescuing Stitch

Military Romance

Guardian Personal Protection Specialists

Sybil's Protector

Lyra's Protector

The One I Want Series

(Small Town, Military Heroes)

By Jet & Ellie Masters

EACH BOOK IN THIS SERIES CAN BE READ AS A STANDALONE AND IS ABOUT A DIFFERENT COUPLE WITH AN HEA.

Saving Abby

Saving Ariel

Saving Brie

Saving Cate

Saving Dani

Saving Jen

Rockstar Romance

The Angel Fire Rock Romance Series

EACH BOOK IN THIS SERIES CAN BE READ AS A STANDALONE AND IS ABOUT A DIFFERENT COUPLE WITH AN HEA. IT IS RECOMMENDED THEY ARE READ IN ORDER.

Ashes to New (prequel)

Heart's Insanity (book 1)

Heart's Desire (book 2)

Heart's Collide (book 3)

Hearts Divided (book 4)

Hearts Entwined (book5)

Forest's FALL (book 6)

Hearts The Last Beat (book7)

The LaRouge Triplets

Asher

Brody

Cage

Billionaire Romance
Billionaire Boys Club

Hawke

Richard

Contemporary Romance

Cocky Captain

Romantic Suspense

EACH BOOK IS A STANDALONE NOVEL.

The Starling

~AND~

Science Fiction

Ellie Masters writing as L.A. Warren

Vendel Rising: a Science Fiction Serialized Novel

Books by Jet Masters

If you enjoyed this book by Ellie Masters, the LIGHTER SIDE of the Jet & Ellie writing duo, and aren't afraid of edgier writing, you might enjoy reading BDSM themed books written by Jet, the DARKER SIDE of the Masters' Writing Team.

The DARKER SIDE
Jet Masters is the darker side of the Jet & Ellie writing duo!

Romantic Suspense
Changing Roles Series:
THIS SERIES MUST BE READ IN ORDER.
Book 1: Command Me
Book 2: Control Me
Book 3: Collar Me
Book 4: Embracing FATE
Book 5: Seizing FATE
Book 6: Accepting FATE

HOT READS
A STANDALONE NOVEL.

Down the Rabbit Hole

Light BDSM Romance
The Ties that Bind

EACH BOOK IN THIS SERIES CAN BE READ AS A STANDALONE AND IS ABOUT A DIFFERENT COUPLE WITH AN HEA.

Alexa

Penny

Michelle

Ivy

HOT READS
Becoming His Series

THIS SERIES MUST BE READ IN ORDER.

Book 1: The Ballet

Book 2: Learning to Breathe

Book 3: Becoming His

Dark Captive Romance

A STANDALONE NOVEL.

She's MINE

About the Author

Ellie Masters is a USA Today Bestselling author and Amazon Top 15 Author who writes Angsty, Steamy, Heart-Stopping, Pulse-Pounding, Can't-Stop-Reading Romantic Suspense. In addition, she's a wife, military mom, doctor, and retired Colonel. She writes romantic suspense filled with all your sexy, swoon-worthy alpha men. Her writing will tug at your heartstrings and leave your heart racing.

Born in the South, raised under the Hawaiian sun, Ellie has traveled the globe while in service to her country. The love of her life, her amazing husband, is her number one fan and biggest supporter. And yes! He's read every word she's written.

She has lived all over the United States—east, west, north, south and central—but grew up under the Hawaiian sun. She's also been privileged to have lived overseas, experiencing other cultures and making lifelong friends. Now, Ellie is proud to call herself a Southern transplant, learning to say y'all and "bless her heart" with the best of them.

Ellie's favorite way to spend an evening is curled up on a couch, laptop in place, watching a fire, drinking a good wine, and bringing forth all the characters from her mind to the page and hopefully into the hearts of her readers.

FOR MORE INFORMATION
elliemasters.com

facebook.com/elliemastersromance
x.com/Ellie__Masters
instagram.com/ellie_masters
bookbub.com/authors/ellie-masters
goodreads.com/Ellie_Masters

Connect with Ellie Masters

Website:
elliemasters.com
Purchase Direct:
elliemasters.com/shopify
Amazon Author Page:
elliemasters.com/amazon
Facebook:
elliemasters.com/Facebook
Goodreads:
elliemasters.com/Goodreads
Bookbub:
elliemasters.com/Bookbub
Instagram:
elliemasters.com/Instagram

Final Thoughts

I hope you enjoyed this book as much as I enjoyed writing it. If you enjoyed reading this story, please consider leaving a review on Amazon and Goodreads, and please let other people know. A sentence is all it takes. Friend recommendations are the strongest catalyst for readers' purchase decisions! And I'd love to be able to continue bringing the characters and stories from My-Mind-to-the-Page.

Second, call or e-mail a friend and tell them about this book. If you really want them to read it, gift it to them. If you prefer digital friends, please use the "Recommend" feature of Goodreads to spread the word.

Or visit my blog https://elliemasters.com, where you can find out more about my writing process and personal life.

Come visit The EDGE: Dark Discussions where we'll have a chance to talk about my works, their creation, and maybe what the future has in store for my writing.

Facebook Reader Group: Ellz Bellz

Thank you so much for your support!

Love,

Ellie

Dedication

This book is dedicated to you, my reader. Thank you for spending a few hours of your time with me. I wouldn't be able to write without you to cheer me on. Your wonderful words, your support, and your willingness to join me on this journey is a gift beyond measure.

Whether this is the first book of mine you've read, or if you've been with me since the very beginning, thank you for believing in me as I bring these characters 'from my mind to the page and into your hearts.'

Love,
Ellie

THE END